The Very Best of
BLACK BOB
THE DANDY WONDER DOG

WAVERLEY
BOOKS

Published 2010 by Waverley Books, 144 Port Dundas Road, Glasgow, Scotland, G4 0HZ

The Very Best Of Black Bob – The Dandy Wonder Dog © 2010 DC Thomson & Co., Ltd
Black Bob® © DC Thomson & Co., Ltd. 2010

The publishers gratefully acknowledge the assistance of Morris Heggie, the editor of *The Dandy* from 1986–2006;
Dave Torrie who joined the staff of *The Dandy* in 1961 and was the editor from 1982–1986;
Ray Moore for the compilation of additional material – *A Dog's Life*

ISBN: 978-1-84934-028-1

Printed and bound in Scotland by DC Thomson & Co., Ltd,
West Ward Works, Guthrie Street, Dundee DD1 5BR

EVERYONE LOOKED UPON BLACK BOB AS A FRIEND, ESPECIALLY THE PUPPIES AT THE FARM. BOB ALWAYS FINDS TIME TO ROMP WITH THEM.

HERE IS ONE OF BOB'S MOST NERVE-RACKING MOMENTS. A FLIMSY BRIDGE CAUGHT FIRE WHEN HE WAS CROSSING IT. BOB ESCAPED DISASTER BY INCHES.

WHILE HE WAS IN ARGENTINA BOB MET A MAN COLLECTING ANIMALS FOR ZOOS. THE CLEVER COLLIE WAS A BIG HELP. THIS WAS ONE QUEER ANIMAL HE DUG UP—AN ARMADILLO.

ANOTHER THRILLING ADVENTURE TOOK PLACE IN SOUTH AMERICA. BOB FOUND HIMSELF ADRIFT ON A LOG RAFT IN A RAGING TORRENT. LUCKILY FOR BOB THE RAFT DIDN'T BREAK UP.

BUT NO MATTER WHERE HE HAS BEEN; WHAT HE HAS DONE; OR THE STRANGE THINGS HE HAS SEEN, BOB IS ALWAYS GLAD TO GET HOME. AND HE'S SURE OF A GREAT WELCOME FROM HIS MASTER — ANDREW GLENN.

Contents

BLACK BOB

Introduction by Morris Heggie, the editor of *The Dandy* 1986–2006

Black Bob arrived in *The Dandy* comic on November 25,1944. This first series was text stories of approximately 3000 words per episode. A pen and ink illustration was used as a header to start off the story.

At this time *The Dandy* was one of a number of children's publications produced by Scottish publishers DC Thomson Co., Ltd. Amongst other titles were household names like *The Beano*, *The Wizard*, *The Rover*, *The Hotspur* and *The Adventure*. In 1944 the comics were run by skeleton staffs as so many of the editorial team, including *The Dandy* editor Albert Barnes, were off on active service. The introduction of new stories to keep the comics fresh was down to group editor RD (Bert) Low and in *The Dandy's* case, stand-in editor Johnny Hutton.

They relied heavily on the talents of a small group of freelance authors to provide the week on week episodes that kept the pages filled. Unlike the comics of today there was a lot of reading in an early *Dandy*.

Towards the end of summer,1944, freelance author Kelman D Frost was visiting the headquarters of DC Thomson in Dundee, Scotland from his home in Hampshire. He and RD Low were good friends, having worked hand in glove on countless stories over the years. On this trip they took some time off to go walking in the Angus glens, to the north of Dundee where RD had a house. They used this relaxed time to discuss new storylines and work out a timetable to provide the material the comics needed. RD would tell Kelman the type of series he was planning to run, working out a synopsis of how he saw it developing. Armed with this information Kelman would then produce the written stories that made up the series.

JUST STARTING—The Adventures Of Scotland's Wonder Sheep-Dog!

BLACK BOB

KIDNAPPED! · BOB BREAKS FREE · LOST IN LIVERPOOL · ON THE WAY HOME

The Prisoner.

BLACK BOB poked his soft, black nose between the wooden bars and sniffed anxiously.

He could not tell where he was, or why he was there. He had never been shut in a box before and he did not like it. There thick stick in it and—Whang !—Black Bob had received a blow on the head which had knocked him senseless.

When he had recovered his wits he was in this box, with a strange collar round his neck, and the feeling that he was being driven along in a motor-lorry. All night they had travelled southwards and all night Black Bob had tried to escape, without any success. Soon after dawn the lorry had stopped in a yard in a great city and the box had been lifted out by two strange men.

Bob tucked his tail down and scampered on to the pavement. He had forgotten he was no longer in the country. The road was busy with traffic. There were lorries and cars, buses and trams, horses with carts and many other vehicles. There were so many whirring wheels that he got giddy looking at them and sat down on the pavement to steady himself.

The next moment he got a kick in the ribs and a man almost stumbled over him.

" Hey, get out of the way, you brute !"

The discussions on this visit were around the great popularity of the new MGM film adaption of Eric Knight's book Lassie Come-Home. It had launched the previous year and been a huge success with both adults and children. RD was looking for a dog hero story that would also incorporate the beautiful scenery of the Scottish glens-similar to the surroundings they were walking amongst. Within weeks of his return home to Hampshire Kelman Frost had sent in the first three episodes of Black Bob. This first series would run to 8 episodes in total.

A new story coming in to the Dandy did so without much advertising, just a little mention in the previous issue and a topline saying 'Starts today'. Such was the popularity of this comic that stories became nationally known almost immediately.

On the week that Black Bob launched in *The Dandy* sales reached 824,000 copies. Due to wartime paper shortages the Government only allowed 850,000 copies to be produced.

even the cleverest man overlooks?—Hi

BLACK BOB
THE WISEST SHEEP-DOG IN SCOTLAND !

Every boy and girl is sure to be thrilled by the amazing adventures of Black Bob as he finds his way through England to his home in the hills.

Black Bob will be the pet of every reader of "The Dandy."

His True Story Starts
IN A FORTNIGHT !

Announcement in **The Dandy** *of November 11, 1944. The Dandy was fortnightly due to wartime paper shortages.*

No. 280—NOV. 25th, 1944

"BLACK BOB"—Great New Dog Story Starts Inside!

KORKY THE CAT

KORKY'S SINGING IS VERY FUNNY, HE GETS EVERYTHING BUT MONEY. BUT THE THINGS HIS LISTENERS THROW, BRING HIM QUITE A BIT OF DOUGH !

Etcher's proof:
A proof sheet from the printworks which the editor had to approve and initial before the print run could go ahead. This one signed by RD Low

Early Jack Prout artwork. Story supplements like this were a common addition to DC Thomson's women's publications.

Courier Home Guard: Jack Prout is second from the right on the back (fourth) row.
Dudley D Watkins is second from the right on the second row.

One of the foundation blocks in the success of Black Bob was the wonderfully atmospheric artwork used in the story title drawings.

This was the work of Manchester born Jack Prout, a DC Thomson staff artist who worked in their Dundee art studio. Jack had first joined the firm in 1923, aged twenty-four and worked mainly for DC Thomson's women's magazines. His weekly workload would see him illustrating scenes from perhaps three differing stories. With such a high demand and emergency wartime staffing, the Dundee studio artists had to be flexible. However, in 1944, his talents as a doggy artist were discovered by The Dandy.

Jack had served in the First World War, where he was wounded. During the Second World War he was in The Courier Home Guard Company which was made up entirely of DC Thomson staff. Along with him in this company was the renown illustrator Dudley D Watkins, who was the mainstay of the firm's notable comic strips like Desperate Dan, Lord Snooty, The Broons and Oor Wullie. After a day at the drawing board the men would leave the studio, get into uniform and turn out at company HQ. Much time was spent in exercises and in drills preparing for the defence of the town should invasion occur.

This is a Manchester edition of The Weekly News, another edition was titled The Glasgow Weekly News.

1946

In 1946 everything changed for Black Bob and his creators. DC Thomson's newspaper come magazine, the Weekly News, decided to run Black Bob in picture strip format every week. The Dandy editorial, now back to full strength after the war, reworked the prose stories into picture and text scripts. Jack Prout dropped his varied workload to concentrate on drawing the Wonder Sheep Dog.

He was now doing a Dandy heading plus a picture strip every week. Within eighteen months it was decided that Jack should stop drawing in the studio and work from home, where he could better concentrate on Black Bob.

The hare that Black Bob caught made a fine stew —but it landed his pal the tramp in the soup!

BLACK BOB

The Wonder Dog of Britain in Picture Story.   **The first Weekly News strip, October 5, 1946**

BLACK BOB

BLACK BOB was a Border collie. He was five years old and lived with his master, Andrew Glenn, the shepherd, in the hills near Selkirk. He was a champion. He had won many cups and trophies in sheep-dog trials. And no wonder, for he was the wisest, cleverest dog who ever rounded up a shepherd's flock. He was a dog to be proud of, and Andrew Glenn was proud of Bob.

2—It was the day of the All Britain Championship trials. Bob was in wonderful form and carried all before him. And now he sat, proud as could be, as his master walked up to be presented with the Championship Cup. The onlookers cheered and admired Black Bob as he sat there, with his fine black and white coat glistening in the sunlight. He looked every inch a champion.

3—Shortly afterwards Andrew Glenn was approached by two hard-faced men. "Say, mister," said one of them whose name was Jake, and who spoke with a strong American accent, "we want to buy your dog and take him with us to America. Name your own price." Andrew Glenn shook his head. "I wouldn't sell Bob for all the money in the world," he said.

7

1946

The Weekly News was a top selling publication. By the end of 1946, with paper restrictions lifted, it was selling over a million copies every week. It had a great name for light-hearted entertainment and Black Bob shared his page with either a comic strip or a collection of cartoons. Black Bob would run this way for an amazing twenty-one years.

Jack Prout did not draw his nine frame strip as a single page, like most strip artists did – instead Jack drew each frame individually, one single frame on his drawing board at a time. He said that this way he could do each as a single little masterpiece and not be distracted by the rest of the page. He drew the frames slightly larger than the paper used them, and each week he would hand to *The Dandy* editor an envelope containing nine beautiful eight by four inch drawings. *The Dandy* staff would then put the strip together and do the write-up. The type was set separately and stuck with glue to the made-up pages by the cut and paste layout artist. Former chief sub-editor of *The Dandy*, Dave Torrie, would marvel at the speed and rough hand Jack would use to do his pencil sketches which he would then show to editor Albert Barnes for approval. If changes were to be made he would do them instantly as the editor watched. All the intricate detail and rendering was added when doing the final inking.

The linework required to get the effect of the shaded cottage interior must have been painstaking to do.

The Weekly News *was always topical so their choice of picture strip was show biz orientated. Mary Ellen was a current music hall hit and sheep-dogs were all the rage at the cinema due to the Lassie movies. Six Lassie movies appeared during the forties.*

Set square, ruler, scalpel, scissors and glue were the tools of the cut and paste layout artist.

1949

With his terrific tales appearing in two national publications, Black Bob's popularity grew rapidly. No great surprise then that The Dandy editor Albert Barnes started to put together a collection of Black Bob's picture and prose stories for the Christmas market of 1949 (the book would be officially dated 1950). DC Thomson had very successful Dandy and Beano annuals that were much sought after as Christmas gifts. This one hundred and twenty-eight page book would be titled simply BLACK BOB The Dandy Wonder Dog, and was an unusual oblong shape which suited the proportion of the Weekly News artwork. Albert mixed text and strip stories, broken up with various doggy features. All the story artwork was by Jack Prout. This was the first of a series of books-in all eight were produced between 1949 and 1965.

After the restricted space of small frames, Jack Prout would have enjoyed doing a large close up scene like this.

Note: These books are quite collectable now and fairly hard to identify which year is which, the covers being quite similar. The trick is to look at the back cover-they had different scenes on them.

The MAD BAD DOG of Tinker's Hill

Albert Barnes would work out art dimensions and pagination for his Black Bob book on a dummy copy

BLACK BOB SPOTTERS GUIDE

1950 Back Cover – Bob on hilltop with shepherd Andrew Glen approaching.
1951 Back Cover – Bob with a boy beside him watching over far off sheep.
1953 Back Cover – Bob watches two robins sitting on his food dish.
1955 Back Cover – Bob pulls a tin bath sled with a girl and pup on board.
1957 Back Cover – Andrew Glen sits on a rock with Bob beside him.
1959 Back Cover – Black Bob with three other dogs including a bulldog.
1961 Back Cover – Black Bob lying on hillock, front paws crossed.
1965 Back Cover – Black Bob surrounded by his trophies. This book is very different in that it is regular A4 shape and only ninety-six pages.

Dandy Editor
Albert Barnes

The first Dandy picture story

WELCOME BACK! To your famous old pal, the cleverest collie in Britain.

BLACK BOB THE DANDY WONDER DOG

IN a hill cottage near Selkirk lived the famous collie, Black Bob, winner of every championship in sheepdog contests throughout Britain. His master, Andrew Glenn, had reared him and trained him, and together they spent long hours, summer and winter, shepherding the flocks on the wide Scottish hillsides.

Bob was the most intelligent dog Glenn had ever known, and he had refused many offers to buy him. There was a strong bond between them; the way they understood each other was the talk of all the shepherds and other country folk. And Black Bob was a great favourite with the children in the district.

2—This great adventure of Black Bob begins on the day of the new Championship Trials, in which Bob and his master were taking part. On arrival at the park, Bob was greeted by a crowd of boys and girls who had come to see him and to cheer him on in the contest. A hard-faced foreign-looking man, who had also come to see Black Bob, watched from a car.

3—Bob gave a flawless display of sheep-handling. The great silver cup was his—no doubt about that. He was Champion of Britain for another year. After the presentation, Glenn was stopped by the foreigner from the car. "I'm Jake Cobb," he drawled. "I want to buy your dawg. How much?" Glenn shook his head. "I wouldn't sell Black Bob at any price."

On May fifth 1956 Black Bob's adventures in *The Dandy* were shown in picture strip for the first time. This was a resizing of *The Weekly News* first series and was part of the trend that saw the text stories being phased out in all the comics.

The prose stories had run in *The Dandy* for eleven years, with twenty-one different series, all written by Kelman D Frost. The prose format was deemed boring compared to the exciting graphics of the picture series. Now *Dandy* readers could get a better look at shepherd Andrew Glenn and his wonder border collie plus they would be able to put faces to the various characters that inhabited the villages and glens in the Selkirk hills where Bob lived and worked.

Editor Albert Barnes and his sub-editors in *The Dandy* comic would all write Black Bob storylines. Over the years Bill Swinton, Ron Caird, Jim Simpson, Iain Munro and Dave Torrie would all contribute notable work to keep this magical series at the forefront. (Apologies to the staff writers who I have not mentioned by name – it's my memory!)

Jack Prout continued to do all the artwork which still appeared in *The Weekly News* first then into *The Dandy*. This way of working continued up to September 1967 when the strip was discontinued in *The Weekly News*. However, on occasions, individual stories were now needed for *The Dandy Book* and *The Dandy Summer Specials*.

A camp-shattering stampede of camels, sheep and goats

39

Black Bob in North Africa.

Pandemonium broke out in the Arab camp when Black Bob stampeded the camels, sheep and goats right through the middle of it.

Comics nowadays would not show boys smoking. These two 'fly puffers' paid for their stupidity – but not before burning down the haystack.

Everyday scene in Black Bob's glen. It takes a very clever collie to round up a rogue elephant.

A seal in the Selkirk hills and a performing one at that.

Black Bob would find many unusual beasts and people in the Selkirk hills. In addition he would visit and have adventures in many different continents including North and South America, Africa and Australia. I suppose some of the incidents in the stories would be deemed non pc today, like the two schoolboys smoking by a haystack and setting it alight. However, in Black Bob tales there was always a punishment for wrongdoers.

Jack Prout and Tim.

Jack Prout's artwork never varied from its high quality. Some of his most beautiful scenes were taken from real life. This old bridge near Aberfeldy in Perthshire was the inspiration for one particular classic scene. When Jack was unwell or swamped by his workload only one other artist was regularly allowed to put pen to Black Bob. He was another veteran DC Thomson staff artist called George Ramsbottom, 'Rammer' to his pals. On occasions, and these were very rare occasions, George would be called in to draw an episode. His period style, and that period was closer to the twenties and thirties than anything else, fitted with the classic Black Bob look. Jack Prout approved of George's take on his beloved character. These two veterans shared another interest – both were actual dog owners. George had a tiny Chihuahua which I personally remember well. I was office junior in The Rover comic and George would bring artwork in to the office from his studio at home. From his pocket he would produce the Chihuahua which he would put on my desk to jump around while he conducted business with the editor. The little beast would often pee against the old mug holding my pencils. Jack Prout owned a dog too, yes, you've guessed it, a black and white border collie called…wait for it….Tim! You might have thought Jack would have seen enough black and white collies on his drawing board to last him a lifetime but that was his breed of choice. Jack reckoned that The Dandy and Weekly News editorial led him a dog's life with all their changes to his pencil roughs so he might as well have the real thing to take his mind off it.

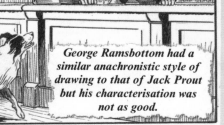

George Ramsbottom had a similar anachronistic style of drawing to that of Jack Prout but his characterisation was not as good.

A single page story drawn by George Ramsbottom.

BLACK BOB

PROFESSOR BURTON was a familiar figure on the hills near Selkirk. Every week-end he came to search for traces of Pictish and Roman dwellings. One day, Andrew Glenn and Black Bob found him digging beside the banks of Torry Water. He was very excited. "I've just found the site of a Roman camp!"

2—Glenn congratulated the professor then he and Bob went on their way. Later, however, Black Bob was near the river again. Suddenly he heard an excited shout. The professor climbed out of a hole holding a big earthenware vase. But in his excitement he missed his footing. He plunged into the river.

3—At once Black Bob dashed to the rescue, but the professor shouted to him, "Never mind me, Bob! Save that vase!" The professor was more concerned about it than about his own safety. Black Bob saw that the professor was swimming quite well, so the collie leapt into the water and swam after the vase.

4—But what the professor didn't know was that the Black Pot lay just ahead. This was a whirlpool that sucked the water into an underground channel and emerged under the Falls of Torry, half a mile away. Black Bob had recovered the vase when he saw the professor being swept into the centre of the whirlpool.

5—The professor was not a strong swimmer and he was drawn nearer and nearer to the centre of the whirlpool. Finally he was dragged under the surface and whirled towards the hole in the river bed. Then he felt Black Bob's teeth grip his trouser leg.

6—Black Bob swam strongly away from the centre of the whirlpool, dragging the professor slowly behind him. It took the plucky collie a long time, fighting against the powerful current, but at last he managed to drag the professor ashore.

7—But instead of being pleased at his escape. Professor Burton could only sit and call himself stupid names for losing the vase. "It's probably smashed to smithereens by now," he groaned. But Black Bob had dived back into the river.

8—The collie emerged with the precious vase from the river, where it had sunk when he had gone to the professor's aid. The professor was overjoyed. Later, when he wrote a book about his finds, the professor presented a copy of it to Bob's master.

Next week—The start of an exciting new story. Three pages of Wild West adventure! Watch for CRACKAWAY JACK.

Unlike Black Bob, 'Tim' was not a highly trained dog. Dave Sutherland, a Beano staff artist (the pen behind The Bash Street Kids) recounted this anecdote to me recently. Dave was a neighbour of Jack's in the Barnhill area of Dundee. On a Friday night Dave and some pals would call in to Jack's house to take him down to the local pub for a pint. Jack would take the collie and between chasing after him and stopping traffic to road train him, the pub was almost closed before the men got to it. Tut! Tut! What would Black Bob have thought of it all? Dave recalls his pals saying "Next week bring Jack but no the dug".

The funsters in the DC Thomson art department made a licence for Tim to keep a pet artist – namely Jack and the licence was signed with Black Bob's pawprint. As this indicates Jack was a popular figure and even when he was getting older still liked to have fun with his mates. He did a drawing for Albert Barnes showing how Black Bob should really look after all his scrapes and near death experiences – another good laugh in the office.

First Name *Tim*

Surname *Prout*

Full Postal Address *11 Navarre St Barnhill*

Description *Black + White Collie* is hereby authorised to keep *one artist* in Great Britain, from the date hereof and until and including the last day of *Nov.* next following. Granted at *11* hours *25* minutes *a* m. o'clock at *The Dandy* office and with the full authority of *The Weekly News* by *Black Bob.*

HIS MARK—

REASONS FOR KEEPING AN ARTIST
(Reasons to be stated in full.)

This artist is reputed to be a dog-lover, and to have the right knack. He has lived, eaten and slept with a black and white collie for upwards of 20 years.

Penalty for refusing to show this Licence to Black Bob, Rin-Tin-Tin, Sooty, Harold Wilson, or any other official Dog, or for keeping an Artist above six months old without licence, £5.

DESCRIPTION OF ARTIST—

NAME *Jacko*

COLOUR *Process White*

AGE *Yes, very*

TEETH *Maybe*

EYES *Bloodshot*

HAIR *All over*

HABITS *Dirty*

DISTINGUISHING MARKS *Ink, Beer, Baccy stains*

SEX *Past it.*

Jack officially retired six months after the weekly picture strips were stopped. He still did individual Black Bob sets for *The Dandy Book* and *Summer Special*. From time to time he would do a new character for Albert Barnes-his last one was the unusual Tomtin and Buster Brass. Jack was drawing animals again but this time they were mechanical.

The old series were reprinted in *The Dandy* weekly until July,1982. One of the reprint stories had Black Bob in Argentina at the time of the Falklands War between Britain and Argentina. Dandy chief-sub Dave Torrie recalls getting a letter from an anxious reader asking if Bob would be safe in that country while the conflict was going on. He replied that not to worry, Bob was a great survivor.

This set was done for the Dandy Summer Special in 1976 when Jack was 77. Although getting on in years he was drawing as well as ever.

This is one of the pages from the Bob in the Argentine story that unfortunately was running in The Dandy when the Falklands War broke out.

18

BLACK BOB
CHAMPION OF CHAMPIONS

ANY SIGN OF THAT MISSING RAM, ANDREW?

Andrew Glenn, Scotland's top sheep-dog handler, was helping neighbouring farmer Geoff Billingham to gather his sheep! At his side, as always, was his faithful collie, Black Bob.

AYE! I CAN SEE THE OLD RASCAL ON A ROCKY LEDGE UP ON SCAR PIKE!

A sharp whistle from Glenn sent Bob in pursuit of the fugitive ram!

The clever collie soon had the ram cornered, but the shepherd was worried in case it slipped off the narrow ledge.

Both colour and speech bubbles were added to this original Bob for the 1991 **Dandy Book.** *Andrew Glenn had found his voice after 47 years.*

When I took over as *The Dandy* editor in 1986, I tried hard to recreate a modern classic Black Bob series. I tried to persuade Paddy Brennan who was a wonderful animal artist to accept the commission but after doing pencils he never continued, saying he loved the original Bob and couldn't get close to it.

For the 1989 *Dandy Book* I persuaded the talented Australian artist Peter Foster to do a Bob set. His work did not feel like Black Bob so I retitled the story Rip. *Dandy Book* 1990 and I got together with artist Keith Robson. Keith and I are old friends and he knew exactly what I was looking for so he did not do it!

When an artist of the calibre of Keith says forget it - you have to listen. We changed tack and did Young Black Bob who was from the same lineage as the original Bob and owned by Andrew Glenn's nephew. Good, but a compromise.

1991

In the 1991 *Dandy Book* I reprinted in colour an original Jack Prout Black Bob story. It was the best....though I have not given up on a new Bob yet. Jack Prout died in September 1978. This book is very much a tribute to him, RD Low and Kelman Frost, Albert Barnes and the talented Dandy staffs that put this classic series together.

Bob was wise in the ways of sheep and men. The exciting stories showed the bravery and intelligence of the champion dog. The charm of the drawing highlighted the bond between this dog and man.

No wonder so many young readers wanted a pal just like Black Bob.

Morris Heggie, Editor

THE BRAVERY OF BOB

AWAY in a hill cottage, in the Border country between Scotland and England, lived Black Bob. His master, Andrew Glenn, was a shepherd on a large sheep farm, and with him Bob spent the long days, summer and winter, spring and autumn, tending and watching the flocks on the wide hillsides. Bob was a champion amongst sheepdogs. He had the "eye", the power to command the sheep. Time after time he saved them from foxes and killer dogs, and from danger in storms, floods and blizzards. Bob was a famous winner in sheepdog trials, far above other dogs in cleverness and knowledge, and his master had refused many offers to buy Black Bob. There was a strong bond between them; the way they understood each other was the talk of all the shepherds and country folk. And Black Bob was a great favourite with the children around Selkirk, near where Glenn and Bob lived.

2—This great adventure of Black Bob begins on the day of the big Championship Trials, in which Bob and his master were taking part. It was an autumn day, and the sun shone on the busy scene when they arrived at the park. Bob was greeted by a crowd of boys and girls who had come to see him and to cheer him on in the contest. But there was one other who had come to see Bob—a hard-faced, foreign-looking man who watched from his car.

3—Bob was the holder of many a championship trophy. But in this Trial he was to compete for the Supreme Championship of All Britain. Bob put up a masterly show. He "gathered" his sheep and obeyed correctly Glenn's signals to bring the little flock through the obstacles on the championship course. In the "shedding ring" Bob's job was to separate five marked sheep from the flock. In record time he did it and chased the unmarked sheep away.

21

4—Other dogs went through their paces, but in the end it was Black Bob's championship—no doubt about that. He looked every inch a champion as he sat there waiting while his master stepped up to receive the handsome silver cup. How the people admired him! And what a magnificent collie he was, in his black and white coat, with his deep chest, his wide forehead, and those big brown intelligent eyes. He was the pride of Andrew Glenn's heart.

5—Glenn gave the cup to the secretary for safe keeping while he went off for some tea. On the way he was stopped by the hard-faced foreigner who had watched him arrive. Another man was with him. "My name is Cobb—Jake Cobb," the man said in an American drawl. "What d'you want for this dawg of yours? Name your price." "Nothing doing," said Glenn. "Not at any price. I wouldn't part with my Bob for all the money in the world."

6—Glenn never dreamed that his next few minutes with Bob were to be the last for a long, long time. He went into the tea tent, leaving Bob with Tommy Gray to look after him. Tommy knew Bob well. He was proud to be given this little job, and he paid no special attention when the two flashy men approached. Suddenly one of them grabbed him from behind. The other, Jake Cobb himself, whipped out a sack and pulled it over Bob's head.

7—There was a whiff of something in that sack which put a quick end to Bob's furious struggling. The two men bundled him into their car, and by the time Bob's head cleared he was many miles from Selkirk. He tried to rise. But he was bound and cramped inside the sack. Tearing and slashing with his teeth, he made a hole in it and got his head out. He was on the floor of a fast-moving car—and still securely tied, his legs bound together with cords.

8—But no cords could hold Black Bob for long. He gnawed them through in half an hour and stood up. He knew very well how to open a car door, and when the car slowed to round a sharp corner he rose on his hindlegs. It was now or never! He was pressing down the door handle when the man Cobb saw him. "Hi, look!" Cobb gasped. "I knew I heard that handle clicking!" He seized a big spanner, whirled round in his seat, and struck Bob over the head.

9—Black Bob lay senseless for hours, and even when the car stopped at last, at a quayside in Liverpool, he was still dizzy and could scarcely stand. A rope was tied round his neck, and he was dragged along the jetty towards a flight of steps. Down below was a small rowing-boat, and a cargo ship lay at anchor in mid-river. "Make it snappy with that boat, Lew," Cobb shouted down to his companion. "This dawg's got a wicked look."

10—The cargo ship anchored in the Mersey was ready to sail for America. The two men hustled Bob on board, and he lay on the deck as though exhausted—but all the time looking around through half-closed eyes. "He'll be worth a packet o' dough over in the States," said Cobb. He was less watchful now. And Black Bob took his chance. Suddenly he was up and away, to leap clean over the side in a reckless dive into the river below.

11—The water was icy cold, but it put new life into Bob. When he came to the surface he headed for the shore. It was a long swim, but he stuck it gamely, and when the Americans started after him in the row-boat he swam all the faster. The shore at last! Bob snarled at his pursuers, then turned and ran along the shore till he found a place to climb the sea-wall. His master would be desperately anxious. Somehow he must get back home.

The danger of the runaway cart-horse

12—Black Bob got away from the riverside as fast as his tired legs would take him. He spent the night in an empty stable, and headed out early, fresh and strong, seeking the road that would lead homewards. But soon he was lost in the maze of Liverpool's streets. Bob always knew his way on the open hills, but here he was bewildered. Time and again he paused uncertainly. Then at a street crossing there was a sudden commotion.

13—A little way along the street, men were shouting. A woman screamed, and there was a great clatter of hooves. A runaway horse! Something had startled the animal, and it was bolting with the lorry swaying behind. Black Bob was nearly run down. The crowding people, the rushing traffic of busy Liverpool—it was all so new and strange to him. Then he seemed to rouse himself from his daze, and with a great bound flung himself clear.

14—On rushed the runaway, with a policeman tearing after it. Bob saw that there was no one in charge of the terrified animal, and that the policeman couldn't overtake it to bring it to a halt. In a flash Bob sized up the danger, and he set off in chase. He ran fast, much faster than the cart-horse, and, after a quick spring, caught up and made a snatch at the trailing reins. He got hold of them at the first attempt and gripped them firmly in his mouth.

15—Bob tugged and strained back on the reins, and he had his work cut out to keep clear of the wheels of the cart. He was dragged slithering along the roadway on his haunches. But the horse felt the pull, and its wild gallop eased down a little. Unaided, Bob might never have stopped the runaway, but the horse began to tire quickly. The gallop slowed to a lumbering trot. Black Bob held on, and, before long, horse and cart came to a standstill.

16—The policeman came panting up to seize the horse's head. Bob dropped the reins and walked on, his job done. But he hadn't gone far when a second policeman caught up with him. "You're a mighty brave dog," said the constable in a kindly voice. "I wonder what your name is?" He examined the disc attached to Bob's collar. "Black Bob," he read. "Owner: A. Glenn, Ettrick Farm, Selkirk, Scotland. Well, you're a long way from home!"

17—"Come on, boy, come with me," said the constable, and he talked in such a friendly way that Bob made no effort to escape. The man took him by the collar and led him round the corner to a police station in the next street, where a uniformed sergeant sat writing at a desk. The constable coaxed Bob on to a stool, and then told his story. The sergeant wrote down quickly the details of Bob's gallant deed, and took a note of his name and address.

18—"These sheepdogs are valuable, Jim," said the sergeant. "We'll have to keep him here until . . ." He broke off as two men entered. "That's our dawg, officer," said one of them—and he spoke in drawling American tones. The hair round Bob's neck fairly bristled. He whirled round and snapped at the man's outstretched hand. For the two newcomers were the Americans who had kidnapped him, Jake Cobb and the man called Lew!

19—The policemen were startled to see Bob behaving so strangely. But Black Bob wasn't going to allow himself to be claimed by these hated men. The door was shut, but there was an open window high up behind the sergeant's desk. Bob made a great spring to the top of a cupboard, and from there he scrambled out through the bars. The appearance of the Americans was enough to set Bob off on the run again, desperate to get back to his master.

20—It was a big leap down to the pavement and a hard landing. But Black Bob got clean away. "Stop that dog!" someone shouted inside the police station. There was a constable at the entrance, and he took up the chase at once. Bob glanced back. The constable was a good sprinter, and because of his quick start he was only a few yards behind. Two other policemen were getting into a car outside the station. Bob ran his hardest.

21—In the next half-minute Black Bob got well away from the running man. But now the police car came and picked up the constable, and then made up on Bob at top speed. Still Bob kept running, trying hard to escape. He reached a place where the road crossed the railway, and there ahead of him appeared two more policemen to bar his way. At the same time the constable on the footboard of the car was reaching out to grab him.

22—Black Bob was in a very tight corner. Then something happened that startled him. A train whistle screeched right below him, and a cloud of black smoke belched up. It was a north-bound train passing slowly under the bridge. Bob jumped on to the parapet, and with his quick wits saw a chance. The constable made a dash from the car to grab him. But Bob was ready. Just as the constable's hand was out to take hold, Bob leaped from the parapet.

23—It was a well-judged jump. Black Bob landed safely on a carriage roof, and held on as the train jolted along. It was a mixed train, goods trucks as well as passenger coaches, running on a branch line. It steamed through the outskirts of Liverpool and went rattling merrily along into the country. But after a few miles Bob realised something was wrong. He saw smoke and flames start to pour up ahead. One of the trucks was on fire.

24—Black Bob knew that fire meant danger. He knew, too, that someone must be warned. Away up in the front of the train Bob could see two men. He barked loudly, but they did not turn round. He saw he must get nearer to them. So he set off, jumping from roof to roof, with smoke and sparks streaming along at him. Bob hated and feared fire, but on he went till he came to the blazing truck. He paused for breath, braced himself, then leapt.

25—Through the roaring flames went Black Bob. His eyes nipped and watered, his coat was singed, his paws scorched, but he got over to the next truck. From there he made his way towards the engine, and soon he reached the coal tender. The driver and firemen were staring ahead and didn't hear Bob's bark. Bob reached out a paw and scratched at the driver's shoulder. The man looked round, and when he saw Bob up there he fairly gasped.

26—"Gosh!" he yelled. "Look—a dog!" Then he saw the blazing truck and applied the brakes at once. Bob was nearly toppled down from amongst the coal as the train halted beside a small station. The driver and fireman pelted back along the line. The guard brought a couple of fire extinguishers, and they all began fighting the blaze. Bob saw a porter in the station getting out a hose. He ran over to the platform and grabbed the nozzle.

27—The truck was still blazing when Black Bob reached it, dragging the hose behind him. He dropped the nozzle at the engine driver's feet as the water began to come on. "See that!" the driver shouted to the guard. "That's a clever dog, that is—and brave, too. Watch him!" But Bob turned away and ran off along the railway track. All around him were fields and trees. He was back in the country again. Now he could head for home.

Cheerful chums - the cripple and the collie

28—For the next two days Black Bob travelled steadily north. On the third morning he came to a quiet river somewhere beyond Blackburn. And he stopped when he saw a one-legged man there. Bob was suspicious of strangers. But there was a friendly look in the eyes of Jim Wilson, the cripple tramp. "Hello, boy," he grinned. Bob wagged his tail. This man looked hungry, and Bob was hungry, too. He turned away to hunt.

29—Bob snuffled up and down the river bank, and then all around a big clump of bushes. Cripple Jim Wilson watched and wondered. "What's he up to? He's a friendly-looking fellow." All he could see of Bob now was the wagging tail above the bushes. Then Bob came into view again with a great bound. He was after something. It was a hare! "Go on, boy!" cried Cripple Jim. "Catch him!" And Bob vanished into a little wood.

30—Cripple Jim thought he had seen the last of Black Bob. He sat down for a bit of a rest, for he had come a long way that morning looking for work. But a moment later he sat bolt upright and gasped. For there was Bob coming out from among the trees, with his tail wagging and with the hare limp in his jaws. Bob laid the hare at the tramp's feet. "Well, I'm blowed!" said Cripple Jim. "Just as if you knew I was starving."

31—The tramp soon got a fire going and set the hare a-roasting. How eagerly Bob sniffed the good smell! "Strikes me you're as hungry as I am!" Jim chuckled. And he was right, judging by the way Bob wagged his tail when he was at last given a big, juicy leg. They crunched and chewed and had a grand feed. Then a sound made Bob lift his head. Here was danger again, for a man who had crept up on them was pointing a gun at the tramp.

32—Black Bob sprang up with a growl. "Caught you!" snapped the man to Cripple Jim. "I'm the gamekeeper here, and I'm after poachers like you. Using a dog to help you, too!" He glanced at Jim's crutch, then suddenly flung it into the river. "You won't get far without that," he said, and stumped off with Bob snarling at his heels. "The police will pick you up," he growled over his shoulder. "I'm off to phone for them now."

33—Black Bob kept after the gamekeeper as far as the main road. A car was passing, and two men in it seemed to recognise Bob. But Bob turned away without noticing them and went straight back. Cripple Jim was hopping awkwardly along the river bank, trying to keep abreast of his drifting crutch. Bob plunged into the water. "That's the stuff, boy, fetch it!" pleaded Jim. Bob seized the crutch just as the two men from the car appeared.

34—They were the two Americans, Jake Cobb and his companion, Lew. They had been scouring the countryside for Bob, and thanks to that chance glimpse of him by the main road, they now grabbed him again as he scrambled out of the water. "Beat it!" Cobb told Cripple Jim. "He's our dawg." Cobb tied a string to Bob's collar, and Jim "beat it"—but only because he saw two policemen coming. The Americans were taken aback.

35—Of course, Cobb knew nothing of the gamekeeper's phone message about a poacher with a dog. The two policemen had come in answer to that, and now they questioned the prisoners. "Sure, this is our dawg," said Jake Cobb angrily. "Right," was the reply. "You're under arrest for poaching." Black Bob felt Cobb's grip on his leash slacken. He took his chance, broke away, and raced after Cripple Jim. He was free again.

29

The clue at a Lancaster crossroads

36—Black Bob was a good friend to Cripple Jim Wilson during the next week. Jim was going north and, although it was a slow business, Bob travelled with him. They were near Lancaster when a notice on a tree caught Jim's attention. "Blowed if you ain't the living image of that dog," he said to Bob. "Here, let's see if there's a name on your collar." Sure enough, Black Bob's name and address were on a disc, the same name as on the notice.

37—"Come on, boy," said Jim. "Let's head for a police station." He didn't like the idea of parting with such a grand pal as Bob had been, but he was a good-hearted man and he knew he ought to get Bob sent home to his master. He led Bob across an open common towards a nearby village—but neither of them saw a bull on the common. The bull eyed them and pawed the ground. Then down went its head, up went its tail, and it charged.

38—There was a strong wind, but it was blowing the wrong way for Bob to get the scent of the bull. It was already very close and coming at them fast when Bob looked round and growled in alarm. Cripple Jim got a nasty fright. He started to hobble off quickly—but he hadn't a chance. The end of his crutch caught in a rabbit hole and snapped in two. Down he went, and he hit his head on a stone and lay still. Bob swung round, barking furiously.

39—Black Bob had often rounded up cattle before, and now he knew exactly what to do. His violent barking turned the bull away, and as it wheeled past him he gave it a sharp nip on the foreleg. Then he was after it like fury, snapping at its legs, nipping with his teeth, and harrying it across the common. The bull was frightened now, and Bob drove it in front of him through an open gate into the empty field beyond, the field from which it had strayed.

Cripple Jim's good deed seems a bad deed to Bob

40—Bob chased the bull well into the field, then turned back to the open gate. Some careless person must have left it open, and the bull had wandered out on to the common. Bob knew that if he pushed against the gate with his paws it would swing shut. So up he got on his hindlegs—but the gate was heavy and it needed some push! All his weight would scarcely move it at first, and then it went with a rush and the latch clicked into place.

41—Black Bob turned back to Cripple Jim. He whined, and licked the tramp's face, but Jim didn't move. Bob tugged at Jim's jacket, but still he didn't move. How could he help his friend? Bob looked round and saw a drinking trough over by the wall. He lifted Jim's cap, ran over to the trough, and filled the cap with water. Back at Jim's side, he lowered his head so that the water splashed down on his friend's face. Cripple Jim stirred at once.

42—The cold water brought him round and he sat up. "Gosh, Bob," he said, "what happened to the bull?" He broke off as he saw the bull safely shut up. "Well, I'm blowed!" he gasped. "No wonder you're a champion!" But Black Bob was off again. This time the clever collie was searching around in a wood on the edge of the common. And when he came back he had a new crutch for Jim—a branch shaped just like the broken crutch.

43—"You think of everything, Bob!" said Cripple Jim, as he took the rough crutch from Bob's mouth. They set off once more for the village. But when Jim went to the police station Bob began to tug on his lead and try to break away. Inside the open door was a man wearing policeman's uniform, the same kind of blue uniform worn by the men who had chased Bob out of Liverpool. In Black Bob's doggy mind that uniform meant danger.

A lorry ride to a lordly mansion

44—"What's wrong with you, Bob? What's come over you, lad?" Cripple Jim couldn't imagine why Black Bob should suddenly fight to get free. But fight he did, until the string tied to his collar snapped. Bob saw a passing lorry, and a quick leap landed him on the back of it. He felt sorry to leave Cripple Jim. But little did he know that by taking him to the police the kindly tramp had really been doing his best to get him home to his own master.

45—As the lorry left the village and sped along a country road, Black Bob was happy to be free again. Five or six miles from the village the driver honked his horn and slowed down. Then the lorry swerved sharply through big iron gates into an avenue leading to a great mansion house. "Hullo there, Harry!" the driver shouted, and Bob saw the gatekeeper wave before turning to close the ornamental gates. He was shut inside.

46—Black Bob sniffed the air eagerly now. There was a homely smell about the parklands here. There were sheep somewhere near. Bob knew it. Sure enough, when the lorry swept round a curve the sheep came into view, lots of them, dotted over the grass. Near at hand was an ornamental pond, and a little girl playing with her doll's pram beside it. Suddenly Bob growled, for a fierce-looking ram was charging at the girl. Bob leaped off the lorry at once.

47—The little girl had her back to the ram and did not know of her danger. Bob tore across the grass to head the ram off. He ran his fastest, head stretched forward, tail streaming behind him, legs going like pistons. He went ripping over the grass like a streak of lightning. But the ram had too big a start. It had almost reached the girl, when Bob gave a warning bark. The girl looked round and cried out. But she couldn't get out of the way

A good job Bob was there!

48—The ram hit her quite a solid thump. Over she went with a great splash into the pond. She struggled in the water, screaming at the top of her voice, while the ram stood there snorting. The water was deep and the poor kid was really terrified. Black Bob dashed up to the edge of the pond and leaned over to catch hold of her dress in his teeth. The girl screamed again. But Bob strained back on his hindlegs and began to drag her out of the water.

49—Black Bob pulled the girl on to the grass and stood over her to protect her from the ram. She lay pale and still, with the water oozing from her clothes. Meanwhile the ram was eyeing Bob up and down and pawing the ground. Was it going to attack again? Black Bob didn't give it, the chance. He had not forgotten any of his sheepdog training. He knew how to deal with an angry ram. A growl rumbled in his throat—then he rushed at the ram.

50—Black Bob's sudden rush and fierce attack frightened the ram, for it turned to run. Bob went after it, to put a real scare into it. A sharp nip on the ear did the trick, and Bob had no difficulty in chasing it back amongst the grazing sheep. It wouldn't give any more trouble. Out of the corner of his eye Bob saw servants running to pick up the little girl. She was beginning to stir by now, and actually she was more frightened than hurt.

51—Two more servants came and coaxed Bob into the great house. Bob was willing enough to follow them, for he was hungry. A grand lady was waiting for him there, and what a fuss she made of Bob when she had seen the girl safely off to bed. She noticed his paw was bleeding, and bandaged it up while she sent the butler for food for him. Bob was happy. He had seen sheep again, and to him that meant he was getting nearer home.

52—Black bob wasn't so happy in the days that followed. He was kept in the great house and given everything he could possibly want—the best of food and plenty of it, and a warm, comfortable sleeping-basket. He had everything—except the one thing he wanted most, his freedom. Always the little girl of the house and the butler were with him. The two of them combed and brushed Bob every day, like a prize dog being fussed up for a pet show.

53—Bob was a great hero to the little girl, and he liked her. But how he hated the butler, especially on those daily walks when the snooty fat man took him out on a leash with a yapping Pekinese. Bob wearied to be off on his own again. Unfortunately, everyone was so proud of Bob for saving the little girl's life that they made him one of the pets of the house, without bothering to find out whose dog he was or where he came from.

54—One evening, a week or so later, Black Bob was lying down in front of the drawing-room fire. The little girl and her mother were listening to a programme about sheepdogs on the wireless. The sounds of bleating sheep, the whistles and signals of the shepherds and the barking of the dogs took Bob back to his home in the hills. He lay thinking about that far-away cottage he knew so well and longing to be back with his master, Andrew Glenn.

55—All night long Bob scarcely slept a wink. And in the morning he dodged the fat butler and got out through a window. He found a gateway where he tried to squeeze through the bars, but couldn't. Bob listened. What was that? Footsteps on the road outside! He nipped away to hide, and an errand boy came to the gates and pulled a long bell-chain. Bob watched how the gatekeeper came in answer to the bell, opened the gates, then closed them again.

56—So that was how to get the gates opened! Bob eyed the bell-chain. It was too high for him to reach, but he searched around under the trees until he found a hooked branch. When all was quiet he ran over with it to the gates. Holding one end in his mouth, he reached up and pushed the hooked part through the ring. Then he pulled down on it hard. Bob heard the bell ringing in the lodge. Quickly he hid again behind the big tree, then waited.

57—It was a minute or two until the gatekeeper came out from the lodge. He was mumbling to himself about being disturbed so often at this early hour. Then he noticed something unusual. "That's funny!" he said. "There doesn't seem to be anyone here. Still, maybe it's a lorry-driver, and he's gone back to his lorry out on the roadway. I'll open the gates and have a look." He swung one gate open. And Black Bob was ready!

58—The open gate gave Bob the chance he had been awaiting for many days. He bounded forward from his hiding-place, his heart in his mouth in case the man should hear him coming and shut the gate. But before the gatekeeper knew what was happening, Bob ran through his legs, knocking him on his back. The man gave a yell as he fell, but there was no one near to hear him. In a flash Bob was through the gates and out, with a clear road ahead.

59—Nothing could stop Black Bob now. He was free! Away down the road he looked back, and there was the gatekeeper sitting on the road, scratching his head. Bob gave a happy bark and carried on at full pelt. He was off to find his way north again. The little girl would soon forget him. A life of luxury and ease was not the thing for Black Bob. He wanted to get home to the rough but glorious life in the hills, with his own master to care for him.

Two weary waifs

60—Andrew Glen sat brooding far away in his cottage. His wonderings and fears about his beloved Black Bob turned to despair as the weeks dragged past and never a clue reached him. He had done so much—searched for miles around and got the police all over Britain to watch out. But without result. Yet all this time Bob was travelling steadily homewards. He was trotting along one morning when a cry sent him running to a river bank.

61—It was the cry of a small boy in distress that drew Bob to this narrow but deep river, some miles from Kendal in Westmorland. The lad was struggling in the water close to a rotten old plank bridge, which had collapsed under his weight. On the bank was a little girl, and she gave a glad shout as Bob ran past her to the end of the broken bridge. Bob stepped gingerly on to the sloping plank. It held firm, and he crept down towards the boy in the water.

62—Bob wasn't afraid of getting wet, but the banks of the river were steep, and the only easy way out was up the plank. Bob edged his way down until his forepaws were deep into the water. Then he braced his hindlegs, reached out, and grabbed hold of the boy's jacket. A strong heave and he pulled the boy on to the creaking plank. The boy got a grip on the wooden cross-slats and helped by dragging himself up. He was a plucky little chap.

63—When the boy was clear of the water Bob let go his hold and backed away upwards. The boy scrambled after him on hands and knees, and they both reached the bank in safety. The little girl was crying now, and the boy tried to comfort her. "I'll soon get dry," he said, scoffing at her fears. "But what will Mummy say?" the girl sobbed. "Oh, I wish we could find our way home, Jimmy. I'm tired, and it seems ages since we had breakfast."

36

64—"Come on. Buck up, Sis," said Jimmy. "We'll find our way somehow. Just you sit down for a minute till I get rid of some of this water." He led his sister under a nearby tree, then wrung the water out of his clothes and sat down beside her. Black Bob stayed to watch over the two children, and presently he noticed they were sound asleep. They were lost and so tired that they couldn't keep awake. Gently Bob covered them over with leaves.

65—By this time Bob was as hungry as a hunter, and he wondered what he could get to eat. He ran out of the wood and stood looking all round him. Away in the distance he could see a small town, and he decided to try his luck there. Off he went, following a road that brought him through the outskirts into the main street, where all the shops were. A good smell attracted him as he prowled along, and he saw a baker putting out a board of meat pies.

66—Bob waited until the man disappeared into his shop. There was no one else near, so Bob crept up to the window and, rising on his hindlegs, he snatched a pie in his mouth. He was just turning away when the baker saw him and gave a shout. Bob scudded off along the street, followed by the baker shouting at the top of his voice. Someone tried to head Bob off, and Bob swerved away from him and went streaking out along the country road.

67—Black Bob was swift. He got clean away into the open country and slowed down to a brisk trot. He could have stopped and eaten the pie himself, but he was going to share it with his two young pals. He trotted back to the woods and barked and barked until the two waifs wakened. Bob placed the pie in front of them, and they both gave cries of delight. Then the three fairly wolfed that meat pie between them, they were all so hungry.

68—Black Bob knew that children didn't usually sleep and eat out in the open like this. He knew they stayed in houses, and he wanted to help Jimmy Gray and his sister to get home to their own house. No doubt it was in the town where he got the pie. So after the pie was eaten down to the last crumb Bob took little Betty on his back. And with Jimmy walking alongside they set off on that cold afternoon through the woods to the main road.

69—"See, Betty, we're on the right road at last!" Jimmy cried. "He's a clever dog, isn't he? He knows the way to our home better than we did ourselves!" They came to a place where they could look down over the town, and Betty pointed eagerly. "I can see our chimney smoking," she said. "Come on, let's hurry." But Jimmy was eyeing the playground at the foot of the hill. His clothes were pretty well dry by now, and he fancied a spot of fun.

70—"Never mind going straight home, Sis," said Jimmy. "Let's have a go on the roundabout." Betty was a little doubtful at first—but she liked the roundabout! So all three of them scampered down to the playground, and the two children jumped on to the roundabout and sat down, puffing and panting. Then Jimmy got hold of Bob's tail. "Right, boy, run!" said Jimmy. Bob started to run round and round pulling his two chums after him.

71—Even Betty thought this was good fun. But her brother soon tired of it. He jumped off and ran over to the chute. Up the steps at the back he went, then whizzed down the long slope to the bottom. Black Bob fancied the idea of having a slide, and the children watched as he ventured up the steps. He came down the chute with a rush, and he liked the thrill so much that he had turn about with Jimmy. How Andrew Glenn would have chuckled to see him!

72—Betty didn't like the chute. She wandered off to the swings and shouted for Jimmy to come and give her a push. Jimmy came at last, and Bob watched him swing her backwards and forwards. She seemed to have forgotten all about going home. But evening was coming on, and Bob knew it was time for the children to go. Their house might be a long way off yet. So Bob walked up behind Jimmy, caught hold of his jacket and tugged.

73—Jimmy wondered what Black Bob wanted at first. Then he saw it would soon be dark, and he and Betty came away from the playground with Bob at their heels. They walked down a long street, and when they turned the corner at the end, there was their house across the road. Betty gave a cry. "Look, Jimmy! There's Mummy at the window. I think she's looking for us." She was—for they had been away so long that she was very worried.

74—"We'd better run," said Jimmy, and he took his sister's hand and dashed off towards the row of houses on the other side of the street. Bob's tail dropped as he watched them go. They seemed to have forgotten him completely now that they had found their home. They hadn't even said good-bye to him. Black Bob suddenly felt very sad. What good fun he'd had with Betty and Jimmy! Now they had left him—and he would miss them.

75—Bob walked across the street. Maybe they meant him to follow? Perhaps the door was left open for him. But when Bob reached the fence round their garden the gate was shut. So they didn't want him after all! Bob walked slowly off along the street. And he was so miserable that he didn't hear the children coming after him a few minutes later. They came running with their father, Mr Gray. They were looking for him, to take him back to their home.

76—What a grand welcome Black Bob got when he was brought in triumph into the Grays' home. It turned out that Jimmy and Betty had been away since morning, away to visit their Granny. They got lost on the road, and it was all thanks to Bob that they were now safely back home. In the snug kitchen the table was set and ready, but before Mrs Gray sat down with the others, she prepared a special plateful of bones and scraps of meat for Bob.

77—Bob licked up every morsel, then lay down before the fire, content. The Grays seemed pleased to have him in their home, and Bob stayed for the next few days, glad to rest before setting out north again. He went around with the children, and even took part in their games. Best of all he liked the football games Jimmy played with his pals. He liked to keep guard in goal with Jimmy, to jump for the shots that flew out of the boy's reach.

78—"Well saved, Bob!" shouted Jimmy one day, when Bob sprang up and caught the ball in his mouth just as it was whizzing through the goal. Some of the other boys raised a cheer. But one big lad among them, a newcomer called Bully Briggs, didn't like Bob stopping a goal being scored. He grabbed Jimmy by the shoulder and swung him round. "Get out o' here!" he roared, shaking his fist. "And take that dog with you. He's spoiling our game."

79—"Oh, no he isn't!" said Jimmy very pluckily. "He's a good dog—and he's a better sport than you are." Jimmy struggled in the big lout's grasp, but he didn't stand much chance. The bully drew back his fist. And it was then that Black Bob took a hand in the trouble. He stalked up behind the bully and let out a deep growl, at the same time putting a paw on the bully's leg. Bully Briggs looked round and his jaw dropped.

No dogs allowed in this friendly home

80—One look at Black Bob's angry face was enough for the bully. He let go his hold on Jimmy and turned to run away. But Bob didn't let him off scot free. He bounded forward and sank his teeth in the bully's trousers. There was a ripping noise, a frightened yell from the bully, and then Jimmy and his pals had a good laugh. For Bully Briggs ran off with a piece missing from the back of his trousers! That was a lesson for him.

81—It was at dinner time next day that Black Bob's rest in the Grays' home came to an unexpected end. Mr Wicks, the town's rent collector, called, and the first thing he saw when he was invited in was Black Bob. "What's this?" he said. "You know the rules, Mr Gray. You can't keep a dog here! You'll have to get rid of him." Mrs Gray protested, "Have a heart, Mr Wicks!" But it was no use. Wicks threatened to report them.

82—The Grays were glum and sad, though they had known Bob must go back to his master sometime. Mr Gray was a lorry driver, and he was going up north through the Lake District to Carlisle that afternoon. He asked his wife for sandwiches, then said, "Wait a minute. Where does Bob belong?" He looked at the disc on Bob's collar. "Selkirk! Right! I'll take him along and set him on the road for home. Tie up some bones for him, Ma!"

83—The thought that Bob was going to his proper home cheered Jimmy and Betty up a little. Soon Bob and Mr Gray were ready to go, and they were saying their good-byes. It was a wrench for Bob to have to leave this happy family. He felt quite sad as he "shook hands" with Betty, Jimmy and their mother. But he knew from the way Mr Gray had spoken that Jimmy's father was going to help him to get back to his master.

84—Black Bob left Mr Gray's lorry on the outskirts of Carlisle. In his doggy way he knew he was much nearer home, and he set off eagerly, heading across country. The night was cold, but Bob found a cosy barn where he slept through the shivery hours. He was off again early, and well out on the Cumberland moors when he came on a gipsy camp. Bob nosed around hungrily. Nearby, two of the gipsies were having trouble with a young horse.

85—The gipsies were trying to break in the horse. But it was a fiery, spirited animal, and it threw its rider and went off at a gallop. The two gipsies were left behind. But Bob was on the move. He was quick to see that if he could stop this horse and take it back to the gipsies, maybe they would give him something to eat. So he went off with a rush to get in front of the galloping horse and try to head it back towards the gipsy camp.

86—The horse flashed along, with mane and tail streaming in the wind. Bob got in front of it, quick as could be, and started barking his loudest. The horse paid no attention. Straight on it came at a furious pace, and Bob had to dodge its flying hooves. There was only one chance now. The trailing rein! Bob sprang in quick and snatched hold of it in his mouth. Then he kept pace with the horse, tugging and straining to pull it up.

87—But it was no good. This horse was too wild and strong to be stopped by a dog. It ran on and on, till it ran itself out and stood snorting and blowing and stamping the ground a mile or more away from the gipsy camp. Bob kept a tight grip on the rein, and after the horse quietened down a bit, he started to lead it back to the camp. The two gipsies were amazed at the sight of the horse, which had not been broken in, walking quietly at Bob's side.

88—"That dog's mighty clever, Joe," said one of them. "He should be worth a bit o' money. Wait till he brings the horse right here, then grab him." And that was what happened. Joe's pal picked up a knotted stick and waited while Bob walked the horse over to him and gave him the rein. The gipsy promptly set about the horse with his stick. Then, before Bob could move, the other gipsy, the man called Joe, slipped a rope through Bob's collar.

89—"Got you, my beauty!" said Joe, and then tied the struggling Bob to the wheel of a waggon. He returned to his horse-breaking job, and other gipsies came to look at Bob and to discuss how much money they would get by selling him. So the afternoon wore on, and the gipsies gathered round the camp-fire for their supper. Bob sat hungry and bewildered. But no rope was going to hold him. He pulled it taut, and started tearing at it with his teeth.

90—When the rope was frayed, Bob strained back and pulled on it. It snapped, and he was free! He stood for a moment, nostrils twitching. He could smell something good cooking. He crept up on the camp-fire. One of the men was frying pieces of rabbit over the fire. Bob ran forward and leapt—straight into the middle of the circle. He landed beside the fire, snatched the biggest chunk of rabbit from the pan, and was off in a flash!

91—What a hue and cry! The gipsies were after Bob quickly enough. They didn't like the idea of losing some of their supper—and a valuable dog into the bargain! But Bob had a good start on them, and was soon safely hidden in a clump of ivy. In the gathering darkness the gipsies could not find him. So Black Bob sure enjoyed that rabbit, taken right from under the very noses of the gipsies who had tried to make him a prisoner.

92—During most of the next day Black Bob plodded over the moor, and it was late in the afternoon when he reached a little village. It was a drenching day, and poor Bob was all wet and bedraggled, and feeling real sorry for himself, when he walked past the village school. There was a rush of feet and a lot of shouting. Bob looked round to see the school just coming out, and two of the youngsters, a boy and a girl, were walking up the road behind him.

93—"Hullo, collie!" said the girl. "Where are you off to?" Bob wagged his tail. These two seemed to be going his way, so he trotted beside them. They talked to him and patted him, until they came to a bridge they had to cross. And here they gasped, for the bridge was nearly down. The river was in spate and the bridge was sagging partly under water. "Look, Jack, we'll have to get our boots and stockings off for this!" said the girl.

94—Ethel Jackson was her name, and she was a spunky lass. She got Jack ready for the crossing, then tied the laces of her own boots together and slung them around her neck. Bob watched these preparations with an understanding eye. Picking his way carefully he started on to the bridge. Ethel followed, gripping the hand-rail with one hand, and hanging on to the strap of Jack's bag with the other. It wasn't very easy though, for the bridge was slippery.

95—Black Bob slid and slithered on the sloping planks and kept looking back to see that the children were all right. But when they reached the part of the bridge where the river was breaking over it in a knee-deep torrent—just about halfway across—disaster came. The strap of Jack's schoolbag gave way, and he fell into the river. Ethel was left clutching the strap. She slipped and staggered backwards, but managed to keep her feet.

Double rescue - a boy and a pair of boots

96—Bob heard Ethel's cry of alarm, and he got back as quickly as he could. Ethel had made a quick grab and caught hold of young Jack, keeping him from being swept away down-river. Bob got a grip on Jack's coat, and between them they tugged him to safety. The little chap's teeth were chattering with cold, but he did his best to help by getting his knees on to the bridge and scrambling up. Then Ethel noticed her boots floating away.

97—"Oh, look, look! There go my boots now!" she cried, and they were well out of her reach before she could do anything to save them. But Bob spotted them and kept an eye on them. He guided the children safely to the other bank, then jumped into the water and swam after the floating boots. Luckily, he was going with the current, and anyway Black Bob was a strong swimmer. Only his head showed where he was to the children on the bank.

98—At last Bob caught up with the boots, and he seized hold of the lace which held them together. Then he turned and swam for the bank. This was not so easy, for the current was strong and Bob was swept along with it. But by paddling like fury he made some headway, and then a side-current swirled him in to the bank where the children were waiting for him. He "gave" the boots to Ethel, and she knelt down and patted him.

99—"Come on in, lad—come in with us," said Ethel, when they reached the Jackson cottage. Black Bob didn't need much coaxing. He was glad to get in out of the wet. Mrs Jackson came running to greet her soaking, bare-footed children, and there were tears of gratitude in her eyes as she fondled Bob's ears after hearing Ethel's story. Soon Ethel and Jack were sitting at the fire, muffled in blankets, with Bob between them, steaming in the heat.

100—Black Bob was welcome in the Jackson house, but he stayed for only one night. The next morning was cold, but clear, and Bob could see high hills not far away. These were part of the Cheviot range on the Scottish border, and the wind from them seemed to bring the smell of his own homeland down to him. Mrs Jackson gave him a good feed, and then he was off to the hills. But the sky turned leaden grey and a snowstorm started to come on.

101—High up in the hills the wind was bitter and the snow drove into Bob's face in a blinding flurry. He kept on, climbing until he topped the ridge, then scrambled down through deep snow on to the road in the valley beyond. All at once he stumbled over something in a snowdrift. It was the body of a man, lying very still. Bob sniffed around cautiously. Nearby was a bicycle and a postman's cap and bag. Bob whined, then began to lick the man's face.

102—The man was breathing, but Bob knew there must be something wrong. After a few minutes the man's eyes flickered open. He tried to sit up, and his face twisted with pain. "My—my right leg—it feels as if it's broken," he groaned to himself. "That—that time the bike skidded—I must have done it then. How am I to get out of this blizzard?" He dug his hands into the snow to lever himself up and Bob took hold of his collar and tried to help.

103—It was a long struggle, but in the end Bob's help enabled the postman to reach the shelter of a wall. Screened from the icy wind and the driving snow, the man took a close look at Bob. He knew a good sheepdog when he saw one. "Look, boy," he said through clenched teeth. "Fetch my bag—that's a good dog!" And while Bob dragged the mailbag over to him, the postman scrawled on a piece of paper a few lines asking for help.

Battle through the blizzard

104—He strapped the mailbag on to Bob's back, and pushed his message under the strap, where it held firm. "Right, boy—off you go," he said to Bob. "There's the road—over that way." He pointed across the snow. Bob ran a few steps, then looked back and whined. The man waved him on urgently. So Black Bob set off in the direction the man was pointing. He knew he was being sent to get help—and he must be quick about it.

105—The valley road was difficult to make out at first, but Bob found it and followed it. He faced the blinding snow again and moved on through deep drifts, sometimes so deep that the snow came up to his haunches. There had been a big fall since the postman came up this way. Bob struggled forward as fast as possible. He must get help to the injured man he had left back there. At last he saw snow-covered roofs ahead, the roofs of a village.

106—A bright light streaming from an open shop door attracted Bob, and he staggered inside. It was the general store and post office combined. The postmaster unstrapped the bag, handing the postman's note to his wife. "That'll probably say how this dog got hold of one of our mailbags, Martha," he said. His wife read the note. "Listen to this, Jim," she cried. "Turner, the postman, has had an accident. We must get help to him at once."

107—No doubt about it—Bob saved that postman's life. A search party turned out with horse-drawn sledge, blankets and everything that might be needed. Bob led the way and they found the postman stiff with cold and just about at his last gasp. But by the time they got him within sight of the village he had recovered sufficiently to lean out and pat Bob. "I don't know whose dog you are," he said, "but you've done a grand job to-day."

108—Everyone admired Black Bob's gallant and intelligent part in the rescue, and every home in the village would have been proud to take him in. But the old postmaster claimed him, and he fed Bob and gave him a warm basket for the night. Bob wouldn't stay any longer. He was eager to press on—and in spite of the snow, on he went throughout the next day. By evening he was weary and hungry again, and followed four children towards a big farmhouse.

109—The children were excited, and all were dressed in their party best. Bob lingered outside while they laughed and joked their way up to the house, and he saw how they were welcomed in by a smiling lady. The door closed, and Bob ventured up the drive to one of the windows. Standing on his hindlegs, he looked in to see a crowd of children round a loaded table having a great feast. Bob didn't know it, but it was a children's Christmas party.

110—This was Christmas Day—and here was Bob just dying for a spot of dinner, Christmas dinner or any kind of dinner. Inside, the children were eating tarts and jellies and cake, and Bob watched so intently that he didn't notice a farmhand come round to the hen-run to feed the hens. The man stopped short inside the hen-run. Two of the chickens were dead and there were lots of feathers lying about. He looked up at the house—and saw Bob!

111—"Harry! George! Quick!" yelled the farmhand. "There's a dog been at the chickens!" He ran towards Bob. And Bob whirled in alarm. Two other men rushed from the house. Bob dodged them all and shot off down the drive. As he passed the hen-run he saw the dead chickens. Surely these men didn't think he had done that? Bob knew better than to touch farmyard fowls. But he couldn't tell the men that, so he kept on running.

Black Bob foxes a fox

112—It was a stern pursuit, and Bob was lucky to get away, for one of the men had a gun. However, they lost his tracks among a lot of marks in a field, and Bob hid in safety in a nearby wood. Poor Black Bob! He didn't know what to do now. He couldn't go back to the farm for food, and there was nothing to eat out here in the snow. Then suddenly he saw a fox sneaking down the road quite near him. It had a dead chicken in its mouth.

113—Black Bob gave a low growl. There was the chicken-killer! He had caught it in the act of making off with one of its victims. His master, Andrew Glenn, had sometimes been pestered with foxes coming after his chickens, and these raiders never lived to do more raiding if Black Bob was near. Now Bob crept towards the bank that overlooked the road and waited for the wily killer. When the fox was right underneath him Bob leapt.

114—And that was the end of the killer. A quick struggle and the brute was dead. Bob seized it by the brush and dragged it over the snow all the way back to the farmhouse door. The children were shouting and laughing and playing games by now, and Bob had to bark loudly to make himself heard. Then the door opened, and the smiling lady appeared with a bunch of children. She gasped when she saw Bob with the dead fox lying at his feet.

115—The farmer himself came hurrying out. "Why, that's the dog we chased half an hour ago," he whistled, and he was about to grab his gun when he saw the fox. "So that's the killer!" he said. "Well done, boy. I think you've earned your Christmas dinner to-night." And Bob was taken in and treated like a lord in the room where the Christmas tree stood by the party table. The children gave him all the titbits, and Bob had the time of his life.

116—The people at the farm were kind to Bob, and he stayed with them for a couple of days until the thaw came. Then he set off eagerly for home, anxious to be back by his master's fireside. He was in Scotland at last, and only thirty miles or so from Andrew Glenn's cottage. But the going was heavy with mud and slush, and he made slow progress. Night fell, and he was passing a farmyard. Suddenly he saw a burst of flame from part of the steading.

117—Fire! Bob surveyed the scene from the top of a wall, sniffing the smoke. He could hear the stamping and bellowing of frightened animals. Fire in the cowshed! The farmer's cows were in a panic. Bob barked furiously at one of the farmhouse windows until it was thrown open and a pyjama-clad man looked out. "What are you makin' such a row about?" he began, then broke off. "Great Scott!" he yelled. "The big cowshed's on fire!"

118—Seconds later the man came running out. "Rouse the men, Mary!" he shouted over his shoulder. "I'll go and get the animals out." He had taken time to put on a pair of boots, and he rushed for the cowshed, with Bob racing alongside him. The farmer quickly unbolted the big door and flung it wide. A great cloud of smoke billowed out to meet them, and inside there was a loud crackling and a deep orange glow. The fire had got a good hold.

119—The animals were stamping about in a frenzy, and the farmer dived in amongst them to free them. They were all haltered and firmly secured to the wall, and what a job he had undoing the ropes and chains and getting them out of their stalls. He freed them one by one, and that was when Black Bob took over and helped by chasing the frightened beasts in the right direction, out through the doorway of the cowshed, from the smoke into the clear night air.

Reward for a fire-fighter - a jolly good scrub

120—The cows milled around helplessly in the smoke, and they needed a lot of driving. The gallant collie kept after them gamely, however, and when he got the last cow out to safety, he was glad to be outside himself for a moment. His eyes were nipping with the smoke, and his coat was singed. But while the farm-hands ran with buckets to put the flames out, Bob did a strange thing. He upset a bucket by the water-trough and rolled in the water.

121—Then the farmer and his fire-fighters got a shock. Several of them were standing inside the cowshed door, emptying water on the flames as quickly as other men could carry the buckets up to them—when suddenly Black Bob ran past them. Straight through the flames he leapt before they could stop him. The farmer gasped. "Come back, boy!" he yelled. "We've got all the animals out. There's nothing left in there now." But Bob paid no attention.

122—Bob knew better than the farmer what was in the cowshed, and that was why he had rolled in the pool of water—to save himself as much as possible from the flames. He was gone for what seemed ages to the men—two long minutes—three—four minutes. Then the men gave a shout as they saw Bob reappear at one of the little windows of the cowshed. And he had a puppy in his mouth! He had heard it whimpering, and had gone back to get it.

123—With Bob and the puppy safe, the men worked tirelessly to get the fire under control. An hour later the farmer was able to let up and get his scorched hands bandaged. Afterwards he suggested a bath for Bob. "He's caked with soot and dirt, Mary, and a dog like him likes to be clean. That's the least we can do for him after all he's done for us." So Bob had a good wash in a tub in the cosy farmhouse kitchen, and a grand feed to follow.

124—"Where's that dog that got me out of bed last night, Mary?" said the farmer next day. "He's a smart one—reminds me now of Black Bob, the champion from over Selkirk way. Remember, he was stolen not so long ago. Let's have another look at our helper." But it was too late! Black Bob was gone. In fact, Bob had already travelled far, and by now was very thirsty. He barked outside a lonely cottage, hoping for a drink.

125—But there was no sign of life, no sound of anyone coming to the door. When Bob stood up on his hindlegs and pushed against it, the door swung slowly open. Bob ventured inside, and then stood still a moment when he saw an old lady lying stretched out on the floor. Bob gave a bark, but the old lady lay quite still. He went slowly towards her and barked again. Her eyes were shut, her face was pale, and she seemed deaf to the noise Bob made.

126—The fire was burning, the kettle singing, and the remains of a meal lay on the table. This kitchen looked very much like any other cottage kitchen, but Bob knew there was something far wrong here. He went whining to the door, and trotted round to the back of the cottage. There wasn't a soul anywhere in sight. Back at the front door he glanced into the room. The fireside brush caught his eye, and he unhooked it from its stand and ran outside with it.

127—Bob's instinct was to take the brush to the nearest house. There, perhaps, someone would recognise it as the old lady's, and come to see why he had it. But things didn't work out that way. The nearest house was a farm more than a mile away, and when Bob trotted into the dairy, the dairywoman whirled on him. "Get out o' here!" she shouted. "Coming sneaking over my clean floor—and with a dirty, sooty brush, too! Be off with you!"

"Good for you, doggie!"

128—The dairywoman brandished a big wooden spoon and rushed at Bob—and Bob dropped the brush and ran. He was bewildered by the woman's behaviour. What had he done wrong? He ran all the way back to the old lady's cottage and found her still lying on the floor, exactly as he had left her. Bob grew desperate. Then he saw her hat on a chair. There was a basket handy, so he put the hat in it and set out once more, basket in mouth.

129—It took Bob a good ten minutes to get back to the dairy. And when the woman saw him at the door she reached for her big wooden spoon at once. "What! You back again?" she cried. Then she broke off as she saw the hat. "Why," she said, "that's like old Miss Tait's hat. Now how did you come by that? Maybe that was her brush you brought. I wonder—can there be anything wrong with the old soul? I'll better see Sandy about this."

130—She stumped off into the adjoining house, shouting for her husband. Bob could hear them talking together, and a few minutes later they both came out, dressed for the road. Bob barked as he saw the man getting his pony and trap ready. They set off at once with Bob leading the way back to the cottage. "See, he's going to Miss Tait's house sure enough," said the dairy-woman anxiously. "Hurry, Sandy! Use your whip, man, and hurry!"

131—Back inside the cottage with help at last, Bob watched as the old lady was lifted into bed. The dairywoman bathed her forehead till she came round. Then she told them of the dizzy turn she had, and how she must have fainted. "It was lucky you came," she said. "There was no luck about it," said the dairy woman. And she went on to explain what Bob had done. "Good for you, doggie!" said kindly Miss Tait—and that was praise enough for Bob.

132—Home! There it was at last, down in the glen. Bob hadn't lingered in Miss Tait's house. In his own way he knew his master's cottage was just a few miles off; and he was so eager and excited that he covered those few miles very quickly. Bob barked wildly in sheer happiness. Here was the goal he had been aiming for through all those adventurous weeks on the road from Liverpool. Bob went rushing down the hill towards the home he loved.

133—But a terrible welcome awaited him. The next thing Bob knew was a bang, and a shower of lead pellets went whistling past his head. Bob slithered to a stop, then wheeled about and ran for his life. Another bang rang out and Bob gave a yelp as the shot zipped around him. He didn't know who was firing at him or why, but the safest thing was to get away and hide. Down near the foot of the hill the man lowered his gun. It was Andrew Glenn!

134—"Drat it!" the shepherd muttered. "I've missed the brute." It was lucky for him that he missed—and he didn't know it. He had no idea that the dog he fired at was his own Black Bob. He was out after another dog altogether, a sheep killer. And in the evening light he had not recognised his long-lost Bob. The collie hid in safety among some rocks far up the hill. All at once he stiffened. Down below a dog was chasing his master's sheep!

135—Bob sprang up with a snarl, baring his teeth as he saw this strange dog pick out one sheep from the rest of the flock. It ran along behind the sheep, snapping and snarling, and chased the luckless animal till it fell. The whole thing happened so quickly that the killer was on top of the sheep and sinking its teeth into its prey while Black Bob was still scrambling down from his hiding-place. Bob leaped to the ground, unseen by the strange dog.

136—Glenn's faithful collie went at the killer with so fierce a rush that the brute was knocked spinning yards away. The sheep scampered off, and Bob flew past it and threw himself at the killer's throat, fighting like a fury. This was happening when Andrew Glenn arrived on the scene. He was trailing the dog he had tried to shoot, and he heard the scuffle. He came running up and rushed in to crack the killer over the head with a stick. That finished it.

137—At close range Glenn didn't mistake the killer, although in the whirl of battle he did not recognise the other dog. But when this other dog came leaping up at him to lick his face, he gasped. "It's Bob—Bob back home!" The shepherd's face was a picture of amazement. "Where have you been, you old rascal? I thought I'd never see you again!" Bob's tail wagged furiously as his master's rough hands seized him and held him tight.

138—It was quite a while later that master and sheepdog set out down the hillside together for home. Black Bob would run on ahead for a bit, then dash back to Andrew Glenn's side and jump up and try to catch his stick. They came down to the back garden of the cottage, and Bob reached it first, away ahead of his master to unlatch the gate in his old familiar way. Key in hand, Glenn followed him up the path, and Bob nearly went frantic with joy.

139—Inside the cottage Bob looked all around. It was still the same, with Bob's dish in its usual corner and the bowl of fresh water beside it. After a big supper the shepherd sat down and got his pipe going. Bob sat with his head on his master's knee. "Well, I don't suppose I'll ever know where you've been all this time," said Glenn, "but it's grand to have you back." And Black Bob wagged his tail to show how glad he was to be home.

BLACK BOB AND THE TOWSY TINKERS

FOOLISH FIRE TRICKS

The morning was bright and sunny, and the wind that rustled the heather was a hot wind from the east. The ground was bone dry and the dust rose under the feet of Andrew Glenn and Black Bob as they headed for a distant pasture where the sheep were grazing.

Black Bob walked a few paces behind his master. He did not scamper or circle about as he usually did, for he knew there was much work to be done on this very hot day. There had been no rain for weeks, and, as the grass on the hills had been burnt up by the sun, the sheep were at pasture on a big moor. The grass here was scant, but there was enough to keep the sheep from going hungry.

The shepherd looked at the cloudless sky and shook his head.

"No sign of rain yet, Bob," he said. "Everything is getting terribly parched. Some of the streams have even dried up."

Bob looked up at him and wagged his tail. The collie liked to hear his master talking to him in that deep, kindly voice of his. Glenn had got into the habit of speaking to the sheepdog, and he did this often when they were alone.

Their path lay along the bottom of a gully on the edge of the moor, which stretched away for many a mile, but they could still see the top of Gorsehill over the ridge. Gorsehill rose to nearly two thousand feet and was the highest hill in the neighbourhood.

Suddenly Black Bob stopped, turned his head, sniffed the wind, and rushed up the slope on their right. Once at the top, he stared out over the wide moorland and started barking loudly.

The seven little tinkers

"Hullo, what's Bob seen?" muttered Andrew Glenn, and he made his way up the slope to where the dog stood.

One glance was enough to show Glenn the reason for Bob's barking. A column of smoke was rising from a clump of blazing gorse near a narrow stream. Dancing round this bonfire like Redskins were seven ragged, grimy boys ranging in ages from five to twelve. Two of them were barefooted, and Glenn recognised them as tinkers from a camp about half a mile away across the moor.

The gusty wind was fanning the flames and spreading them rapidly. But the young tinkers did not seem to realise there was any danger. They were laughing and shouting, and the more the fire spread the more excited they became. They were lighting matches and throwing them about all over the place.

"The little monkeys!" growled the shepherd. "They'll have the whole moor on fire in a few minutes!"

He began to run across the moor towards the boys, and Bob followed him. The tinkers whirled round when they heard the shepherd and his dog approaching.

"What's the big idea?" snapped Glenn as he came running up. "Don't you know the flames will spread and set the moor ablaze? Now beat out that fire. Hurry—don't stand there staring!"

He snatched up a branch which lay nearby and began to beat at the burning gorse. Blue smoke billowed around him as he fought the tongues of flame. Sparks were flying in all directions.

The seven boys just stared. They made no attempt to help.

"Don't you see the danger?" cried the shepherd. "This fire of yours is a menace to the whole countryside. Look, it's spreading over there! Come on, do something."

It was then that Andrew Glenn saw a bucket standing nearby. Apparently the tinker boys had been on their way to the stream for water when they started playing around with matches.

"Get that bucket filled! Be quick!" said Glenn sharply. "Don't just stand there like a lot of dummies."

"We were doing no harm!" growled the biggest of the boys.

"No harm my foot!" snorted the shepherd, and he threw down the blackened branch, seized the bucket, and ran with it to the stream. A few moments later he was back with it brimming full and hurled the water into the heart of the fire.

There was a loud sizzling and a cloud of steam shot up. The flames died down. But one bucket of water was not enough to quench the blaze. Back went Andrew Glenn again and again, until only one smouldering patch remained.

He emptied the bucket over it with so much force that it not only put out the glowing gorse, but splashed the boys as well. They began to mutter, and one shouted angrily. Andrew Glenn wiped the sweat from his brow as he turned towards them.

"Well, that's the fire put out," he said wearily. "But boys of your age ought to know better than to start fires when the moor's as dry as this. If the wind had been blowing the other way your own camp would have been in danger. Didn't you know that?"

FIRE THREATENS THE FLOCK

Suddenly there was a savage growl behind Glenn, and two mongrel dogs rushed out of the heather and hurled themselves at his legs. In a flash Black Bob leaped to defend his master. He faced the mongrels, snarling and showing his teeth so fiercely that the mongrels came to a halt and stood whimpering.

A sharp whistle caused the dogs to draw away. A tall, powerfully-built man dressed in ragged blue trousers and a khaki shirt, with a red scarf knotted round his neck, strode towards the group. He was a tinker from the camp.

"What's going on here?" he demanded.

"He threw water over us, Dad!" wailed one of the boys.

"I didn't—but it's just what they deserve!" snorted Andrew Glenn, whilst Black Bob kept a wary eye on the mongrels. "They set a light to these bushes and the flames were spreading."

The tinker spat scornfully on the ground.

"What of it?" he growled in a surly voice. "They were doing no harm to anyone. You've no right to bully my kids. You leave 'em alone in the future, d'you hear?"

Black Bob crouched, ready to fly at him if he lifted his stick. Andrew Glenn held his temper in check with great difficulty.

"Look here, if you're going to camp on this moor you'll have to

Shepherd and tinker in a stiff tiff

tell your kids not to play around with fires," he said. "There's a big flock of sheep over on the other side of the moor, and a farm down in the glen, not to mention my cottage. All of these might have gone up in smoke if this fire had spread. Haven't you ever seen a moor fire, man? Your own commonsense should tell you to stop your boys playing with fires."

"I've seen plenty of moor fires, and I know as much about 'em as any thick-headed shepherd," retorted the tinker. "I need no advice from the likes of you. Give my kids back their bucket and leave 'em alone in future!"

Glenn tossed the bucket down. There was an angry glint in his eyes, but he had no wish to start a quarrel with this man.

"Well, I've warned you!" he said quietly. "And I'm glad you know all about moor fires. In that case you won't be very anxious to have one here. Come, Bob, we're late!"

He turned on his heel and strode away, followed by the growling of the two curs and the giggling of the boys. Black Bob followed with a backward glance at the dogs.

It had been an unpleasant encounter, and Glenn hoped he would see no more of the tinkers.

The morning passed swiftly, for there was not a moment when Bob and his master were not kept busy. Most of the grass was dry, tasteless stuff, burned yellow by the sun, and the sheep were wandering far and wide in search of fresh green patches. Black Bob was for ever circling and bringing them back. Andrew Glenn too was continually on the alert, and quite often he climbed to the top of a hillock to see how the flock was faring.

It was one of the hottest days Glenn had ever experienced on the hills, and by noon the shepherd was only too glad to sit down in the shade of a rock beneath some cliffs, and rest while he ate his sandwiches. Black Bob came and sat near his master, but all the time he kept one eye on the sheep grazing in a nearby hollow. Now and then Glenn tossed him a morsel of sandwich.

Once the meal was finished, Andrew Glenn leaned back and lit his pipe. He usually had a ten-minute smoke after his dinner, but to-day he took only a few puffs at his pipe before his eyes closed and his head drooped. The heat, and the hard work, had made him very sleepy. He fell into a doze.

Black Bob was watching his master. When he saw the pipe drop on the ground, he carefully picked it up, and placed it on a big flat rock where there was no chance of it being crushed by the shepherd's foot. Then Bob lay down nearby, and in a few minutes he, too, was dozing.

When Bob awakened, he sat up with a start, and with the feeling that something was wrong. And there was! A strong smell of burning came to his nostrils, and the sky overhead had grown dark. Looking up, he saw an immense cloud of black smoke drifting over the moor. The moor was on fire!

A big patch of heather and gorse was blazing furiously. Bob could see tongues of flame leaping along the ground, and spreading like wildfire across the moor. The wind was driving the fire straight towards the flock of sheep, and ahead of them was a steep cliff which no sheep could climb.

Bob pawed at his master's arm, barking loudly. Andrew Glenn opened his eyes, and blinked in surprise for a moment. Black Bob barked more urgently. The shepherd looked away beyond him towards the part of the moor from which the smoke was rising, and immediately he realised the danger. His face became grim.

"So the tinkers have done what I warned them against!" he muttered. "Bob—the sheep! Quick, lad—quick!"

Black Bob was off like the wind, racing towards the hollow where he had left the sheep grazing. Some were already on the move, and in a few minutes there would be a stampede away from the oncoming flames. But Glenn knew there was no escape for the sheep in that direction. Right in their path was the steep cliff.

The fire was sweeping round the hollow in a wide semi-circle. Soon the advancing flames would be licking along the bottom of the cliffs away to the east. But to the west there was still hope. The fire was still a fair distance away from the base of the crags. The sheep would have to be driven out through that ever-narrowing gap, otherwise they would be trapped between the hungry, crackling flames and the cliff face.

They would be too afraid of the fire to turn and head through the smoke towards the gap by themselves. Black Bob would have to drive them through it.

59

The rude awakening for the sleeping shepherd

Glenn woke from his nap to find Bob pawing at his sleeve. Then he saw why the collie had wakened him—the moor was ablaze and the flames were sweeping towards them.

THE BATTLE WITH THE BLAZE

Andrew Glenn hurried towards the sheep, and once when the wind parted the smoke, he saw a group of figures standing on a ridge beyond the fire—watching. It was the tinkers—twenty or thirty of them, men, women and children. They were making no attempt to put out the flames.

"Huh, we'll get no help from them!" muttered Glenn, grasping his stick more firmly.

He could hear Black Bob barking. The collie had reached the sheep in the hollow, and was trying to get them on the move. The sheep were bleating fearfully, and running hither and thither. The gap through which they must be driven had narrowed to a hundred yards.

For several minutes the barking and the bleating continued without Glenn being able to see anything. Then out of the smoke came half a dozen frightened sheep, running for their lives. Behind them streamed the others, driven on by Black Bob.

Never had Black Bob moved so quickly. He raced along behind the fleeing flock, hurrying on stragglers, and heading off the sheep that tried to turn back. The flames were advancing fast, and it was touch and go whether the flock would get out in time.

Andrew Glenn did his bit, shouting, waving his stick, and making every effort to drive the sheep in the way they should go. Thanks to his efforts, the leaders swerved in the right direction, and a few minutes later both man and dog were running along at the rear of the flock, driving them down the steep side of the glen into the valley below.

The whole of Glenn's flock had been saved in the nick of time, thanks mainly to the great efforts made by Black Bob. The grass over which they had just run was already dotted with sparks, and scores of new fires were springing up. If Black Bob had not been so quick, the fire would have surrounded the sheep—all would have perished in the blaze.

Down through the glen raced the frightened sheep, and Bob had to hurry on ahead to prevent them straying too far. He brought the flock to a halt and stood panting with his tongue lolling out when the shepherd arrived and took charge.

"Good work, Bob, good work!" cried Glenn. "I could never have got the sheep to safety without you. But the fire's spreading across the moor. If it comes down into the glen we'll have to move again. Those lazy rascals of tinkers didn't lift a hand to stop the blaze."

The burly, bearded shepherd looked towards the distant Grant Farm. Nobody seemed to be stirring down there.

"I can't understand why Farmer Grant and his men don't notice," he muttered. "They must all be at work in the barns. . . . You'd best run and warn them, Bob. Away you go! Hurry!"

Glenn waved his hand and pointed towards the distant farm as he spoke. Bob wasted no time—off he went like a shot. He leaped a stream and headed at full speed towards the farm.

Five minutes later Black Bob burst into the farmyard. It was deserted, for two men were demonstrating a new milking machine to the farm folk. It had been rigged up in the big cattle-shed, and everyone was there to see it working. Farmer Grant, his son, wife and daughter, and all of his men were present. The hum of the motor which drove the machine, and the voices of the demonstrators had prevented the farm folk from hearing the frightened bleating of the sheep, or the crackling of the moorland fire.

Black Bob charged in at the barn door, barking as loudly as he could. Everyone turned round.

"It's Black Bob, and he's mighty excited about something," declared Farmer Grant. "He seems to want something. What is it, old fellow?"

Bob ran back into the yard, setting up such a loud barking that they all followed. Almost immediately young Jim Grant saw the pall of smoke drifting over the hilltop.

"Look, a moorland fire!" he cried. "The moor's ablaze! And it's a big fire, too, by the looks of it. I'll bet Glenn sent Black Bob to warn us! Everyone turn out with wet sacks and fire-brooms! This is serious!"

"Aye, it's serious, all right!" snapped Farmer Grant. "Away you go, and help Glenn all you can. I'm going to phone for more help. The whole district may be threatened unless the wind changes."

While he dashed away to phone the fire brigade in Selkirk, the local police station and the neighbouring farms, the rest of the farm folk went hurrying off up the hill, carrying sacks and spades.

Black Bob went to the horse-trough and had a long drink, for he was parched with thirst. Then he headed back to find his master. He ran like the wind and was back at his master's side long before the farm folk reached the scene of the fire.

The hour that followed was an exciting one. Not only did everyone from the farm hasten to fight the advancing flames, but some motorists who were passing stopped and joined in, the policeman from the village came up on his bicycle to give a hand, and some Boy Scouts who were on their way back from camp further north were speedily in action.

Farmer Grant arrived, puffing and blowing, to say that no help would come from the fire brigade for some time. It had been called out to deal with a big factory fire in a town some twenty miles away. They would have to fight the fire by themselves until the brigade got back.

The farm-hands spread out in a long line, beating at the flaming heather with fire-brooms and wet sacks. The sheep were as yet in no danger, but Andrew Glenn remained with them, seeing to those that had been hurt in the escape from the flames, and watching the others.

Meanwhile, Black Bob found himself a job. He would drag sacks down to the stream, soak them, and haul them back again to the fire-fighters. He did this dozens of times, and good work it was, for nothing was more effective against burning heather than the wet sacks.

A couple of lorries arrived from the village with a crowd of volunteers aboard, but even with these extra helpers the fight was a grim one. The heat was tremendous, and every now and then some of the fire-fighters had to stagger out of range to cool off and get back their breath. It was hot, tiring work.

Not until the wind began to drop was there any chance of a real breather. Men stepped back and mopped their faces and rubbed their red-

rimmed eyes. Black Bob went down to see if his master needed any help with the sheep. Bob's beautiful, glossy coat was blackened by the smoke and smeared with soot and ash.

Glenn had the sheep under control, but he was looking anxiously at the sky.

"Reckon the wind's changing, Bob," he said. "There's a cloud coming up from the west. Aye, the wind's going round, and that means the fire will sweep back across the moor. I hope those tinkers have noticed their danger."

During all this excitement no one had seen the tinkers. They were the only people in the district who had not given a hand, and many of the village folk spoke bitterly of their laziness.

Black Bob did great work in helping to fight the moor fire which was threatening the farm. He ran backwards and forwards to the burn, wetting sacks for the fire-fighters.

HORSES AND PONIES IN PERIL

Black Bob lay down for a brief rest, and presently heard his master calling up the hill to the fire-fighters.

"Have those tinkers moved their camp yet?" he wanted to know. "They'll be caught if the wind veers round, and it's going round now."

"We can't see the tinkers' camp because of the smoke," yelled back someone. "They haven't helped us, but I reckon they'll have enough sense to save their own skins."

The weary fire-fighters were too overjoyed that the wind was changing to worry about anything else. But Andrew Glenn was still worried.

"There were women and children in the tinkers' camp, Bob, small children, some of 'em. We must make sure they've got away."

Black Bob sensed the worried note in his master's voice, and he wagged his tail eagerly, as if anxious to be off.

Glenn suddenly waved to a man among the crowd on the hill.

"Hey, there, Campbell! Come down and keep an eye on these sheep of mine for a while," he called. "I want to take a look over the burning moor and see what's happened to the tinkers."

Angus Campbell, an old shepherd friend of Glenn's, was tired out by now, and he gladly hobbled down to take Glenn's place.

Glenn and Bob hastened up to the edge of the burning moor, and skirted around it for quite a long way. Bob's master strained his eyes as he peered through the smoke. The wind had swung right round, and was spreading the fire in the opposite direction. New tongues of flame were rising on the far side of the vast, blackened area. The fire had only been smouldering there, but now the wind was fanning it to life again. A clump of dry gorse flamed up and the sparks flew freely.

"I can't see much for smoke," muttered the shepherd. "The waggons and carts were over by that hollow. I expect the tinkers have cleared out by now. For one thing, they'd be afraid that they'd be blamed for starting this fire, and—— What's that, Bob?"

He had noticed that the dog was up on top of a boulder and staring ahead, standing with head and tail rigid as he always did when "pointing". The keen-eyed collie had seen something that the shepherd had missed.

Andrew Glenn peered through the smoke, and suddenly he realised what Bob had seen. Grazing in a hollow, and tethered to stakes driven into the ground, were four horses and two shaggy ponies. They belonged to the tinkers. They were tossing their heads and beginning to tug at their ropes, for they could smell the smoke billowing towards them.

"That settles it!" cried Glenn. "The tinkers haven't moved on yet, for they wouldn't leave their horses and ponies behind. They can't realise their danger. In another twenty minutes this part of the moor will be a raging furnace. What are they thinking about?"

Glenn broke into a run. He cut round the edge of the blackened moor, where it was still burning furiously in parts. Bob followed his master, carefully avoiding the smouldering heather.

Glenn wanted to warn the tinkers of their danger, but when he came round on the far side of the moor he discovered their camp was farther off than it seemed. A good way over the moor stood their carts and caravans, most of them drawn up in a circle. Nearer than the rest was an old motor lorry and a big caravan. A meal was being prepared, and the tinkers were all seated round a camp-fire, obviously unaware of the approaching flames.

Glenn gave a gasp of dismay. "They don't know they're in danger," he muttered. "They've left their horses right in the path of the fire. Why did they tether them so far from their camp?"

He saw the reason for that almost at once. Around the camp there was little grass, only heather and gorse, but there was plenty of logs for the tinkers' fires. So the tinkers had tethered their horses and ponies in this hollow where they could graze on the good, green grass which grew there.

By now the animals were getting frantic, and were making wild efforts to escape. A sudden gust of wind had carried flames to within a hundred yards of them. This belt of fire was rapidly spreading. Andrew Glenn watched it with growing horror.

"The poor brutes will be trapped and burnt to death unless something is done for them," he cried. "Come on, Bob, we'll have to get them out of there!"

THE CRY OF A CHILD

Andrew Glenn went across the moorland at a run, but a moment later tripped and fell heavily. He had put his foot into a rabbit hole, and when he tried to rise he discovered he had hurt his ankle. It was agony to set his foot to the ground.

White-faced and gasping, he looked at the approaching flames, then at the distant camp where the tinkers were having their meal. The chances were that they still had not noticed the change in the wind. They believed the flames were being carried away from them and that they had nothing to worry about.

Could he send Black Bob to warn them whilst he tried to get to the horses? No, he decided he would hobble on to the camp and warn them himself. Bob would have to try to save the horses.

Bob had been watching the horses with his bright, eager eyes. Glenn only had to point towards the struggling animals and the dog darted away, running in a wide circle to avoid the advancing wall of flame.

Every minute the wind strengthened from the west. It was the whole of the wide moor that was threatened now, and not the farms and cottages in the glen. The tinkers were camped in the centre of the moor, and unless Black Bob saved their horses it did not look as though they would get clear.

Andrew Glenn hobbled and stumbled over the rough ground towards the tinkers' camp. The fire-fighters on the other side of the rising clouds of smoke knew nothing of the tinkers' plight. Anything that was to be done must be done by the injured shepherd and his dog.

Black Bob had never run faster. He could hear the neighing of the panic-stricken horses as he came racing up. They were doing their utmost to break the ropes or uproot the stakes, but so far not one of them had succeeded.

Bob ran with his ears flat, his tail streaming out behind him. Then suddenly he halted in his tracks. He had heard a cry from nearby—and it sounded like the cry of a small child!

He listened, heard it again, and went into action. Straight for one certain clump of coarse grass he headed, and there found a child sprawling face down on the ground. The kiddie was exhausted and sobbing bitterly.

The child was at the toddling age, and had probably wandered out from the tinkers' camp an hour or more ago. In course of time the toddler had wandered as far as this, and here he lay, too tired to go any farther. Nobody at the camp had missed him.

Black Bob did not hesitate. He got a good grip on the child's vest and lifted him from the ground. The toddler's legs and arms dangled like those of a doll, and he was red in the face, but he stopped sobbing out of sheer fright and hung there in silence.

Holding his head high, Bob stumbled after his master.

He could not bark to attract attention without setting down the child,

**Black Bob picked up the little toddler
by his vest and carried him away from the advancing flames.**

and so he had to catch up with Glenn before the shepherd realised what was happening. Andrew Glenn turned in astonishment.

"Bob—the horses—where——? What have you got there?"

Black Bob gently placed the toddler at his master's feet, where the little chap instantly burst into a loud wailing. Then the collie turned about and headed back towards the hollow where the horses and ponies were tethered.

Meanwhile, Andrew Glenn snatched the child in his arms and hurried on towards the tinkers' camp, shouting as he went. Surely the tinkers must have noticed their danger by now?

But Glenn was almost up to the camp before he saw them leap to their feet and look towards the approaching fire. For the first time they were aware of their danger.

They saw Glenn and rushed towards him. He thrust the crying child into the arms of the first woman he saw.

"Here, look after this poor little kiddie," he said. "My dog found him on the moor—and it was lucky Bob happened to spot him, for the little fellow would have been burnt to death in another five minutes. . . . Didn't you notice that the wind had changed? It's driving the fire straight for your camp."

The tall tinker who had been so rude to him that morning shook his head in dismay.

"We did not see it," he gasped. "Now it is too late to save our caravans. Our horses are over there, and we'll never get them out in time. We must leave everything and run!"

Andrew Glenn's foot gave him great pain when he put any weight upon it, but he limped across to the tinker.

"Wait, there's still a chance!" he said, shaking the man in an effort to put some spirit into him. "My dog has gone to try to free the horses. Get all your things loaded on the carts and waggons in readiness to move off. If Bob can free the horses you should be able to get away."

When they realised there was still hope the tinkers got busy. The carts and caravans were loaded. Some of the men started to beat back the fire, others ran to a motor lorry parked near the hollow. They were too late. There was a blinding flash as the petrol tank exploded. The men were driven back. Flames licked towards a caravan parked alongside and next minute, that too caught alight—and there was no water nearby to deal with the blaze.

Meanwhile half a dozen of the tinkers were manhandling the other caravans out of the path of the flames.

Three even set off to try to help Bob. They dodged round the outskirts of the fire looking for a way into the hollow. But always the acrid billowing smoke drove them back, spluttering and coughing. Glenn watched them anxiously, and wondered if he had given Black Bob too difficult a task. Supposing the gallant collie was overcome by the choking smoke! What then?

Glenn clenched his fists and waited.

Although Black Bob had saved the tinker's child, the delay almost cost the lives of the horses and ponies. By the time the sheepdog reached the grassy hollow where they were tethered, sparks were falling among the surrounding bushes. The frenzied animals were rising on their hindlegs and beating the air with their forelegs as they neighed in terror. One of the horses had dragged up its stake and bolted.

But the tinkers had used strong wooden stakes, driven well into the ground. None of the other animals could pull up the stakes, neither could they break the thick, strong ropes attached to them.

Black Bob seized in his mouth the rope of the biggest and most powerful horse. He attacked it with his strong sharp teeth, biting and gnawing with all his might. The struggling horse dragged him this way and that, and he narrowly escaped death beneath its pounding hoofs. All around him were maddened beasts fighting to escape.

A glowing spark fell on Bob's back and scorched him. Fires were springing up in the bushes. In a few minutes Bob and the horses and ponies would be surrounded by a mass of flames.

But the rope was giving. All of a sudden it parted and the big horse swung around and vanished through the smoke. Black Bob started gnawing at the rope belonging to a shaggy pony.

Fortunately the pony was tethered by a fairly thin rope, and Black Bob's sharp teeth bit through it in record time. The maddened animal, with sparks burning its back, ran for its life.

There were still two horses and one pony left. Black Bob caught at a third rope, but before he could get to work with his teeth, a spark landed on the pony's back. With a shrill whinny the pony reared itself up on its hindlegs. At the same time, it threw its head back and the tether went as

taut as a bowstring. The terrific jerk yanked the long wooden stake out of the ground. The pony was free!

Away it went in a mad gallop, dragging the rope and stake behind it.

By that time the heat was almost unbearable, and wreaths of hot, choking smoke swirled around Black Bob as he made for the next horse. Through the smoke he could see leaping yellow flames, tipped with

Sparks, flames and smoke were everywhere. Black Bob pulled the horse's tether and held it over a blazing bush so that the rope began to burn through.

orange. There were ugly, brown patches where Bob's glossy coat had been scorched, and his paws were stinging.

He managed to get the horse's rope in his teeth, but there was no time to bite it through. Instead he held the rope over a burning bush. The horse tugged in the other direction; Bob hung on, and the rope was stretched across the flames.

Wise Bob – how he made use of a burning bush

The tinker dived for the trailing tether of the fleeing horse. He missed and went sprawling all his length. Glenn, despite his sore ankle, jumped at its head.

The dazed, almost suffocated dog saw the rope turn brown as the flames licked around it. In a matter of seconds it had burned right through and parted. The horse vanished through the smoke.

A minute later Glenn saw it come careering out of the hollow in a panic-stricken flight. One of the tinkers made a dive for its trailing tether. He missed, and went sprawling all his length. Then as the frightened horse raced past Glenn the shepherd seized the rope. In spite of his injured ankle he hung on grimly.

"Whoa, lad," he shouted. "Steady." Trembling violently the horse came to a standstill, and Glenn led it towards one of the caravans.

THE TINKERS LEARN THEIR LESSON

That was the fifth horse—there was only one more to be freed and it seemed as if Black Bob was too late. The poor creature was on the verge of collapse. It was down on its knees, with a helpless, staring look in its eyes, when Black Bob gave a desperate tug at the rope.

Once again he decided to burn through the halter, and he dragged the rope into the burning bush. Thirty seconds later the rope parted. But the horse did not bolt as the others had done. It seemed about to sink to the ground. It was almost overcome by the smoke.

Back Bob is scorched, limping and dead-beat – but all the horses are safe

Black Bob grabbed its broken halter between his teeth.

Holding this firmly in his mouth, he tugged fiercely until the horse came to its feet. Then he began to lead it up the side of the hollow. At the top they came to a narrow belt of burning grass, and for a moment the animal refused to cross it, neighing in alarm as it threw itself back on its haunches. Bob tried to urge it on, and burnt his paws on a red-hot branch. But he still kept his hold on the rope, and tugged and pulled for all he was worth.

Then, suddenly, the horse seemed to realise its danger. It bounded for-

The frightened horse neighed in alarm. It jibbed and refused to follow Bob through the patch of burning grass.

ward and cleared the blazing grass with one mighty leap. Bob jumped with it, still holding the halter in his mouth.

Behind them the flames roared through the grassy hollow. Black Bob had got the horse out just in the nick of time.

Presently he saw the caravans and lorries with men surging round them. They had caught the horses and ponies Bob had freed, and were harnessing them to the laden vehicles. Whips were cracking as the first caravan moved off, crammed with tinkers and their belongings. The other lorries and caravans followed.

Only the biggest and heaviest of the lorries remained behind, and when the tinkers saw Bob arriving with the last horse they could hardly believe their eyes.

Andrew Glenn was there when Bob handed over the horse to its owners. The shepherd was horrified to see his dog's condition, with scorched patches of fur everywhere, one ear singed, both eyes bloodshot, and two paws so badly burnt that Bob winced each time he set them down.

"Poor old fellow! You didn't spare yourself!" muttered the shepherd. "We'll have to do something about these paws of yours. I wonder if the tinkers have any bandages?"

The tinkers didn't. But they gladly gave Glenn some handkerchiefs which he tore into strips and tied round Bob's paws. Then he lifted the collie on to the lorry and climbed up beside him.

The tinker driver cracked his whip, and the horse started off at a cracking pace. Two vehicles had been lost—the motor lorry and a caravan.

Behind them the moor was red with flame, and a great cloud of smoke entirely hid the hill in the background. This time there was nothing to stop the fire. It would spread over the moor, and devour everything until it came to the river, where it was bound to die out. But there were no sheep or other living things in its path, thanks to Black Bob. Hundreds of acres of heather would be blackened and charred, but the following spring it would come up better than ever.

As for the glen, the wind had carried the fire away from there, and neither Farmer Grant's property nor the shepherd's cottage was threatened.

The tinkers drove along at a breath-taking pace, the lorry rolling and pitching, until they reached the track where the caravans were waiting. The tinkers were thankful to have escaped so lightly, and everyone had an admiring word for the dog which had done such good work.

69

The happy end to a dreadful day

Black Bob and his master rode on the lorry to where the moorland track joined the road that led to the glen, and there Andrew Glenn said they would walk. He lifted the sheepdog down.

The tinkers crowded round to thank the shepherd for what he had done for them, and the swarthy man who had quarrelled with Glenn that morning, held out his hand.

"I'm ashamed of myself, mister," he said in a shamefaced way. "You were right and we were wrong. Ye'll never have cause to complain about us again if we come to camp in these parts. You and your dog have taught us a lesson. I'm sorry for everything."

Andrew Glenn shook hands with him, and he turned for home, for the shepherd knew that his friends would be worried about him, and he was anxious to get back to see about his sheep.

Bob limped at his side, and looked up at Glenn.

"Well, here we are—a couple of cripples," said the big shepherd with a wry grin. "But we did good work! I'll bet those tinkers never start another fire on a moor in dry weather."

When Glenn and Bob got back home, they found Farmer Grant and his son awaiting them. Black Bob's paws were smeared with a soothing ointment, and then Andrew Glenn's ankle was bathed and tightly bound up. The scorch-marks would remain for some time on Bob's back. But eventually his coat would grow in as long and as silky-smooth as before. Until then it would be a reminder of how Bob and Glenn fought the most terrible moor fire ever seen in that part of Scotland; and how they taught a lesson to a tribe of towsy tinkers.

BRAVE BOB'S ISLAND ADVENTURES

THROUGHOUT the length and breadth of the land there was no collie better known than Black Bob. As a sheepdog Bob had become famous, for no other dog was his equal at handling sheep, and he had won many championships at sheepdog trials in both England and Scotland. But to Andrew Glenn, his master, Black Bob was more than a sheepdog—he was a pal and a trusted friend, and many were the adventures they had been through together. In spite of all the fame that had come to them, the shepherd and his dog still lived in their little cottage in the hilly Border country near Selkirk. Here they worked together tending the sheep, clipping and dipping them in summer and guarding them against the ever-present dangers of storms, foxes, killer dogs and sheep-stealers. For miles around they were known and liked by the country folk, because the kindly shepherd and his famous collie were always willing to lend a hand to any of their neighbours.

So one day, when young Tom Laird, a crippled ex-serviceman, found himself in need of help he went to Andrew Glenn. Tom had a small sheep farm, but he had fared badly in the last few years. First one trouble then another beset him; storms, floods and blizzards had all taken toll of his stock, until Tom despaired. Now he had been given the chance of taking over a small croft on Birsay, an island off the west coast of Scotland. Tom had farmed on Birsay before, and he felt that he would have more success there. It was going to be a big undertaking to shift all his implements and livestock to his new home. That was why he came to Andrew Glenn. He wanted the shepherd to help him move all his farm animals. And Tom Laird had come to the right man. The shepherd thought it over for a few days, then he made up his mind to give all the help he could to Tom. And that was how another great adventure started for Black Bob and Andrew Glenn.

2—The next few days were busy ones for Andrew Glenn and Tom Laird and his wife, for there were many things to be done before they could set off. They planned to go by road to a west coast seaport, so lorries were ordered and the route mapped out. Then they had to arrange for a steamer to take them from there to Birsay Island. Even things like pots, pans and food had all to be packed into crates, for there were no shops on lonely Birsay.

3—But at last the day of their departure arrived and Glenn, pack on back, set off for Tom Laird's little farm, with Black Bob trotting at his side. As Glenn reached the service road leading to the farm a sports car drew up and a man got out. He was a surly-looking fellow with a black patch over his right eye. He came over and stopped Glenn. "If you intend going to that island," he muttered, "take my tip. Stay here." With that he turned away.

4—Glenn stared, surprised, then he shrugged his shoulders and went up the road to join Mrs Laird and Tom. The animals were all being loaded on to the lorries, and Black Bob soon got a job helping with the sheep, while Glenn helped the Lairds to load the last of their cases on to the furniture van. The shepherd said nothing about the stranger, and in a few minutes something happened which drove the man's queer words clean out of Glenn's mind.

5—In the excitement no one noticed Tom Laird's little daughter Peggy had slipped away, and it was fully five minutes later before they realised she was missing. When their shouts brought no answer they grew alarmed. Here they were starting on a long, arduous journey, and little Peg had vanished. Panic seized the mother, but Glenn kept his head. He whistled for Bob. "Fetch Peggy," he coaxed, and Bob at once started to nose out her trail.

6—Some distance away over the fields was a disused quarry. It was a dangerous spot and Peggy was forbidden to play there, but on the previous day she had disobeyed and gone to it, with her beloved dolly. Now she remembered she had left the dolly behind, so the little mite stole away to the quarry. She found the doll, but slipped on the grassy lip. By a miracle she caught hold of a bush and was hanging there when Bob came running up.

7—Peggy was pale with fright. She cried out when she saw the sheepdog running round the brink towards her. "Hurry, Bob," she sobbed. But the collie saw her danger. He was running as fast as his four legs would carry him. Bob reached the top of the slope, directly above the little figure. Beyond was the terrible drop to the quarry bottom. The grass was slippery, but with great caution, inch by inch. Black Bob began to make his way down.

8—The little girl watched wide-eyed as Bob crept towards her. At last Bob was near enough to grab her coat. Now came the tricky part. The collie braced himself to take the strain, then he began to pull her, step by step, up the slope. It was hard going. Little Peggy helped as much as she could, digging her toes into the ground and clutching at tufts of grass with her right hand—in the other she still held her precious dolly.

9—Bob and Peggy were breathless by the time they reached level ground, and Bob stood there with his tongue lolling out, waiting till Peggy had recovered from her struggle on the slope. Bob and Peggy were already great friends and had often played together. So once Peggy was all right again she climbed on Bob's back. The collie picked up her doll and set off back to the farm, where the anxious mother ran and met them with outstretched arms.

Off on the road to the Isles

10—Now that Peggy had been found there was nothing more to delay them. The men quickly stowed the last few odds and ends aboard the lorries, while Mrs Laird took a last look round just to make sure nothing had been forgotten. The great moment had arrived. The Lairds set off in the furniture lorry, leaving Glenn and Bob to follow in the trucks carrying the animals. They were off on the long road by mountain and loch to their new island home.

11—All that day the lorries rumbled on through the countryside, heading for the little seaport where they were to embark for the Isle of Birsay. The narrow, twisting roads were a big strain on the drivers, but at last they had only twelve more miles to go. It was then that disaster overtook them. The driver of the lorry in which Bob and Glenn were travelling swung out to take a sharp corner. They were halfway round when the lorry gave a sudden lurch.

12—It swayed for a moment then stopped. The edge of the road had given way and canted the lorry at a dangerous angle over the drop into the loch below. It seemed about to topple over. Glenn's first thought was for the animals in the back. "The sheep, Bob," he shouted. "Quick, boy." In a flash Bob was out of the cab. A flying leap took him on to the back, where he began pulling at the pin holding up the tailboard of the lorry.

13—The other side of the tailboard had been loosened by the skidding, and as the pin came away in Bob's teeth the back fell with a crash. The sheep took their chance and poured down the ramp. The damaged lorry had slewed right across the road. The second lorry couldn't get past, nor could it turn to go back for help. And, what was worse, the furniture lorry was miles in front, and there was no way of letting Tom Laird know they were in trouble.

74

Glenn and his dog on a long foot slog

14—The driver shook his head as he looked at the lorry. "It's hopeless," he declared. "The axle's broken. It will take a crane to shift it." Here they were, stranded, and less than an hour's run from their destination. Glenn thought hard for several minutes. "We'll unload the second lorry and go on foot," he decided. But when the animals were released they scattered in all directions, with Black Bob and the two drivers in pursuit.

15—The animals were frisky after being tied up for so long and it was a hard job catching them. However, in the end they managed to get the pigs and cow tethered. Once this was done Bob and Glenn turned their attention to the sheep which had strayed down to the loch. Night was falling as the clever collie, obeying Glenn's whistled orders, herded them into the shelter of a stone wall. When they had done this the men prepared to spend the night in the open.

16—They lit fires to warn motorists that the road was blocked, then settled down in the shelter of a cliff. They would need all the rest they could get for the journey ahead. Though less than an hour's run in a lorry, it would take many hours of slow, patient walking to herd the stock over these last twelve miles. Black Bob squatted down in front of his master. At times the collie seemed to doze, but always one alert brown eye stayed open—watching.

17—The next morning dawned bright and clear and the men were early astir. After washing in the cool waters of the loch they breakfasted on some sandwiches which the drivers had with them. In less than half an hour they were ready for the road. And a queer sight they were. The two lorry drivers led the way with the two horses, each horse carrying two crates of fowls. The cow, pigs, and sheep followed; Bob and Glenn bringing up the rear.

75

18—Black Bob was kept busy. He raced hither and thither rounding up the sheep and pigs, and keeping them on the move. All went well till they came to where a cliff flanked one side of the road. Suddenly there was a rumble above them. Then, with a roar, a deluge of stones and earth, loosened by recent rains, cascaded on to the road. The leading horse snorted and reared wildly up, throwing the startled driver clean off its back.

19—Everything went wrong at once. The loose earth engulfed some of the animals, the others scattered. The leading horse, badly frightened, stampeded down the road. It was a bad moment. Then Bob acted. He leaped over the rubble and set off after the horse to try to stop it. The men could do nothing to help him. They had their hands full keeping the rest of the livestock from getting out of control. Only Bob could stop the runaway horse.

20—About a hundred yards down the road was an opening cut into the cliff. At one time it had been used by roadmen for storing stones and gravel, but now Black Bob put it to a new use. He put on a spurt and nipped in front of the horse, barking so furiously that the animal was forced to turn into this opening. It came to a stop, trembling with fear. Bob stood by, keeping it penned there till Glenn ran up and calmed the frightened beast.

21—Glenn led it back to the landslide. Here there was trouble in plenty. A quick count showed that two sheep and a pig were missing, buried under the landslide. Glenn thought of Tom Laird waiting. To try and dig out the sheep would make them even later, and by now the animals were probably dead anyway. Glenn made up his mind. "It's hopeless," he said. "We'll have to go on and leave them." But Bob was sniffing and digging at one spot.

The bully bars the bridge

22—As Glenn turned away he felt a tug at his coat. It was Bob. "What's the matter, lad?" Glenn asked. Bob whined, then pulled Glenn towards the rubble. The shepherd realised the clever collie was trying to tell him something. "Quick, boys," he shouted excitedly. "I think Bob's heard the beasts." With that Glenn dashed after Bob who led the way back to the fallen mass. Here Bob started to scrape feverishly at the loose earth.

23—They had no tools so, using flat stones, and at times their bare hands, Glenn and one of the drivers dug into the loose earth where Bob was scratching. In three minutes they got through to the animals. They were in a small cave below the overhanging bank. Encouraged by this find, the men worked on, enlarging the hole until it was big enough for them to get at the animals. Then at last, Glenn was able to lift them out, one by one.

24—Time was precious so they pressed on till they came to where a side road turned off over a wooden bridge. One of the drivers knew the country well. "We could take a short cut through here," he said, "and save nearly two miles. Let's try it." Glenn agreed. But as they started across the bridge a burly man in plus-fours stepped on to it and levelled a gun at them. "There's no road this way," he snarled. "Turn back, or I'll start shooting."

25—"But we'll do no harm," protested Glenn. "We only want to take a short cut." "I don't care," shouted the man. "This is a private estate, and you're not crossing this bridge with your travelling menagerie." For a while Glenn argued with the man, but it was useless. Glenn turned to the lorry drivers. "Carry on by the main road," he said. Disappointed, they turned away while the shepherd gave the man with the gun a proper telling off.

26—The road skirted the river for half a mile, then crossed it by a bridge, and the travellers came to a high stone wall which ran along the left-hand side of the road. It was evidently the boundary wall of the estate which the man on the bridge had mentioned. Here they were stopped again. But this time it was by a kindly old lady. "And where are you bound for?" she asked. There was something about her that made Glenn take off his cap before he told her their story.

27—"Oh, but you would have been quicker taking the short cut across the bridge just down the road," she said with a smile. "Yes," replied Glenn, "but a big gardener fellow wouldn't let us cross it." "Oh, I see," she said reflectively. "I know who that was. Well, just come with me." So saying, she produced a big key and opened a gate in the wall. Then she pointed up the drive. "Just go up here," she said, "and straight over the lawn."

28—Glenn was surprised, even doubtful, but the lady insisted, and her tone of quiet authority convinced Glenn that it was all right. They went up the drive, with the lorry drivers leading the way, and Glenn and Bob coming along behind with the old lady. But just as all the animals were crossing the lovely lawn there was an angry shout, and a man raced towards them. Bob growled angrily. It was the gardener who had stopped them on the bridge.

29—Suddenly his face fell. He had just seen the old lady as she came round the corner of a brick wall. "That's quite enough, Innes," she said quietly. Shamefaced, the man took off his cap and twisted it nervously in his hands, for Glenn's friend was none other than the owner of the estate, a Mrs Leslie. She soon gave Innes a piece of her mind, and told him what she thought of him for his ill-tempered conduct, and for refusing to help Andrew Glenn.

30—Once she had given Innes a good telling off, the old lady guided the travellers through the well-kept parks to a gate on the other side of her estate. Here Glenn thanked Mrs Leslie, for she had saved them a long hard tramp and brought them to within a mile of the seaport. They tramped on, and at last came in sight of the sea. Down below was the harbour with a ship moored against the quay—the ship that was to take them to Birsay.

31—In half an hour the cavalcade of sheep, pigs, a cow, and horses arrived at the quayside where Glenn told the Lairds of their adventures. The farmer was relieved to see his livestock safe, and soon the work of loading the farm implements began. The animals were rested in a nearby yard, all except the cow. It wandered on to the quay, but nobody paid any attention to it. Certainly not Bob. He was too busy watching Peggy playing with her doll.

32—Suddenly there was a loud bump and a rumbling noise as a big herring barrel came rolling down the jetty. The cow had come to some barrels piled up one on another, and in trying to scratch its neck on the upper barrel had knocked it over. Now the barrel was trundling straight for Peggy. Bob heard the noise and, turning round, he saw the oncoming barrel. Bob couldn't stop it, but he did the next best thing. He sprang straight at the little girl.

33—The barrel was a big, heavy one, and it gathered speed as it rumbled over the square setts of the jetty. Peggy had her back turned, and was so intent on playing with her doll that she did not realise her danger. But Mrs Laird did. She gave a shrill scream of fear and both men turned, only to realise they were helpless. But Black Bob's leap carried him to Peggy's side, and he knocked her sideways out of the path of the rolling cask.

34—Black Bob was just in time. The barrel went rumbling past, right over the spot where Peggy had been standing only a second before. It missed them by inches, but crashed right over the top of Peggy's doll, smashing it to fragments. And that was all the damage that was done. Andrew Glenn saw to that. He rushed over, and with the aid of his crook he slowed down the runaway barrel. Then he rolled it over to the harbour wall.

35—The Lairds ran to Peggy, and they found that the little girl was none the worse, so they turned their attentions to the work ahead. There was no time to waste, and Birsay was a nine hours' voyage out into the Atlantic. The skipper was anxious to get away before the weather broke. The barometer was falling, and he did not want to be caught in a storm amongst the scattered islands off the west coast with this strange deck cargo aboard.

36—The rest of the implements and furniture were soon taken aboard by the ship's deckhands, who toiled hard, helped by the two lorry drivers. Then came the difficult task of coaxing the animals aboard the ship. The cow was the first to be herded up the gangplank, and Black Bob played a big part in getting it aboard. In the bustle no one noticed the man watching them from the shadow of the harbour wall. A man with a black eye-patch!

37—Once the cow was on deck the sheep were driven on to the quay, then Bob started to herd them up the gangway. It was here the trouble started. Just as the leading ewe was about to step on to the deck, there was an outburst of furious barking and a fierce-looking Scotch terrier appeared at the top of the gangplank, barring the way. The frightened sheep turned back, only to find that they couldn't get past the other sheep pressing on from behind.

38—The narrow plank became a jumbled, jostling mass of terrified beasts, all trying to go in different directions. Andrew Glenn saw the danger. At any moment one of the sheep might be pushed off the gangplank into the water, where it would be crushed between the ship and the quay. "Quick, Bob," shouted the shepherd, "shift him." With a single bound Black Bob leaped from the quay right over the rail and landed on the deck of the ship.

39—Bob turned on the Scottie. It took one look at him then raced off down the deck with Bob right behind it. The little fellow tore into the galley and dodged under a table, where the cook grabbed hold of it. "You'll be better locked up, Dusky," he said. "I can see you're just going to be a nuisance." His job done, Black Bob went back to the gangway. The collie's action had again prevented trouble, perhaps even saved the lives of some of the sheep.

40—Everything went smoothly after that and within an hour all the livestock were safely aboard. They drove the sheep into a makeshift pen; tethered the horses and the cow; and put the pigs in a big wooden crate. The gangway was raised and they were ready for the next stage of their journey. The hardest part was over and Glenn and Bob had done much towards its success. Now, if all went well, the Lairds would soon be seeing their new home.

41—The mooring ropes were cast off, and slowly the ship nosed its way out of the narrow harbour entrance. Then it headed north-west, out into the open sea. From the stern the travellers waved good-bye to the three lorry drivers. But in the failing light they did not see the sinister figure standing behind the men. It was the man who had warned Glenn not to go to Birsay and who spied on them on the quay. The man with the black eye-patch!

42—During the night the wind rose, and by dawn heavy seas were rolling in from the Atlantic. The little ship was buffeted by the huge breakers, and the animals on deck had a terrible time as she pitched and rolled from side to side. Glenn and Bob tried hard to calm the frightened beasts, but as they worked there was a shout from the bridge: "The rudder chain's snapped." The little ship was helpless, at the mercy of the wind and waves.

43—Suddenly a shudder ran through the ship. She had run aground on a small sandbank. Here they were, stuck fast on one of the shoals around Birsay. All morning the seas broke over the ship, then about noon the storm began to die away. By now the tide was on the ebb, and when Glenn and the skipper looked over the side they could see the sandbank. One look was enough to tell them that the ship could not be moved until the tide rose again.

44—But the ship would have to be lightened first. That meant unloading all Tom Laird's livestock and implements. It was bad luck. But for the storm and the sandbank they would have sailed on till they came to a better landing place than this rugged stretch of coastline. Now everything would have to be ferried over to a rocky beach. It was going to be a tricky job as the dinghy was too small to hold the cow and the horses.

45—The only thing to do was to let the two horses and the cow swim ashore. Once this was decided the dinghy was launched. Then while Glenn lowered two pigs and the lamb into it. Tom Laird attached long ropes to the cow and the horses. This was to make them follow the dinghy, for, if left to themselves, there was no saying to where the animals would swim. When this was done Glenn and the Lairds rowed away until they were clear of the ship.

The queer invasion of Birsay by swimming animals

46—Black Bob did not go in the dinghy. He stayed aboard the ship to help coax the animals over the side. It was no easy task. The beasts were still nervous, and clearly they did not like the idea of plunging into the sea. But the deckhands tackled the job gamely, though they were not used to handling animals. They thought nothing of unloading crates. Livestock, however, was a different matter, and the three big animals gave them no end of trouble.

47—Most of the work fell on the clever collie, and in the end the deckhands stood back and left it to Bob. He seemed to be everywhere. Barking at the heels of first one horse then the other, he drove them down the sloping deck towards the water until at last one of the horses plunged in. Once they saw the big beast swimming, the second horse and the cow followed. Black Bob leaped in after them and the strange procession got under way.

48—The dinghy gradually drew away from the ship, with Glenn leaning over the stern shouting words of encouragement to the swimming beasts. Getting them safely ashore would see the worst part of the job over, but there was still a lot to be done in the few hours left before high tide. With only one small boat, it would take many trips to and fro before all the farm implements, furniture and food could be brought from the ship to the beach.

49—Glenn did not row very fast in case he tired the animals, so it took some time for the dinghy to reach the island. But at last they reached the beach and stepped ashore. When Black Bob felt stones under his feet he gave an excited bark. He was glad to be on firm ground again. He quickly paddled through the shallow water and watched as Tom Laird lifted little Peggy out of the boat on to the beach of their new home—Birsay Island.

Animals, implements, fowls and furniture - all are safely ashore

50—When the two horses and the cow were safely ashore Glenn rowed across to the ship for another load. Two of the sailors rowed back to the island with him. This saved a lot of time. The two sailors took over the job of ferrying the gear ashore, leaving Glenn, Bob and the Lairds free to carry it up the beach away from the incoming tide. In this way they made good progress, and load after load was transferred from the ship to the beach.

51—Bob and Glenn had to make one more journey to the ship to bring the sheep ashore. They loaded as many as possible into the dinghy, then the rest swam for it with Bob. This was the last trip. Glenn had kept his promise, and all Tom Laird's implements and livestock were ashore on Birsay. But now that Glenn saw all the difficulties facing Tom Laird, he decided he couldn't leave the farmer just yet. He would stay for a few days to help him.

52—The Lairds were already on their way to Corbie, the little croft, less than a mile inland, so Glenn sent Bob after them with the sheep. The sailors helped the shepherd to put together a cart which had been brought ashore in pieces. Next they loaded it with furniture and harnessed a horse. Then Glenn set off. Once he was on his way the sailors got into the dinghy and rowed back to the ship, which was getting up steam, ready to sail on the high tide.

53—Like all island crofts, Corbie was small and compact, but Tom Laird and his wife weren't very happy about their new home when Glenn arrived. There was a gaping hole in the roof where the winter gales had torn it open. "We'll have to put that right at once," said Glenn. "It might rain to-night. A tarpaulin will do just now." "You're right," said Tom Laird. "I'm glad you're here to help me. We wouldn't have managed without you and Bob."

The Lairds have a new home - but nothing to eat

54—It was now nearly eight o'clock, and nobody had eaten since leaving the ship. So, while the two men got busy tying a sheet of tarpaulin over the hole, Mrs Laird began to prepare a meal. She got out the pots—and then she found that the big packing case containing their store of food was missing! Mrs Laird cried out in dismay. "What are we going to do?" she shouted to the men. "There's no food here. We have nothing to eat."

55—Without a doubt the food had been left in the ship, for both Glenn and Mrs Laird remembered seeing it in a dark corner on deck. The position was serious, for at any minute now the ship would leave and would not be back for a fortnight. The two men climbed down off the roof and put on their jackets. "Let's go to the beach and shout to the ship," said Glenn. "We'll just have to hope that they hear us. We'll take Bob, too. We may need him."

56—They hurried to the beach and shouted till they were hoarse, but there was no answering signal from the ship. The crew were below decks and did not hear them. "We'll have to send Bob," said Glenn. Quickly he scribbled a note and put it in his rubber tobacco pouch. While Tom Laird tucked it in Bob's collar, Glenn pointed out to the ship. "Go on, Bob," he said. To add to their troubles, the tide had begun to carry off some of their goods.

57—As Black Bob swam off towards the ship Andrew Glenn waded in after him to salvage the floating cases. Though the shepherd said nothing, he was very worried. It was asking a lot of Bob to expect him to do this, but it was their one chance. The tide was at the full—the ship was clear of the sandbank and ready to leave. Unless Black Bob caught up with the ship they were all marooned on the island without a bite to eat.

58—Black Bob swam on steadily, and soon he was out of sight of the two men on the beach. Luckily the sea was calm and Bob made good progress. At last he was near enough to hear the throb of the engines. The ship had got clear of the sandbank and was getting under way. Bob put on a terrific spurt and at the same time he barked for all he was worth. A sailor's head appeared over the stern, and next minute a rope came swirling down towards Bob.

59—Bob gripped the rope between his teeth and the seamen began to pull him out of the water. Once he was on deck they saw the rubber tobacco pouch tucked in his collar with the note inside it. None of the crew had noticed that the food crate had been left behind, so they lowered the dinghy and put the missing crate aboard. Two of the hands started to row ashore, while Bob stood in the bows, still panting after his long and tiring swim.

60—On the beach Glenn and the Lairds were peering anxiously into the darkness, looking for some sign that Bob was safe. At last they heard the splash of oars and saw the dim shape of the dinghy. Mrs Laird ran down the beach and hugged Bob when he came ashore. The sailors lifted out the food crate and waved goodbye as they rowed back to the ship. Once again Bob had helped in a real bit of trouble, and Glenn felt proud of his well-trained collie.

61—Glenn and Laird carried the crate back to Corbie, where Mrs Laird got busy rummaging through it. Soon she had some food ready, and they all gathered round the table in the kitchen. Here, in the flickering light of a candle, they had their first meal on Birsay—a hearty feed of soup, tinned meat, bread, jam and tea. After their hard time they felt it was the best meal they had ever eaten. Bob was not forgotten, for Peggy gave him some titbits.

Who is the midnight prowler on Birsay Island?

62—By the time they had finished it was nearly eleven o'clock and bedtime. There was no room in the cottage for Glenn and Bob to sleep meantime, but the hardy shepherd thought nothing of spending a night in the open. With a sheet of tarpaulin and some branches he fixed up a tent-shaped shelter. He rolled up his jacket for a pillow, crawled under a rug, and settled down for the night with his faithful collie, ever watchful, stretched out at his side.

63—Andrew Glenn was tired after his strenuous day and soon fell asleep. For several hours all was quiet, and only the distant sound of the sea broke the silence. It was about three o'clock when Bob suddenly jumped up, growling. Glenn woke immediately. Outlined by the moonlight on the side of the tent was the shadow of a man. A quick glance told Glenn that it wasn't Tom Laird. Then who could it be, prowling around at this time of night?

64—"Who's there?" shouted Glenn. There was no reply. Glenn started to scramble into his clothes while Bob ran out barking. "Stay here, Bob," Glenn ordered, for he did not want the dog to run into an unknown danger. When Glenn got out of the tent there was nobody to be seen, but Bob was sniffing at something on the ground. Glenn picked it up. It was a black eye-patch, and Glenn was sure that it had not been there when he went to bed.

65—"I'll tell Laird about this at once," he decided. Putting on his boots, he went over to the cottage and woke them up. "What do you make of this?" he asked as he showed them the black patch. But they, too, were puzzled. As far as they knew there was no one on the island except themselves, yet here was someone stealthily spying on them at dead of night. Pondering over this queer mystery, Andrew Glenn went back to his tent.

66—Andrew Glenn lay awake for nearly an hour, wondering if the man would return. But as the minutes ticked past and nothing happened the shepherd dozed off. Soon he was sound asleep. He awoke to find Black Bob pawing at his shoulder. It was morning, and promised a bright, fresh day to follow. Andrew Glenn dressed quickly and hurried across to the cottage for his breakfast, for there was a lot to be done this morning—their first on Birsay.

67—But just as he was about to enter he stopped abruptly. There, hanging from a nail on the cottage wall, was a piece of cloth. "Come here a minute, Tom," shouted Glenn. The Lairds came running out. "Look," said Glenn. "It looks as if our prowler left this behind him too." Tom Laird frowned. "I think we'll look round the island after breakfast." "Right," replied Glenn. "Meanwhile I'll hang on to the eye-patch and this bit of cloth."

68—They went into the cottage and sat down to their breakfast. The men were strangely silent during the meal. Uppermost in their minds was the mystery of their stealthy visitor. When they had finished, Laird attended to the two horses, the cow and the pigs, while Bob and Glenn drove the sheep out on to the hillside. But when they came to a plank bridge over a stream the leading ewe stopped. It stared down at the plank and refused to move.

69—The bridge was too narrow for the others to get past the leader, so the whole flock came to a stop. But Glenn and Bob, in their long experience with sheep, had met this bother before. Sheep were often nervous when confronted with something that was new or strange to them. Glenn waved his crook towards the leader. Quickly the collie leaped on to the backs of the sheep and made for the one causing the trouble. He reached it and snarled fiercely.

70—The sheep, startled, jumped forward and crossed the bridge, with Bob chasing it. The others followed. Glenn looked around till he found a suitable spot for the sheep to graze, then left them there and went back to the Lairds. It was several years since the farmer had been on the island, but he still knew his way around. He pointed to a hill behind the croft. "We'll get a good view from there," he said. So they all set off up the slope.

71—From the top of the hill they could see the whole of the island. Below them lay Loch Shay, with the rugged slopes of Ben Var looming over it. But what caught the eye was a big house in a wood near the sea. "Would it be someone from there who was prowling around last night?" asked Mrs Laird. Tom shook his head. "No," he said. "That's Dun House and it's been empty for years." The house certainly looked bleak and deserted.

72—After a good look round they left the hill to go back to Corbie. Suddenly Glenn stopped as a thought struck him. "A man warned me not to come to Birsay just before we left home," he told the Lairds. "He had a black eye-patch and was wearing a brown suit, just like this bit of cloth I took off the nail. I'll bet it was the same man." But before he could say any more there was a scream from Peggy as a huge black mastiff leapt over the wall.

73—Peggy ran to her mother screaming with fear, and both Glenn and Laird turned to see what was wrong. They saw the huge, powerful brute standing at bay, with its teeth bared and its tail lashing from side to side. Black Bob had stopped its rush by getting between it and Peggy. Now the collie was advancing, ready for a fight, with his eyes glued on his enemy. Here was another mystery. Where had this big, ugly brute of a dog come from?

74—Andrew Glenn was sure that the dog belonged to the one-eyed man. What was his idea in getting his dog to attack them? Was he trying to frighten them? If that was the game it didn't work, for it was the mastiff that got the fright. Bob made a quick rush and bowled the brute over. There was a furious fight for a few minutes, but the mastiff was no match for the brave Bob, and suddenly it ran away, yelping and yowling with fear.

75—As it tore past some bushes a man dashed out and made off towards the cliffs. "By jove," said Glenn, "that fellow is in a mighty hurry. Come on, Bob. Let's get after him. He shouldn't be here, whoever he is." With that he raced off in pursuit of the fleeing man. Tom Laird started to hobble after them, but Glenn waved him back. "You stay there and look after Mrs Laird and Peggy," shouted Glenn. "Black Bob and I will handle this."

76—The man ran to the clifftop and vanished. Glenn guessed there must be a path leading down to the water's edge. Sure enough there was, but Glenn and Bob reached it too late. From below there came the sound of an engine and a fast-looking motor boat sped out to sea. In it were the man and his dog. They had escaped and there was no way of giving chase. It was a very worried Glenn who walked back and told the Lairds what had happened.

77—It was all very mysterious. But there was much work to be done on the croft, and for the next few days they were too busy to worry about their queer visitor. The cottage was repaired and fields ploughed up. Then the men decided that they would have to build a pier so that when any boats called stores could be landed more easily. At low tide Glenn got busy driving piles into the beach, while Laird brought big planks from the farm.

78—It was a hard, tiring task, for the pier had to be a solid structure to withstand the fury of the winter seas that would sweep round the little island. Cartloads of stones were built in round the wooden piles to serve as foundations; then stout battens were nailed on top, and by the time the tide rose the pier had begun to take shape. There wasn't much work for Black Bob, but the collie did all he could to help, and took a great interest in what the men were doing.

79—All went well until Glenn started laying planks across the top of the beams. It was then that an accident happened. The shepherd was right out on the end of the pier, putting a plank into position, when he stepped back. Bob and Laird heard a shout. They whirled round, just in time to see Glenn toppling backwards. He had put his foot on the end of a loose plank and it had tilted up, throwing the shepherd off his balance.

80—Glenn hit the water with a splash and disappeared under the surface. Laird and Bob hurried out to the end of the pier. They reached it just as the shepherd came to the surface. Glenn was senseless and blood was streaming from a wound in his scalp. He had hit his head on one of the planks as he fell. Quickly Tom Laird grasped Glenn under the armpits while Black Bob crouched down, almost overbalancing in his eagerness to help.

81—Tom pulled Glenn in until Bob was able to grab his master's waistcoat. Then between them they dragged the shepherd on to the pier. The farmer frowned as he bathed Glenn's forehead. It was a bad knock, and it was fully five minutes before Glenn recovered. He was still dazed and had to lean on Tom Laird for support as they walked back to Corbie. Here Mrs Laird took command. Skilfully she bandaged Glenn's head and sent him to bed.

82—It was three days before Glenn was able to get up and about. Even then he had to take things easy. By this time Tom Laird had finished the pier and was busy cutting and stacking peat for their winter fires. Glenn and Bob were sitting watching him when suddenly the shepherd pointed out to sea. "Look," he cried. "The ship's coming back." There, rounding Cape Hoye, was the little steamer which had brought them to Birsay.

83—The ship was returning with stores of food and other things they needed. There would be letters, too, their first since coming to this lonely island. The men shouted to Mrs Laird, then they all hurried down to the pier and waited eagerly while two sailors rowed towards them in the dinghy. They were towing another small boat behind them. Tom Laird had ordered it to be sent, knowing it would prove useful in his new life as an island farmer.

84—Presently the dinghy drew alongside the pier and the work of unloading began. First two crates of food and a portable wireless were landed, then a sewing machine and a wringer for Mrs Laird, and a bundle of newspapers and letters. While Glenn and Mrs Laird read these, Tom examined his rowboat. It was a staunch little craft. "We're all right now, Andrew," he cried. "We can go fishing. Aye, and visit our neighbours on the other islands."

85—Mrs Laird was pleased, too. The sewing machine and wringer would save her a lot of hard work. So it was a happy family that made its way back to the croft. Force of habit made Glenn glance over at the sheep grazing on the hillside. A speck in the sky caught his attention. He stopped Tom Laird. "I don't like the look of that bird," said the shepherd. "It looks like a golden eagle." "I wonder if it's after the sheep?" said Laird anxiously.

86—They weren't left in doubt for very long. As they watched, the big bird swerved and dived towards the sheep grazing on the hillside below it. Quickly Glenn put down the sewing machine he was carrying. "Hurry, Bob," he shouted. But Black Bob was already racing through the heather at top speed towards the flock. Glenn snatched up a stick and followed him, shouting for all he was worth to try to frighten the eagle away from the sheep.

87—The huge bird was not to be scared off so easily. It plummetted down at tremendous speed, never wavering for an instant. The frightened sheep heard Glenn's shouts and scattered in all directions, but the eagle had picked out a lamb grazing some way from its mother. The lamb ran off, trying to dodge the eagle. But the bird pursued it relentlessly. Then, with a harsh cry, it dropped like a stone and buried its talons in the lamb's back.

88—Black Bob put on a terrific spurt to reach the eagle. It was already getting ready to fly off. With powerful beats of its huge wings it rose into the air, lifting the bleating lamb with it. At that moment Bob jumped and just managed to grip the eagle's leg in his teeth. The bird's wings threshed madly in the scuffle that followed and it struggled desperately to shake off the collie. But Black Bob held on grimly to the eagle's scaly leg.

89—The extra weight proved too much for the mighty bird and the three bodies fell to the ground in a jumbled mass. Glenn came racing up and struck at the eagle with the stick. Blow after blow he dealt it, until finally the eagle lay dead. Glenn and Bob sat back, panting, as the lamb scampered off to rejoin its mother. It was a mighty good job they had been able to destroy this bird of prey before it wrought havoc with their flock.

90—Next morning Glenn and Bob rose before dawn to go fishing in the new boat. It was a lovely morning and by the time the sun rose Glenn had a dozen fish lying in the bottom of the boat. This was enough so he rowed back, hoping Mrs Laird would fry some for breakfast. But Glenn got a shock when he reached Corbie. Bowls of porridge and cups of tea were steaming on the table. But there was dead silence in the house—and no sign of life.

91—Glenn was puzzled, then it struck him that the Lairds might be out in the steading somewhere. He ran out to the stables. The Lairds weren't there—nor were the horses. They had all disappeared. By this time Glenn was really alarmed at this sensational upset. Something startling must have happened to make the Lairds leave without having any breakfast. Yet there was no sign of a scuffle or fight. Was the mysterious stranger behind this?

92—Glenn and Bob had another look round and found that the cow and the pigs had vanished, too. The sheep usually grazed on a hill near the cottage, but there was no sign of them either. "There's something mighty queer about all this, lad," said Glenn, turning to Bob. "Seek them." Black Bob ran around for a few minutes then picked up a scent. He set off inland with Glenn striding along behind him, looking very grim and determined.

93—Bob followed the trail across the island and led Glenn right to the Lairds. They were on a hill near Dun House, the big empty mansion. "You had me worried," said Glenn. "What's been happening?" "All the animals have vanished," said Tom excitedly. "Someone must have driven them away while you were out in the boat. We were sound asleep and didn't hear anything. The queer thing is—they've left no hoofprints—not a trace."

94—Tom Laird was right. There was absolutely no trace of the animals. Even Bob couldn't pick up any scent or trail. They had completely vanished. The men were puzzled. "Let's try the empty house," said Glenn at last. They sent Mrs Laird and Peggy back to Corbie and set off down the hill towards the house. The gates at the entrance were open so they went straight up the drive. Suddenly they stopped. Running to them was a young boy.

95—"Where can he have come from?" asked Laird. "There hasn't been anyone living in that house for years." "Well, the little fellow seems anxious to see us," said Glenn. "Maybe he knows something about the missing animals. Let's go and meet him." They went on up the drive. Meanwhile, unseen by them, two strong hands had grabbed the boy as he ran past a clump of bushes. Before he could utter a sound he was whisked out of sight.

96—By the time Glenn, Laird and Bob reached the spot he was nowhere to be seen. They searched under the bushes that bordered the drive, but couldn't find him. Bob was sniffing around when suddenly he barked. Next minute he came running to Glenn with a boy's shoe in his mouth. "That proves we haven't been seeing things," said Glenn, as he took it from the collie. "There was a boy here right enough." "But where is he now?" asked Laird.

97—"My guess is that the boy wanted to see us," said Glenn. "But someone grabbed him to stop him." "I think you're right, Andrew," said Laird. "It's a bit of a mystery. The only place he can be is in the house. Shall we have a look?" Glenn agreed, so they marched up and knocked loudly on the front door. Not a sound came from inside the big, gloomy mansion, but two shifty eyes were watching them from a small window beside the door.

98—Andrew Glen knocked again, but there was still no answer. They stood back and looked up at the house. By now the face at the window had vanished. There was no sign of life. At length Glenn lost patience. "Come on, Tom," he said. "We'll go in." He pushed open the door, and they entered the stone-flagged hall. "Doesn't seem to be anyone here," whispered Glenn. Just as he spoke, Black Bob started scratching at a door.

99—Andrew Glenn strode forward and cautiously opened the door—expecting trouble. Nothing happened. There was no one in the room. In the far corner was a bed, and near it a table and a chair. But what interested Glenn was a boy's blazer, a cap, a toy yacht, and a cricket bat. "It looks as if the boy we saw slept here," said Glenn. "But he gets precious little to eat." For the only food in the room was a dried-up loaf of bread and a jug of water.

100—"Well, there's not much doubt that there is someone in this house," said Glenn. "Someone who's mighty keen to keep out of sight. Let's look around and see if we can find out what the game is." They left the boy's room and climbed the spiral staircase on the other side of the passage. This led to the top of a turret. It was then they got a surprise. Down below two men suddenly went hurrying across the yard, carrying a heavy bundle.

101—"Get down after them," said Glenn. "We'll ask them what they're doing here. Come on, Tom." They ran down the stairs and out into the yard, only to find that the two men were already out of sight. "This way," shouted Glenn, and raced off down the path the men had taken. It led to the cliffs above a little harbour. As Laird, Glenn and Bob raced along they heard an engine starting. "Hurry," shouted Laird. "They've got a motor-boat."

102—They clambered down a zig-zag wooden stairway that led down to a jetty. But by the time they reached the bottom the motor-boat was heading out through the narrow entrance to the cove. Glenn pointed after it. "That's the same boat that I saw before," he said. "It must have been these men who sent the black dog to attack us." "But what are they up to?" asked Laird. "You'd think they were trying to frighten us away from Birsay."

103—But there was no way of finding why the men were acting so strangely. They had got away. The problem was to find the missing animals. They climbed back up the steps to the house. Then, at the draw well in the yard, Laird stopped. "Look at all this spilt water lying on this path," he said. "That's funny," agreed Glenn. "Unless—yes, that must be it. They've been carrying water to the beasts. They must be around here somewhere."

104—They followed the pools of water down the path towards a derelict summer-house. "They can't be in there. It's too small," said Laird as they hurried along. "You're right," said Glenn. "But that's a stupid place for a summer-house to be. It's right under a cliff, and won't get any sun. Maybe it's a fake of some kind." When they reached the summer-house, they saw that it had four wheels underneath it which were mounted on a set of rails.

105—They pushed, and the summer-house slid easily down the rails. Behind it was a cave—and in the cave were all the lost animals. The beasts' hoofs were swathed in sacking. Little wonder they had left no tracks. "The rogues," burst out Laird. "Maybe they intended to take them to the mainland and sell them." "I've a feeling there's more behind it than that," said Glenn. The two men tried to puzzle it out as they drove the beasts back to Corbie.

There's more than corn in the corn-bin

106—For the next few days Glenn and Laird saw no more of the mystery men, and were able to get on with the work around the croft. Then one morning a motor-boat came into the bay. In it were a police sergeant and a burly man wearing a bowler hat, who looked like a detective—and a nasty one, too. Glenn and Laird just couldn't imagine why they had come to Birsay. "What do you want?" asked Glenn as they helped the men ashore.

107—"We've come to search your croft," announced the detective in a bullying voice. "Information reached us that money stolen from a post office near Selkirk is hidden here." Glenn and Laird were thunderstruck. "That's nonsense," said Glenn. "We've nothing hidden, and you can look anywhere." "Right," said the detective. When they got to the croft the sergeant went straight to the corn-bin in the stable, and raked amongst the grain.

108—"I've found it, Mr Barr," he said. "The phone call was right." With that he held up a brief case. Glenn and Laird stared, baffled. But their bewilderment turned to alarm a minute later—the case was stuffed full of banknotes. Barr gave a satisfied smirk. "This money was stolen about the time you left Selkirk," he said. "We got a phone call telling us to search the corn-bin. So there's no doubt about it. You stole the money."

109—"That case must have been planted there by the people who are persecuting us," protested Glenn, and then told them all that had happened. The detective scoffed. He was going to arrest them, but the sergeant felt they should look at Dun House. They went round in the motor-boat, and made for the boy's bedroom. It had been emptied. Glenn was shaken, and for once paid no attention to Bob, who growled as he looked down the corridor.

110—Glenn and Laird were worried. They simply had to find some way of convincing this bumptious detective that their story was true. "I'll tell you what," said Glenn. "We'll show you where the animals were hidden." But when they got there another shock awaited them—there was no summer-house. Even the rails had been removed. It looked as if the mystery men were going to succeed at last in forcing Glenn and Laird to leave the island.

111—"Your story of mystery men is too far-fetched for my liking," jeered Barr. "You're coming with us in the boat for further questioning." As they went aboard the boat Laird sidled up to Glenn. "I'm sure the men are not far away," he whispered. "When we were in the boy's room Bob growled as if he'd heard a noise. Can't we do something?" "Yes," said Glenn. He pointed to the stairs. "Back, Bob," he ordered, and the wise collie ran off.

112—Bob hated leaving his master, but he was too well-trained to disobey an order, and his instinct told him that Glenn was in trouble. Bob was half-way up the stairs before Barr realised what was happening. "Hey, what's the big idea?" he shouted. "Surely you don't want Bob for further questioning?" mocked Glenn. "N-no, but what good's he going to do?" demanded the detective. "Wait and see," replied Glenn. "Just leave it to Black Bob."

113—"Bah," said Barr irritably. "Why would anyone try to drive you away from the island? It doesn't make sense. Do you think I'm dumb?" Glenn winked at Laird. "Come on, Nicol," went on Barr. "Get going. We've wasted enough time." But just as the boat left the pier, Glenn jumped to his feet excitedly. "D'you hear that?" he shouted. He could hear Bob barking somewhere on the clifftop. Then, as they listened, a shot rang out.

Bob's solo clash with the crooks

114—"Turn back." shouted Andrew Glenn. "Black Bob's in danger. He's found the men and they're shooting at him." "That was a revolver shot, right enough," said Nicol. "I think we should go back and see what's up," he went on, turning to Barr. "All right," said the detective gruffly. The sergeant swung the boat round and headed for the jetty. Glenn was first ashore, and he raced up the steps, anxious about Black Bob's safety.

115—Meanwhile, Black Bob was fighting for his life. In the yard he had found the two men dragging the boy back into Dun House. They had been hiding in the grounds and thought they had been successful in getting rid of Glenn and Laird—until they saw Bob. In desperation one of them fired wildly at the collie. Bob was on him like a flash. He was still struggling with them when Glenn, Laird and the two policemen came running up.

116—The men saw them coming and made a dash for the house. But they had to leave the little boy behind. Bob saw to that, for he got between the men and the boy and wouldn't let them near him. Glenn and the sergeant stopped to make sure that the boy wasn't hurt. He seemed to be unhurt, so they left him in Barr's care, and raced after the fleeing men, who were just disappearing through the main door of the big house.

117—As Glenn, Laird and Nicol reached it, the door shut with a slam and they heard a bolt rattling into place. Laird and the sergeant charged with their shoulders. But Glenn saw that the big iron-studded door was too solid to be forced open. A narrow window in the wall gave Glenn an idea. It was much too small for a man to get through, but Black Bob would manage. The shepherd lifted Bob and helped him to scramble through the window.

100

118—"Open the door, Bob," he ordered. The collie realized what was wanted. Back home in Selkirk, Glenn had trained him to open gates and doors, and now his master wanted this one opened. Bob landed in a small cloakroom, and from there he soon found his way into the hall. He ran over to the door and stood up on his hindlegs. Then he curled his paw round the head of the bolt and pulled it back. The door swung open and the men dashed in.

119—They searched every room, every attic, and even in the cupboard under the stairs, but there wasn't a sign of the men. They had completely vanished. "That's queer," said Laird, scratching his head. "But we have at least proved there are two strange men on the island. Now, do you believe our story?" "Yes," said Nicol. "And I'm convinced there must be a secret passage somewhere in this house. Let's see if the boy knows anything about it."

120—They hurried out through the back door and found the detective coming to meet them. "Did you find them?" Barr asked. "No," replied Glenn. "Never mind, we've got the boy safely locked up," said Barr proudly. "Trust me. He won't escape." "Where is he?" asked Glenn angrily. "He's no crook." Barr was taken aback. "We'll see about that," he said. "I've tied him up in that shed." Glenn's temper rose. "Get him out!" he snapped.

121—Barr opened the door of the outhouse. "There he——" Then he stopped. The boy wasn't there! Laird stifled a laugh. It was funny to see the look of sheer amazement on Barr's face. But Glenn was angry. This stupid detective had undone all Black Bob's good work. The mystery men had got hold of the little boy again. It was maddening, for Glenn felt the little chap, somehow, might provide the key to the whole mystery.

122—Unknown to the four men, there was a secret passage which led from the shed to Dun House and to the jetty. The two mystery men had nipped down this passage, recaptured the boy, and at this very moment were climbing into the police boat. It was Tom Laird who heard the engine starting. "Come on," he shouted suddenly. "They're down at the jetty." Everyone raced to the clifftop, only to find that the motor-boat had already left.

123—"Hurry," shouted Glenn. "We'll maybe catch them farther along." With Bob he led the race along the clifftop. By now the two policemen were convinced that there was something crooked about these two men and were anxious to catch them. But Glenn and the others couldn't keep pace with Black Bob. The collie was soon well in front and level with the motor-boat. Here the cliffs were only fifteen feet high, and as the boat passed Bob jumped.

124—The collie landed right on top of the man standing in the stern. It was the man with the black eye-patch. He staggered under Bob's weight then fell backwards, hitting his head such a thump on the deck that he lay there dazed. The man's body broke Bob's fall, and the collie turned on the second tough, who was standing at the wheel. The crook was scared. "Keep away," he shouted. But Bob did the very opposite. He kept harrying the man.

125—Meanwhile Glenn was running along the clifftop, trying to keep pace with the boat. At the same time he was anxiously watching the fight. There was no way of getting down to help his dog. And it looked as if Black Bob was going to have some trouble, for the one-eyed man was recovering. But as he began to get to his feet he suddenly gave a shout. "Look out," he yelled, pointing over the bow. "There's a rock ahead."

The twist of a wheel makes two crooks reel

126—The man at the wheel had been so busy keeping Bob at bay that he hadn't noticed the danger. Now the rock was only a few yards away. Frantically he swung the wheel to steer the boat away from the rock. Just then Black Bob flew at him and landed on the steersman's back. The man ducked, and Bob thrust out a paw to steady himself. His paw hit the wheel and the motor-boat swung round again, straight for the jagged rock.

127—The tough threw Bob off his shoulders and grabbed the wheel. He was too late. The motor-boat hit the rock with a grinding crash and a gaping hole was torn in the bows. The water poured in. Then the bows slid back off the rock and the boat began to sink. Black Bob had stopped the crooks in the only way possible—by wrecking the boat. But in doing so he had put the little boy in danger, for in the crash he had been thrown overboard.

128—Black Bob saw him struggling in the water trying to keep afloat. The collie dashed to the stern and started to bite and tear at the rope tying down the small lifebelt. There was no time to lose. The boy couldn't swim, and at any moment now the boat might sink, taking the lifebelt with it. Bob slashed desperately at the rope as he felt the water rising round his legs. At last it parted, and Black Bob was able to grasp the lifebelt between his jaws.

129—Bob shoved the lifebelt into the water near the little boy, who grabbed it eagerly. By the time he had wriggled into it Black Bob was in the water beside him, prodding the lifebelt along as he tried to push it towards the shore. Glenn and the others had managed to climb down to the water's edge, and they stood there, watching Bob battling shorewards. All except Detective Barr. "That dog's no use," he muttered. "I'm off to get a boat."

130—The detective was wrong. In spite of the swift currents swirling through the gap Black Bob made good progress. Glenn got into the water and was able to pull in the lifebelt. The boy was safe, but they still had to get hold of the two men clinging to the sinking boat. "I'll go and get a rope," said Sergeant Nicol. "There should be one in the boat-house." He hurried off, and in less than ten minutes he was back with a length of rope.

131—"What's Barr doing?" asked Glenn. Nicol smiled. "He's tinkering with the crooks' boat. We'll have them rescued before he gets it started." But it looked as if Nicol had spoken too soon. He couldn't throw the rope out as far as the boat. Finally Glenn took it from him. "Here, let Bob take it," he said. He put the end of the rope in Bob's mouth and pointed towards the men. Obediently the collie jumped in and started to swim out to the boat.

132—Black Bob paddled out to the men, and they clutched the rope eagerly before plunging into the water. Then Glenn and Nicol started to pull them to safety. Meanwhile the boy had been telling Laird how he came to be on this lonely island. His name was Tommy Matlock, and about two months ago these two men had kidnapped him from his home near Glasgow and brought him to Birsay. Ever since then he had been kept a prisoner in Dun House.

133—Sergeant Nicol looked grim as he heard this. "Looks like a kidnapping case," he said to Glenn. "The black dog, the stolen animals, and the planted money were meant to frighten you away from the island so that you wouldn't find out about the boy." By now the men were only a few yards from the shore. Glenn helped them out of the water, where the sergeant grabbed them. "We'll get the whole story later," he told them. "Meanwhile you're under arrest."

134—They marched the two men up the cliffs. Just as they reached the top they heard the sound of an engine down in the bay. Glenn looked down. There was Barr, standing in the stern of a motor-boat racing out to sea. It was the boat belonging to the crooks. "Help! The steering's jammed and I can't stop her," yelled Barr. "The fool," muttered Glenn. "Now we've only Tom's rowing-boat left to get over to the mainland."

135—There was nothing they could do to help Barr, so they went on up to Dun House. Here Tommy showed them the secret passage. In it they found the black mastiff chained to a wall near all the missing furniture. After that they went back to Corbie, where Mrs Laird soon had a meal ready for Tommy. There was no strong lock-up place on the croft to hold the crooks, so Glenn and Nicol rowed them and their dog out to a rocky islet for the night.

136—On the way Sergeant Nicol got their names. The one with the black patch on his eye was Joe Huggins; the other was Spike Dobson. How they raved when they were left on the little island. But Sergeant Nicol was firm. "The weather's warm. You'll come to no harm," he said. "Anyway, you'll be spending the next few years in a prison cell, so you'd better make the most of the fresh air.' With that they rowed away and left the crooks.

137—It was growing dark as they headed back for the pier. They were talking over the day's happenings when suddenly Nicol gave a shout. "Look, a ship. Let's signal to it." Glenn lit a hurricane lamp that was in the locker. Then he waved it to and fro. If they could get in touch with this ship it would save them a long journey to the mainland in the rowing-boat, for the captain could send wireless messages to report all that had happened, and to bring help.

138—Luck was with Glenn and Nicol. The look-out saw the lantern. Fifteen minutes later they were on board the ship watching the wireless operator tap out the startling message announcing the finding of Tommy Matlock. Within an hour there was a reply. "Police launch on the way. Sir Andrew Matlock arriving later by air." It was a great climax, for Tommy's father was none other than the famous inventor of the Matlock helicopter.

139—Tommy's disappearance was a sensation at the time, for Dobson and Huggins demanded a huge ransom for the boy. Sergeant Nicol made a note of Tommy's story when he got back to Corbie, then they all went to bed. Next morning a motor-boat arrived with Inspector Gray of Scotland Yard along with two assistants. "We found that fool Barr drifting in a motorboat," he said. "But he doesn't seem to want to tell us how he got there."

140—"No wonder," said Sergeant Nicol. Then he reported all that had happened. "This means a long prison sentence for Huggins and Dobson," said the Scotland Yard man when he heard the whole story, "and a ticking-off for Barr." The police left shortly after, and on their way back to the mainland, picked up Huggins and Dobson from the islet. About an hour later a strange machine flew over and landed near the croft. It was a Matlock helicopter.

141—Out of the aircraft stepped Tommy's father and mother, and there was a very happy reunion between Tommy and his parents. Matlock was a fine type of man, and he thanked Glenn and the Lairds for what they had done. Then little Tommy pointed out that it was really the sheepdog who had saved him, so Black Bob got a special word of thanks. After that they all went into the house and had a long talk over a cup of tea.

The end of the tale

142—Sir Andrew was a wealthy man, and he had good ideas on how to reward the Lairds for helping to rescue Tommy. He wanted to help them in their struggle on the island farm. He had a quiet word with Andrew Glenn, and so when the Matlocks left for the mainland Glenn and Bob were in the helicopter with them. As the plane hovered over Corbie they waved good-bye to the Lairds and to Birsay—the place that was no longer an island of mystery.

143—They landed at an airfield near Sir Andrew's home in Glasgow. Then the inventor took Bob and Glenn to a big motor show-room. His idea was to present Tom Laird with a brand new tractor. "My wife is buying some things for Mrs Laird," he said. "I'd like you to take them to Birsay." Glenn agreed to do this. Next day he and Bob caught the boat for Birsay with the tractor and a huge wooden packing-case full of presents.

144—They reached the island, and there was great excitement when the Lairds opened the crate. There was a shotgun for Tom, a watch and a string of pearls for Mrs Laird, a doll and pram for Peggy, and many other things that would provide comfort for them on Birsay. Once the excitement died down Glenn told Laird the latest news. The police had proved that Dobson and Huggins robbed the post office near Selkirk. Then in a desperate attempt to get Glenn and Laird arrested and taken away from the island, they had planted some of the stolen banknotes in the stables. As a result, they were being charged with robbery as well as kidnapping. "Well," said Laird, patting Bob's head, "they won't bother anyone for a long time, thanks to Black Bob." A few days later Glenn and Bob left Birsay on the long journey back to Selkirk—but they were to return again to this island of adventure.

THE FEUD AT THE CLATTERING CRAGS

TWO TROUBLE-MAKERS

Black Bob and his master were hurrying homewards on the path that ran along the foot of the Clattering Crags and led straight down the glen. They were returning from a visit to old Sandy Henderson, the aged shepherd who lived a couple of miles up this way; and Andrew Glenn wanted to be home by tea-time.

Suddenly Black Bob went off at a run. He had glimpsed the long ears of a hare, and he went after the animal like a shot from a gun.

"Run him down, Bob!" called Glenn, with a grin. "Catch him, lad, and you'll be sure of a good supper when we get home!"

But Bob hadn't a chance, and Glenn knew it. The hare had too much of a start, and when it rounded a bend and turned up-hill, it was safe.

Bob went flashing round the bend in hot pursuit—and then he slithered to a sudden and violent stop. Ahead was something that took his mind clean off the hare. It was a dog—a big brown dog, standing on the brink of a burn. It was a stranger to the district, a dog which Bob had never seen before.

It was obviously a working sheepdog, and it was barking and growling at a fat ewe which had fallen into the burn that foamed down the steep hillside. The sheep was one belonging to Farmer Ross, whose lands stretched to this corner of the glen. It was not often that Farmer Ross's sheep wandered right over here, but the ewe was evidently a stray that had fallen into the burn.

The sheepdog's snapping and snarling only frightened the ewe and kept it from scrambling out of the burn by itself.

Black Bob moved forward, and then paused, uncertain what to do. He could have got the sheep out, but this other dog was going the wrong

The surly shepherd and the snarly sheepdog

way about it. The dog was a big, fine-looking animal except for his rather wicked eyes and ragged ears. He looked a fighter who had been often in the wars.

The dog spied Black Bob, and leaped up the bank at once, snarling savagely. Bob saw that the sheep was in trouble, so he stood his ground. The brown dog came at him with a rush. Bob had no intention of getting mixed up in a fight, and now he merely turned his shoulder to the charging animal. Bob caught the dog a glancing blow and sent him staggering.

That seemed to make the brown dog angrier than ever, for he spun around and snapped at Bob's tail. Bob faced him with a low, warning growl.

The brown dog flattened himself to the ground, ready to spring. And that was the moment when Andrew Glenn came round the bend in the path. As soon as he saw what was happening, Glenn gave the low whistle that called Black Bob to heel. The brown dog made another rush as Bob trotted to his master's side, but Bob nimbly avoided him. The shepherd let out an angry shout:

"You're a fierce brute, aren't you? Go on—off you go!"

He waved his arms and stick, and the brown collie circled, still snarling. Then Andrew Glenn caught sight of the sheep in the burn and hastened towards it. Kneeling on the bank, he gripped its fleece with his strong hands and pulled it out of the water on to firm ground. It slumped down on the grass and lay there panting, too exhausted to move.

"So you don't know your job, eh?" said the shepherd. "No well-trained sheepdog would leave a ewe there and start fighting."

There was the sound of heavy footsteps behind them, and a harsh voice growled:

"What's this about my dog? There's no better one in the country. Mac's a dog in a thousand, let me tell ye!"

Both Bob and his master turned in surprise. They found themselves looking at a short, thickset man with a red face and close-cropped hair. He had a broken nose, and his mouth was drawn in a grim line. He was dressed in a grubby, well-worn raincoat, a thick tweed cap, and he carried a stick.

"Hullo!" said Andrew Glenn in a friendly way. "You'll be Duncan Hogg, Farmer Ross's new shepherd? Glad to meet you. My name's Glenn."

He held out his hand, but the other man ignored it. There was a sneer on his lips as he pointed with his stick at Bob.

"If you're Glenn, then that must be the famous Black Bob," he growled. "I'm sick and tired of hearing people praising that dog. And now that I've seen him, I don't think much of him."

THE FLOCK IN DANGER

Hogg chewed tobacco all the time he talked. The brown dog remained crouching at a distance, showing his teeth at Glenn and Bob. The new shepherd and his dog were somewhat alike; both were quick-tempered and touchy.

"Oh, I don't know," replied Andrew Glenn, good-humouredly. "Bob must be a pretty good sheepdog, you know, when he has twice won the Championship of Britain at sheepdog trials."

He spoke with quiet pride, but the other shepherd merely snorted.

"Trials!" he growled. "I wouldn't give sixpence for a trial dog! They're no good for real work on the hills. Over rough country, Mac is the best dog living. We don't waste our time going to trials."

It sounded as though he was trying to pick a quarrel. But Andrew Glenn was not the quarrelling kind.

"Every man to his taste," Glenn said. "By the way, that ewe of yours has been in trouble. I think you ought to have a look at it. I'll give you a hand if you like."

Duncan Hogg's eyes flashed. The two dogs were growling at each other, although Bob did not leave his master's side.

"I need no help, thanks!" the man snapped. "Just leave Mac and me alone—that's all I ask, Glenn!"

"Just as you like," said Andrew Glenn. "But we're bound to meet sometimes on the hills, since our flocks are on neighbouring farms. And I think we ought to be friends. By the way, where are you living? I didn't know Farmer Ross had a spare cottage."

"I've got a cottage all right!" growled Hogg. "I'm living in Greendykes Cottage at the foot of the crags."

Glenn gave a whistle of surprise.

Twenty tons come tumbling down

"Greendykes Cottage!" he said. "I wouldn't feel comfortable in that place, Hogg. The crags aren't safe. There are often rock falls around the cottage, and I remember some years ago, one corner of the roof was smashed in. These crags are well named—and I'd ask to be put somewhere else, if I were you."

"Why don't you mind your own business?" snapped Hogg. "Just because you've lived for a few years in this district you think you know all about it. I can take care of myself without a lot of advice from you."

His tone was heated. Andrew Glenn turned on his heel at once, and snapped his fingers for Bob. It was useless to talk further with a hasty, hot-tempered fellow like Hogg.

Bob watched the other dog out of the corner of his eye, but followed his master. He knew the dog was longing for a fight.

"And the next time you find my dog standing guard over a sheep, just mind your own business!" shouted Hogg.

Glenn did not turn his head. He merely shrugged his shoulders, and muttered to Black Bob:

"It's a pity that Farmer Ross had to employ a man like that, Bob. No doubt he's a good shepherd, but his tongue and his temper will get him into trouble one day."

Presently Glenn and Bob came in sight of Duncan Hogg's cottage. It was a pleasant, old house facing across the glen. But at the back of the cottage was a great, rugged crag of grey rock that rose steeply to quite a height. It cast a sinister shadow on Greendykes Cottage.

Glenn's eyes swept upward to the grassy brow, and his glance lit upon

The cliff face suddenly broke away and a huge mass of rock came crashing down from the Clattering Crags.

half a dozen sheep grazing on a green patch among the crags. Almost at the same moment, a dull, rumbling sound reached his ears. One of the sheep had dislodged a big boulder, which went bounding down the slope towards the other sheep, and sweeping a shower of smaller rocks along in its wake.

Instinctively, Glenn's hand went up in a signal to Bob, and the collie bounded forward. But the sheep were a long way off, and the danger was over within a few seconds of Glenn's spotting it. Heads went up in the little flock, and then the sheep bolted. Fortunately, a few steps carried them out of the path of the landslide, but they scattered in wild alarm as the rumbling went on, and the dust rose in a cloud. Several feet of the crag cracked away when the boulder hit it, and about twenty tons of stones and earth went crashing down into the glen, less than thirty yards from Hogg's cottage.

Black Bob was far up the steep hill by now, heading for the scattered sheep. The landslide was over, but he herded the sheep together, and drove them down on to the moorland in the glen, where they would be safe from any further landslides.

Glenn strode on his way, but as he went he ran his eye over the beetling Clattering Crags, and followed the sweep of the steep rock wall down to where Greendykes Cottage nestled at the foot. Here and there on the land all round were dotted great boulders which had fallen from above. And the more Glenn looked at the cottage, the less he liked it.

Meanwhile, Black Bob came romping back, his good job done, and his master stooped to fondle his ears for a moment.

"Well done, Bob," he said. "But Greendykes Cottage is even more unsafe than I thought it was. Until Duncan Hogg moved in, it stood empty for years. I'm afraid a big landslide will bury it one day. I must warn Hogg when I see him again, though I don't suppose he'll listen to me."

Glenn and Bob continued on their way, and when he came in sight of the pleasant little cottage where they lived, Glenn forgot all about the quarrelsome shepherd and his fierce, brown dog.

During the next week or so Andrew Glenn and Black Bob twice passed Hogg driving sheep up the glen. Each time Glenn tried to warn Hogg of his danger—but the hot-tempered shepherd refused to listen.

THE MIX-UP IN THE MIST

Then came the day when a sudden mist blotted out the hills, and Hogg decided to drive his flock down to a field near his cottage. While he went off to round up some strays, he set his dog to drive the others down to the road at the foot of the hill.

Andrew Glenn was driving some of his own flock along the road with Black Bob's help, when out of the mist dashed about twenty of Hogg's sheep. Driven on by Mac's excited barking, they rushed among Andrew Glenn's flock.

There was a sudden growl from Black Bob, and he dashed to try to cut out the intruders before they could get completely mixed up with his master's flock. Bob seemed to know every one of Glenn's sheep and he set about sorting out the strangers, driving them a little way down the slope, a few at a time, then doubling back for more.

Mac should have remained in charge of his own sheep as Bob sorted them out, but instead he dashed after Bob, barking furiously all the time. As a result, there was a panic among the sheep, and they began to scatter in all directions.

Then someone came striding out of the mist. It was Duncan Hogg, his eyes blazing angrily.

"Are you trying to make off with my sheep?" he demanded.

"Oh, don't be a fool," snapped Glenn. "Your dog drove some of your sheep in among mine. Now Bob is trying to get them out. Why doesn't your dog stand by and guard your sheep as Bob fetches them to him? Doesn't Mac know better than to frighten the sheep?"

The man stopped and glared.

"Mac knows what he's doing, which is more than your show specimen does! Maybe Black Bob has won a few prizes, but not for real work. I'd challenge you to a test if I thought you had the spirit to accept!"

"It's test enough to see them at work now," Glenn said. "Your dog's making the job twice as difficult as it ought to be. If he'd leave Bob alone you'd have all your sheep back in a few minutes."

Hogg fairly bristled.

"What rubbish!" he snorted. "Mac's the finest sheepdog in Scotland. Black Bob is all polish and fancy style. When it comes to a good hard day on the hills——"

Down the hill like a bullet from a gun

"Bob would run him off his feet!" snapped Glenn, stung to the defence of his dog.

Suddenly a solitary sheep came rushing out of the mist and went charging headlong down the hillside. At the bottom there was a steep drop into the river. It looked as though the animal would plunge right over the edge.

Hogg shouted for his dog, but it was Black Bob who went down the hillside like a shot from a gun. It seemed as though he would go headlong into the river, but he pulled up on the very brink of the drop and swung across in the path of the runaway sheep. He crouched and fixed it with his eyes. Several times the sheep tried to swerve away, but each time it found Black Bob facing it. Very cleverly Bob drove it back to the rest of the flock. He had saved it without uttering a bark or frightening it in any way.

"See that?" said Glenn. "That was a champion at work."

"I'd put my money on Mac," growled Hogg. "What about a match between the two dogs for a stake of five quid, Glenn?"

"Nothing doing," said Andrew Glenn. "Bob took part in a couple of competitions only last week and he needs a good rest. Anyway I don't bet—"

"Not when there's a real sheepdog around to challenge your precious Black Bob, eh?" sneered Hogg, and he whistled for Mac to drive the sheep down the road.

Mac got the sheep on the move very quickly. But he snapped at an old ewe which was slow in getting off the mark. Glenn saw tufts of wool flying.

"See that!" he cried. "In a sheepdog trial a dog would lose points or be disqualified for doing that."

Hogg snorted and hastened away. The mist swallowed him up, and for some time afterwards the bleating of sheep and the barking of his dog could be heard. Andrew Glenn waited so as to let the other flock get well ahead before he and Bob drove their sheep down the road. He did not want to have any more trouble with Hogg.

A couple of days later Farmer Grant stopped Andrew Glenn as he and Black Bob came from their cottage after breakfast.

"Good-morning, Glenn! What sort of a dog has Ross's new shepherd got?"

"It's a good sheepdog—but rather rough and fierce. It upsets the sheep more than it ought to, but it's a hard worker."

"Well, Hogg has been urging me to run a competition between the two dogs. He was talking about it to me in Selkirk last night. He says that under working conditions a dog like Bob, who has been trained for sheepdog trials, would come off second best."

"Hogg is talking through his hat," said Glenn. "I'd like to knock some of the wind out of him. But Black Bob has been taking part in too many sheepdog trials recently and he needs a long rest."

"That's a pity, for I agreed to a trial next Saturday afternoon," said Grant. "I've put up a stake of ten pounds, and Hogg has done the same. Surely Bob will win? He's never been beaten yet."

"I'm sorry you've done this, Mr Grant," replied the shepherd. "I don't like the idea. But if you've gone and fixed everything, I can't let you down, and Bob will do his best to win."

"Good man!" exclaimed Farmer Grant. "We've fixed up for Alex Sinclair, the sheepdog trial judge, to come over from Stirling and give the decision. It will be all fair and square. Bob will get an honest deal."

Black Bob pricked up his ears at sound of his name. Farmer Grant patted Bob's head and went on his way, well pleased with the prospect of some excitement the following Saturday.

On Saturday morning Black Bob and his master were working as usual. At midday a car came up the glen with Alexander Sinclair, the famous judge of sheepdog trials, and two of his friends. They went to Farmer Grant's house, and shortly afterwards Farmer Ross and some of his friends arrived.

Over the top of the hill, between the two farms, a course had been marked out. It was over very rough ground, and would test the dogs more than the average sheepdog trial. Hurdles had been erected and some pens had been put up to hold the sheep.

Until Glenn and Bob climbed the hill in the early afternoon they did not know what the course would be like. But when Bob saw the hurdles and the pens and the gate he knew what was afoot. He held his head higher, and his eyes sparkled. He loved competitions.

The other shepherd and his dog were already there, and since they had been working on that part of the hill during the morning, Mac was no doubt familiar with the layout by now.

The test of the hurdles and pens

Two small flocks of sheep had been brought there and were now in pens. Judge Sinclair walked around and satisfied himself that everything was as it should be. Then he called the two men together and explained that the dogs were to do the kind of work they did every day, and in similar surroundings.

The shepherds tossed for choice of flocks and Hogg won. He picked out the sheep from one pen and these were driven about half a mile away and left to graze in a hollow.

When they had settled down Hogg gave Mac the signal, and the brown dog flashed off towards the sheep. For a time Mac vanished from sight, and then he reappeared on the far side of the flock. The watching men heard him bark, and the sheep began to move, rather slowly at first, but speeding up when Mac began to hustle them.

About a hundred yards from the pens there was a steep, sandy bank with a drop of five or six feet to the moor below. It was part of the test to drive the sheep over this.

Mac drove them towards it, never slackening speed for an instant. Normally the sheep would have stopped to look for the easiest way down, but Mac never gave them a chance. He was right on their heels, barking so fiercely that the beasts were panic-stricken. Two of them plunged over the edge, missed their footing, and tumbled to the ground below.

The watching men gasped. Mac was quick, but many felt he had been too quick. No farmer liked his sheep to be treated in that fashion. As it was, the two that fell were limping badly as Mac drove them nearer to the pen.

Hogg moved to the gate and opened it. By whistles alone he got Mac to drive the sheep in through the gate, and this part of the test was done neatly and well. Mac took eight minutes to round up the sheep and drive them into the pen. It was quick work.

Black Bob had waited patiently all this time, but now he looked at his master. The second lot of sheep were let loose and the signal given. Away went Bob in a wide circle that would take him over the hill and round behind the sheep.

As soon as Bob came into view again, he got the sheep on the move. Quickly and expertly he drove them towards the waiting men. Bob did not utter a sound, and it was a joy to see the way he kept the sheep in a small, compact bunch.

Glenn and Bob watched Mac, Bob's rival, driving the sheep over the bank. He frightened them so badly that two of them fell.

When Bob came to the bank he slowed down. The sheep hesitated on the brink, but Bob did not rush them. He circled, gently coaxing the beasts forward until they jumped down the bank.

Bob lost a few seconds here, but at least all the sheep were uninjured and that was important.

Andrew Glenn opened the gate, and Black Bob headed the sheep towards it. Nearer and nearer they came—and then in the last few yards an unlucky thing happened.

A covey of partridges rose from the grass with a sudden fluttering of wings and a chorus of cries—right in front of the sheep.

Mac is quick and breezy: Bob takes it easy

It happened with such startling suddenness that even Black Bob was taken by surprise. As for the sheep, they got the shock of their lives. They panicked, and fled from the spot.

It was a bad set-back for Bob. But in record time he rounded the flock up again, returned with them, and drove them into the pen.

His time was eight minutes and ten seconds—ten seconds longer than Mac took. But the judge said they would each be given ten points because Mac had barked, and Bob had worked in silence.

Meantime, three sheep had been turned loose and allowed to wander right out of sight. Mac was sent after these, and in due course came back with three exhausted-looking animals. One of them had a fleck of blood

Black Bob was putting up a great show in the sheepdog trials. Suddenly a covey of partridges rose with a loud noise and the sheep scattered in alarm.

on its leg. He had been hurrying the sheep by nipping with his teeth. The judge frowned and penalised him one point.

HOGG IN A HUFF

Then it was again Black Bob's turn. Three more sheep had been turned loose and Bob was entirely on his own when he went to round them up. He took a little longer than Mac, but when he returned, all the straying sheep were trotting along in good condition, and again the judge awarded him full marks. That put Bob one point ahead of Duncan Hogg's dog.

Between his turns, Black Bob sat down quietly, but Hogg and Mac paced nervously up and down. They were both rather jumpy.

Hogg didn't have such a cool, clear head as Andrew Glenn. He made more noise, waved his arms about more, and was apt to get flustered and lose his temper. Mac had the fault of snapping and frightening his charges, but he was a very quick worker.

Black Bob needed no more than the lift of a finger or the faintest of whistles to tell him what his master wanted. He never snarled or snapped. He moved about with the swiftness of a shadow.

Black Bob had bad luck in the next test. When Bob was driving sheep into a pen, one ewe became panic-stricken and ran. When Bob turned it back, it injured its leg on the gate-post. That was not Bob's fault, but he had to pay the penalty—forfeiting one point. Bob and Mac now had exactly the same number of points.

Duncan Hogg looked grim. This wasn't to be the walk-over he had imagined it would be.

The toughest test of all was when eight sheep were put in a pen, four with bows of ribbon round their necks and four without any distinguishing marks. The sheepdogs had to pick out the sheep with the bows and drive them back to their masters.

Mac had the first go. Guided by whistles from Duncan Hogg, he picked out four sheep and drove them up to his master. But when the sheep were examined it was found that he had brought three with bows and one without.

That lost him a point. But Hogg was looking pleased, for he knew that his dog had done pretty well.

"Let's see Black Bob do any better!" he challenged.

Andrew Glenn ignored the challenge, but gave Bob the necessary orders. Away Bob went—and back he came with four sheep, all with bows round their necks. Duncan Hogg's face fell.

"Black Bob is the winner," announced Alex. Sinclair. "Even if he hadn't beaten Mac in the last test, I would have awarded the prize to him because of the smoothness of his work. There was real class in his performance."

"I knew it! I knew the local man would win!" snorted Duncan Hogg. "As soon as the name of Black Bob is mentioned, the judges lose their commonsense. Come on, Mac!"

He gave his dog a push with his foot, and stalked away down the glen in the direction of his cottage.

Andrew Glenn shook his head.

"Hogg needs a good fright to bring him to his senses," he said. "I believe he'd be a good chap if he'd only stop imagining that everybody is up against him. He honestly believed that Mac was the real winner, and that Bob was favoured."

"Then he's all wrong!" snapped Sinclair, as they made for the road. "He's a bad loser. I don't know why you employ him, Ross!"

"I can't get anyone else," confessed the farmer, "and he's a hard worker."

ENTOMBED!

Presently the men from Stirling drove away in their car, and Glenn and Bob walked along to their cottage. Farmer Grant wanted to give Glenn a share of his winnings, but Bob's master wouldn't take the money.

In fact, he wasn't too happy about the afternoon's work. He feared he had made an enemy of Duncan Hogg.

"I wish we'd never taken part in the trial, Bob," he said, over his tea. "The glen is too small for Hogg to live here hating us. I wish there was some way of making friends with him. What's that? Thunder?"

Bob's ears had come up sharply. Away in the distance they could hear a loud rumbling, crashing noise. It had been hot and stuffy all the afternoon. Glenn felt sure it was thunder.

But Black Bob was cocking his ears as if he were puzzled by the sounds. When his master settled down in a chair with his newspaper, Bob slipped out of the back door, and hurried down the glen.

Since Hogg came to live at Greendykes Cottage in the shadow of Clattering Crags, Bob always kept away from that end of the glen, although it had once been one of his favourite hunting-grounds for rabbits. But this evening Black Bob was drawn to the crags by some strange feeling inside him. He jumped a stream, and gained the footpath leading to Greendykes Cottage. When he came in sight of the little stone-built cottage, he stared with wide-open eyes.

Something had happened to the cottage. One end of it had disappeared beneath a great mound of earth and rocks. Part of the crag had fallen down and buried it. The noise Glenn and Bob had heard was the crashing down of hundreds of tons of rock.

As Black Bob drew nearer, he saw the full amazing sight. A mass of earth and stones was piled thirty feet high over one end of the cottage, and even the chimneys were buried beneath it.

Black Bob sniffed as he ran to and fro among the stones and rubble. Then all of a sudden, he began to bark loudly.

Someone was inside the buried cottage. Bob fancied he could hear a faint whining. He began to dig desperately.

Earth and stones flew out behind him. He worked at full speed, but the mound of rubble was so great that he made very little impression on it. He must fetch his master.

Bob turned and raced away at top speed.

It was quite a long way to his master's cottage, and Bob was breathing heavily long before he got there. But he did not spare himself. He leapt everything in his path, and did not even wait to open the garden gate. Straight over the top he went, and raced up to the front door.

The door was shut, but he could hear the rustle of his master's newspaper inside. Up on his hindlegs went Bob, and raised the latch with his nose. His weight did the rest. The door swung inwards, Bob landed on all fours, and went panting towards the chair where Andrew Glenn was sitting reading.

The shepherd had removed his boots and was wearing his slippers. Black Bob gave a short, sharp bark, and Glenn looked up in surprise.

Bobs 15-minute race with 15 urgent words

"What's the matter, Bob? What's all the excitement about?"

Bob barked sharply again and then picked up the boots from the side of the fireplace, and dropped them at Glenn's feet.

"What's the trouble? You want me to put on my boots and come out?" said Glenn, as Bob watched him with pleading eyes. "Some trouble with the sheep? Is that it, Bob?"

He began to pull on his boots, while Bob ran to the door, barking as if urging him to hurry.

Andrew Glenn felt fairly certain that something was wrong with the sheep, but once outside his cottage, Black Bob led him away from the fields where they were grazing and turned down the path leading to the Clattering Crags.

The shepherd was hot and panting by the time he turned the bend in the path, and came in sight of Greendykes Cottage. He stopped and gaped for a moment, then he broke into a run.

"A landslide—the very thing I feared!" he gasped. "The cottage is half-buried. This is what Bob wanted to show me. What on earth's become of Hogg and Mac?"

While Glenn scrambled among the rubble, wondering if anyone could be alive, Black Bob went to work. He made for the spot where he had heard the whimpering of the buried sheepdog, and began to dig at top speed.

His master saw him and came to his side.

"Is there someone alive in there, Bob?" he cried. "Hi, Hogg, are you there? Is anyone there?"

He got no reply, but he thought he heard a faint tapping sound. He hunted around until he found a shovel, but it was not much help. He knew he could not move all this rubble single-handed.

Calling Black Bob to him, he took an old envelope and a stump of pencil from his pocket. On the back of the envelope he scribbled:

Landslide at Greendykes Cottage. Come with every man you've got. Bring picks and shovels.—Glenn.

Tucking the envelope into Bob's collar, he pointed down the glen.

"Go to Farmer Grant's. Good boy, go—hurry!"

Away went Black Bob with the speed of a hare.

GLENN'S DARING DEED

The collie took all the short cuts that he knew, but it was at least fifteen minutes later before he arrived at the Grant Farm. Farmer Grant and his family were sitting down to supper when the dog burst in upon them and started a furious barking.

Something was obviously wrong. They jumped to their feet, wondering what it could be. Then someone saw the envelope sticking out from Bob's collar and removed it. When the message was read there was a rush for tools, while Grant hurriedly got out the car.

The farmer and his men piled into the car, and Black Bob jumped up beside them. Away they went as fast as the roads would allow, past Bob's home, and down the main road to where the footpath branched off it.

They could drive no farther than that. There they got out of the car and hurried along, carrying the tools over their shoulders.

When the men got close enough to see what had happened there were whistles of amazement, for no sound of the landslide had been heard at the farm.

Andrew Glenn had stripped to the waist and was digging furiously.

"I believe there is somebody alive in there," he gasped. "We must get them out before they suffocate. It may be the dog, but I thought I heard a man's voice."

The newcomers began to dig with picks and shovels. Tons of earth and boulders were thrown to one side, and the grey stone wall of the cottage came in sight.

Now they could hear Duncan Hogg calling weakly. His dog was whimpering. Hogg called out that one of the beams from the roof had fallen on him, pinning him helplessly to the floor.

The rescuers were careful to prop up their tunnel with logs of wood as they dug towards the trapped man. They did not want another fall to bury them all.

The farmhands sweated and slaved, and at last there was a gap through which Black Bob squirmed. He found himself in what had been the cottage kitchen. The roof had fallen in, and under a heavy wooden beam lay Duncan Hogg. His dog was pinned under the upturned armchair, but seemed more frightened than hurt.

Tons of rubble - but no pick, no shovel

Bob made his way across the wreckage to where Mac was trapped. He licked the brown dog's face with his warm red tongue. This time Mac did not snarl. Instead he licked Bob's ear.

Bob turned now to Duncan Hogg and began tugging at his clothing, hoping to free him. But it was hopeless. Bob could do nothing until Glenn arrived.

There was a fall of stones a few minutes later, but the tunnel still held. At last the hole was enlarged and Andrew Glenn scrambled through into the kitchen. His heart sank when he saw the great wooden beam that lay across Duncan Hogg's back. That would take some moving—and time was precious. A sudden shifting of the rubble might bring down the roof and bury them all.

Glenn saw, too, that he would have to get Hogg out with only Black

Bob to help him, for there was no room for anyone else in the wrecked kitchen.

"I'm going to raise that beam," said Glenn to Hogg. "And then Black Bob will drag you out. Are you in pain?"

Hogg gritted his teeth.

"I think I've broken a rib," he said. "Hurry, Glenn, hurry!"

"All right, Bob!" said Glenn to his faithful sheepdog. "Get ready to drag Hogg out, lad, when I lift this beam."

Bob gave an answering bark. Glenn stooped and got his shoulder under the beam. Then he strove to lift it clear of the helpless Hogg.

Very, very slowly the huge, wooden beam started to rise.

The blood was pounding in Glenn's head, his back felt like breaking, and the strain seemed to be tearing his muscles apart. But he exerted all

Black Bob tugged desperately at Duncan Hogg's jacket to try to free him as his master raised the beam clear of the injured man.

Glenn and Hogg; Mac and Bob – all the best of pals

his strength, and at last raised the beam clear of Hogg.

"Now, Bob!" Glenn gasped. "Get him out now, Bob. Hurry!"

Black Bob needed no urging. He gripped Hogg by the coat collar and began dragging him towards the tunnel. It was hard work moving a heavy man like Hogg, but desperation drove Bob on.

At last Black Bob got Hogg within reach of the rescuers in the tunnel and willing hands seized the shepherd. When they carried him out to safety he lay limp and senseless in their hands.

A few moments later Andrew Glenn and Black Bob appeared. The shepherd was carrying Mac in his arms. The dog was bruised and frightened, but not badly hurt.

Hogg was soon on his way to a hospital near Selkirk in an ambulance. Before he left, he had a few words with Grant and asked the farmer to look after Mac until his return.

This Farmer Grant did. And long before Hogg came back from the hospital, Bob and Mac had become friends. Perhaps Mac knew that it was Bob who brought help to himself and his master in the buried cottage. Anyway, they became the best of pals—and they often went on a rabbit hunt together after the day's work was done.

Duncan Hogg was a changed man. His narrow escape from death knocked all the cockiness and the bad temper out of him. He was most grateful to Glenn, and apologised for his previous bad behaviour.

Farmer Ross gave him a room in the farmhouse during the building of another cottage, and often Hogg would come down to supper at Glenn's home.

While the two shepherds were talking by the fire in the cosy lamp-lit room, their two dogs would either sleep side by side on the hearthrug, or go off in search of a rabbit. Their feud was forgotten, and peace reigned in the glen all the way from the Clattering Crags down to Andrew Glenn's cottage and the Selkirk road.

BLACK BOB'S BIG JOB

IN a lonely valley near the market town of Selkirk there stands a little stone cottage. It is not a big cottage; the windows are small and the furniture is old-fashioned. But to Black Bob, the champion sheepdog, it is the best cottage in the world—it is home. All the year round Bob lives there with his master, Andrew Glenn, tending the sheep on the hills and guarding them from foxes, wild cats and sheep-stealers. Sometimes Bob and his master take part in the sheepdog trials, for Bob is a famous winner at the many trials held up and down the country. In fact, there is hardly a cup he has not won at one time or another. Occasionally Farmer Grant, Glenn's employer, sends the shepherd and his dog off on a job that takes them away from home for a few days or even weeks. It may be to buy some sheep, or just to help out a farmer who is in trouble. But whatever the job is, Farmer Grant knows that Black Bob and Andrew Glenn will not let him down.

One day Grant hailed Glenn as the shepherd was passing the farmhouse. "I've got a big job for you," he said. "I've just had a letter from your old friend, Tom Laird. He's got four prize sheep he wants me to buy. Would you go to Birsay and bring them back?" Glenn did not take long to make up his mind. "Yes," he said. Both Glenn and Grant knew Laird well. Some years before, Tom had left the Selkirk district to take up farming on Birsay, a lonely island off the west coast of Scotland. Glenn had only seen him once since then, so he was glad of this chance to go and visit his friend. Next day Glenn and Bob set off. They went to Glasgow, and from there took a train for the Highlands. It was late before they arrived at the little seaport from which the boats left for Birsay, so Glenn and Bob spent the night in a hotel. Next morning they boarded the boat and it set sail for Birsay. Glenn and Bob did not know it, but they were off on another thrilling adventure

121

2—When Andrew Glenn and Black Bob arrived at Birsay, Tom Laird was waiting on the jetty to meet them. He gave Bob and Glenn a hearty welcome, then they all went to the croft for a meal. Later Tom took Bob and his master into the hills. There was a ram roaming wild there, and Tom, being lame, couldn't round it up, so he asked Glenn to try. The shepherd borrowed Tom's telescope and scanned the hills for some sign of the ram.

3—It would be ten days before the steamer returned to pick up Glenn, Bob and the four prize sheep, but Glenn was not worried about the delay. Instead, he was looking forward to spending the time helping his cripple friend. Yard by yard Glenn scanned the ground, and soon he spotted the ram grazing at the bottom of some crags. Bob and the two men set off across the valley towards it. As they drew near, the shepherd motioned Bob forward.

4—For nearly two years now that ram had been roaming over the island as it pleased. Its fleece was long and shaggy. It was wild right enough—and wary. Whenever it saw Bob it was off like a shot. Bob raced after it, trying to head it back to the croft. Given a straight run in open country, no doubt Bob would have succeeded. But right in front of them was a cliff. The ram reached it first and scrambled up on to a narrow ledge. Bob followed.

5—Along the ledge the chase continued, winding higher and higher up the cliff face. Then suddenly the ledge came to an abrupt stop. The ram turned at bay with its head lowered. But from down below Glenn saw what was happening. He realised that if there was a struggle up there on the ledge both Bob and the ram might be hurt. Glenn gave a short whistle. It was the signal to come to heel. Obediently the collie turned away from the ram.

The sheepdog in sheep's clothing

6—"Let's go back to the croft," said Glenn. "I know how we can catch it. All we need is an old sheepskin and some rope." They returned to the croft and Tom found a sheepskin. Glenn draped it carefully over Bob's back, then they set off back to the hills, with Tom carrying a length of rope with a stick tied to one end. The idea was that Bob would have to get this stick and the rope tangled up in the ram's horns so that it could be recaptured.

7—When they got back to the cliff they found that the ram had descended from the ledge. "Go on, Bob," whispered Glenn, and he pointed to a rock beside the ram. The ram looked up as Bob approached, then went on grazing—it thought Bob was a sheep. The collie stealthily climbed the far side of the rock until he was directly above the ram. Glenn whistled. It was a signal telling Bob to drop whatever he was carrying. At once Bob dropped the rope.

8—As the rope fell down over the ram's horns Glenn tugged at the end he was holding. He gave a shout. "It's worked, Tom. The stick has caught in its horns." The ram was caught. It kicked and struggled, but it was no use. Glenn pulled hard on the rope, and this kept the stick jammed in the ram's horns. Bob jumped down from the rock and ran to his master's side. His job was done, so he started to shake himself free of his sheepskin disguise.

9—Glenn twisted the rope more securely round the ram's horns before setting off back to the croft. It was a tough struggle, with the ram fighting for its freedom all the way. But at length they got it securely penned. "It should be all right now," said Glenn. "A few weeks in the pen will get it used to human beings again, and it will quieten down." And Glenn was right. There was no more trouble from the wild rebel ram of Birsay.

10—Black bob and Andrew Glenn, his master, were used to working in all kinds of weather. But never had they encountered a gale such as the one that struck Birsay Island a few days after their arrival. The storm came whistling in from the Atlantic with hurricane force. Black Bob was nearly bowled over; Glenn's cap went swirling away. Worst of all, Mrs Laird's washing was whisked off the clothes line as if clutched by some invisible hand.

11—"Go on, Bob," Glenn shouted, pointing to the washing. "Fetch it." Away went Bob, running his fastest, while the shepherd set off in pursuit of his cap. Bob found it was a difficult job. Just when he was about to pounce on a towel, a sudden gust of wind swirled it away out of reach again. This happened time after time, but in the end Bob caught the lot and carried them back to Mrs Laird. They were dirty, but at least they hadn't been lost.

12—By this time Glenn had retrieved his cap and was working at the stables. After Bob handed over the shirts and towels, he ran over to help his master. Part of the thatch had already been blown off and at any moment it looked as if more would follow. Glenn was about to throw a weighted rope over the roof when Mrs Laird came running up. "Have you seen Peggy?" she cried. "She's disappeared." "No, she hasn't been here," said Andrew Glenn.

13—Then Glenn turned to Bob. "Find Peggy," he said, and at once Bob ran off. Half a mile from the croft, Bob found Peggy. She was crouched on all fours, crying bitterly. The little girl had run after her handkerchief, which had been blown away, but found that she couldn't fight her way back against this furious gale. She brightened up when she saw Bob and clutched his collar. Then, step by step, Bob dragged her into the shelter of a rock.

Havoc and devastation on Birsay

14—Meanwhile, back at the croft Tom Laird and Andrew Glenn had their hands full. No sooner had they slung ropes over the stable roof and made them secure than they saw the tarpaulin covering of a haystack billowing out as the wind tore at it. In fact the stack itself was nearly toppling over. Tom hurriedly propped up the stack with stakes while Glenn wrestled with the flapping tarpaulin. Then suddenly the henhouse was whipped up in the air.

15—It seemed as if nothing could stand against this gale. The noise was terrific. Above the howling of the wind came the creaking of ropes, the banging of spars of wood, the clatter of loose slates and the crash of falling chimney pots. In the midst of all this, Bob struggled back to the croft with little Peggy hanging on to his collar. It had been tough going, for the wind was so fierce that they had to rest every few yards to get their breath back.

16—Mrs Laird was overjoyed to get Peggy back safely. She took her into the house and Bob went to help the two men. Night fell before they got everything lashed down securely, so there was nothing else they could do but wait till morning. They did not get much sleep that night. Hour by hour the wind seemed to get stronger, and at times the cottage trembled with the force of the gusts. By morning, the wind died down and, after the howling and clatter the night before, the sudden quiet was eerie. A scene of utter devastation greeted them. Big chunks of the stable roof had been blown away. The hay from the stack was scattered all over the island. Even part of the cottage roof had been dislodged. It was a bad setback for Tom Laird. It would take a lot of hard work to put things right again, just when he needed all his time to get his land ploughed up and ready for the crops.

17—For nearly a week Glenn and Tom were kept busy righting the damage done by the gale. Then when things were more or less ship-shape again Tom decided to clear a patch of rough ground as long as Glenn was there to help him. The farmer was anxious to get it ploughed up so that he could sow seed on it, and the two of them toiled hard for a whole day using Tom's powerful tractor to wrench tree stumps and huge boulders out of the earth.

18—It was late in the afternoon before they stopped work, and since Bob had not had much exercise all day, Glenn decided to take him for a walk along the beach before returning to the croft. They had not gone far before Glenn saw what seemed to be a big wooden box or a trunk being washed ashore by the incoming tide. "Come on, Bob," he said. "Let's see what this is." With Black Bob at his heels he set off across the sands.

19—That stretch of beach was soft and yielding, much more so than it should have been. But Glenn was a countryman and unfamiliar with the ways of the seashore. He did not realise he was walking into danger until suddenly he sank into the sand, right up to his knees. He struggled to free his feet. It was no use. He was in quicksands. Bob, a few steps behind, stopped just in time. "Quick, lad," shouted Glenn. "Fetch Tom." At once Bob ran off.

20—Bob raced back to the croft like the wind, and ran up to Tom Laird, barking excitedly. He grabbed Tom's jacket then he began to tug him towards the tractor. All that day Bob had seen massive tree stumps being ripped out of the ground by the powerful tractor. In his doggie way he realised that Glenn was in danger and that he would have to be dragged out. So he pulled Tom over to the tractor. Then he looked appealingly at the farmer and whined.

21—The look in Bob's eyes told Tom Laird there was something wrong. "You want me to come with you, is that it?" he said. He climbed into the driver's seat and started the engine. Never had that tractor been driven faster. There was no road, not even a track, but that didn't stop Tom from following Bob. Soon Tom saw Glenn, sunk almost to his armpits in the quick-sands. Behind the shepherd, the tide was creeping up the beach.

22—Luckily the rope they had been using for uprooting the tree stumps was still attached to the tractor. Tom took it and went along the beach until he reached some rocks. He decided it was unsafe to go any farther. But he was still a good way from Glenn and the only hope was to throw the rope to the shepherd. "Catch this rope, Andrew," shouted Tom. "I'll pull you out with the tractor." With that he sent the rope snaking out towards Glenn.

23—The first throw fell short, but Tom quickly pulled in the rope and tried again. This time Glenn caught it. "Right," he shouted, "start pulling." Tom quickly hitched the rope to the back of the tractor, then he gently eased it forward, taking up the slack rope. When the rope tightened the strain on Glenn's arms was terrific, but inch by inch he was dragged out of the sticky sands. Bob watched anxiously, until at last Glenn reached firm ground.

24—Before they returned to the croft, Glenn looked around to see what had become of the chest. He saw it wedged amongst some rocks at the far side of the bay and decided to have a look at it. They reached it without any trouble this time and Glenn soon opened it. Inside were chisels, hammers, saws—in fact a complete collection of carpenter's tools. Laird whistled with pleasure. It was a lucky find, for the tools would be useful on the farm.

25—Two days later the mailboat dropped anchor just off the island. Some stores and mail were brought ashore in a dinghy and on the return trip the sailors took Glenn, Bob and the four sheep back to the steamer. Glenn made sure that the sheep were safely penned, then he went to the rail to have a last look at Birsay. Presently he heard the ship's engines speed up—they were off on the first stage of their long trip home to Selkirk.

26—The mailboat called at several more islands so it was some hours later before they reached the Scottish mainland. When they went ashore with the sheep Glenn was faced with a problem. The nearest railway station was twelve miles away and just then there was no transport available in the port which could take the sheep to it. There was only one thing for it—they would have to walk. After a meal, Glenn and Bob set off with the four sheep.

27—By the time they got halfway, daylight began to fade, so Glenn, knowing it would be dangerous driving the sheep in the darkness, decided to stop and spend the night at the roadside. Just as he and Bob settled down among some bushes a caravan came trundling along the road. Leading the horse was a surly-looking tinker. As he passed, the man's shifty eyes took in everything, particularly the four prize sheep grazing on the moor near Glenn and Bob.

28—No other traffic passed the shepherd and his dog, and for some hours all was quiet. Then about four in the morning Bob, always on the alert, heard a bleat coming from one of the sheep. He leapt up, barking furiously. The noise wakened Glenn. At once he saw the trouble. The rascally tinker had sneaked back in the dark and had grabbed one of the sheep. "Go on, Bob," shouted Glenn. "Stop him." Away went Black Bob like a shot.

29—Glenn started to run after the collie. But, in the darkness, Glenn didn't see the trailing wires of a broken fence. His left foot caught in the wire. He tripped and fell headlong down a four-foot bank. A sickening pain shot up his leg. Glenn groaned in agony and gingerly tried to stand up. He couldn't—his leg had been badly twisted in the fall, maybe even broken. He lay back against the bank, unable to move and almost sick with the terrible pain.

30—Black Bob came running back to his master. The thief had cleared off in fright. Glenn gritted his teeth. "Get help, Bob," he muttered. "I can't move." Bob whimpered and stood beside Glenn. The collie could see that there was something far wrong with his master. Just then they heard the sound of a motor car engine. Black Bob ran out into the middle of the road and stood right in front of the approaching car, barking furiously.

31—The car came to an abrupt stop. "What's the matter?" began the driver. Then he saw Glenn lying at the roadside. Glenn explained what had happened. "That's bad luck," said the man, who was called McLean. "I'll strap up your leg and take you into town." Bob stood sadly by as McLean helped Glenn into the car. But his ears pricked up as his master spoke to him. "Watch the sheep, Bob," said the shepherd. "Take care of them."

32—Glenn was worried about leaving Bob. "I'll be kept in hospital with this leg," he said to McLean. "I wonder if you could get someone to look after Bob and the sheep till I get out." "Don't worry," replied McLean. "I know a farmer who'll be glad to help." After McLean took Glenn to hospital, he called on his friend. Then together they went back to the spot where Glenn had been hurt. They stood puzzled. Black Bob wasn't there.

A greengrocer loses his greens and his temper

33—The two men climbed up on the banking at the side of the road. By now it was daylight, and they could see a long way over the moors. But there wasn't a sign of Bob—or the sheep. No wonder. Black Bob was already four miles away on the road to the south, driving the sheep in front of him. His master had told him to take care of the four prize sheep, and Bob was doing that all right. He was taking the sheep to Selkirk—all on his own...

34—Bob had never been this way before, but his doggie instinct told him in which direction Selkirk lay, and he was now heading towards that district. On the quiet roads Bob made good progress, but when he came to a busy little township his troubles started. The passers-by stared, the traffic stopped, and the policeman gaped in bewilderment at the sight of this lone black and white sheepdog driving four sheep through the town all by himself.

35—What puzzled the onlookers was the fact that there was no shepherd there. They would have been even more amazed had they known Bob was going to take the sheep all the way to Selkirk. All went well till Bob reached the square. Here there was a sudden burst of excited yapping, and a small dog dashed at the little flock. One of the sheep bolted, with the yapping little brute at its heels. Black Bob streaked after it.

36—Bob soon dealt with the small dog. A snap at the yapper's ears sent it scurrying up a side street with its tail between its legs. Then Bob rounded up the runaway sheep and drove it back towards the main road. Here more trouble awaited him. In his absence the three sheep had been attracted by the array of vegetables outside a greengrocer's shop. When Black Bob got back, there were the sheep, munching contentedly at some cabbages

Bob makes his four sheep vanish

37—Before Bob could get the sheep away from the shop the greengrocer spotted them. "Get out of here, you thieving brutes," he yelled. "Go on, get moving." Bob hustled up the sheep, and they went spanking down the street at a good pace. Unfortunately one of them had got a bouquet of flowers tangled in its horns. It was a very special bouquet, and the green-grocer didn't want to lose it. With an angry shout he pounded after them.

38—Right down the main street went Bob and the sheep and out into the open country. But the sheep couldn't keep this pace for long. Then as Bob came round a corner he saw a flock of sheep grazing on the moor. The shop-keeper wasn't in sight, so Bob quickly turned his four sheep off the road and into the middle of the flock. When the greengrocer came charging round the bend he stopped and stared. Black Bob and the four sheep had vanished.

39—It would have taken an expert to pick the four strangers out of the flock, for by now the bouquet had fallen off. Thoroughly mystified, the man went off back to his shop, muttering angrily to himself. From his hiding place behind some bushes Bob watched him go. Then, as soon as the man was out of sight, Bob got busy. Crouching low, he wormed his way towards the flock of sheep. They all huddled together, eyeing the collie suspiciously.

40—But Bob soon separated them, all the time keeping an eye open for his own sheep. And one by one he singled them out and drove them away from the rest of the flock. It was the work of a champion. Then for the second time that day Bob heard an angry voice bellowing at him. This time it was the farmer who owned the flock. He had come over a hill, and here, or so he thought, was a dog stealing four of his sheep. Things looked black for Bob.

The stowaway sheepdog

41—The farmer ran after Black Bob, shouting all the while, but when he saw he was being left behind he stopped and gave a long shrill whistle. At once a shaggy-coated mongrel and a massive Alsatian came running over the brow of the hill. Cobb, as the farmer was called, pointed towards the fleeing collie. "Go on! After him, catch him," he coaxed. And with excited barks the two fierce brutes went racing after Black Bob and the four prize sheep.

42—Bob snapped at the heels of the sheep to keep them moving, then he turned to face the two dogs with his teeth bared. But Bob was up against it. The dogs leapt at him together. Bob fought back, but step by step he was forced to retreat until he came to the bank of a stream. Again the brutes rushed him, and this time Black Bob could retreat no farther. He was knocked backwards into the water by the combined weight of his attackers.

43—The icy cold water took Bob's breath away, and for a few seconds he floundered about helplessly. Then as he recovered he struggled to the surface and struck out for the bank. But the banks were steep and the current was swift. Bob couldn't get a foothold, and he had to swim a good way downstream before he was able to clamber out. Bob growled at what he saw. The dogs were driving his four prize sheep into a lorry along with the others.

44—Cobb was selling some of his sheep to another farmer, and he never thought of examining closely the four sheep Bob had been driving away. He took it for granted they were his own. However, Bob didn't intend to lose the sheep. Keeping out of sight, Bob made for the lorry. But just as he drew near it started to move off. There was no time to lose. Black Bob shot forward and leapt on to the spare tyre which was fixed under the back of the lorry.

Bob turns the tables in the stables

45—It was a rough ride, but Black Bob managed to cling to his perch until, an hour later, the lorry pulled up at a farm. Before the men got out Bob darted away. Then, from behind a pigsty, he watched the sheep being driven off the lorry into a pen. The Alsatian was in its kennel nearby, and Bob realised that he must get rid of it before he could get near his sheep. Bob ran right in front of the brute and at once it leapt to its feet and chased him.

46—Keeping just in front of the Alsatian, Bob lured it away from the pen and headed for the stables. He had noticed that the stable door was open. Bob raced inside and quickly nipped into an empty stall just inside the door. He stood there stock-still as the Alsatian came blundering in after him. The dog ran a few yards into the stables and then stopped and stared—puzzled by Black Bob's sudden disappearance. It couldn't see him anywhere.

47—The Alsatian had its back to Bob, and as quick as a flash Bob streaked outside, unseen by the dog. Then the clever collie reared up and threw his weight on the stable door. The rusty hinges creaked and the noise made the Alsatian whirl round. It sprang to the door. But it was too late. Black Bob had tricked it. The door slammed shut right in the dog's face. At the same moment the latch fell. The big watchdog was well and truly trapped.

48—By this time all the sheep had been put in the pen and Farmer Cobb and his mongrel had left in the lorry. The sheep's new owner was in the farmhouse, so the coast was clear. Bob quickly opened the gate of the pen, then ran in and picked out his own four sheep. Next Bob drove them out of the pen and away down the road. But Farmer Cobb had done him a good turn after all—his lorry had brought Bob and the sheep thirty miles nearer Selkirk.

All aboard - except Black Bob

49—For mile after mile Black Bob padded south through lonely mountainous country. There was little traffic on the roads to bother Bob and the sheep, so they made good progress. But it was too good to last. In mid-afternoon they were trotting down a slope when Bob suddenly paused and looked, first left then right. Stretching to east and west, as far as Bob's eye could see, was a wide river estuary—and there was no bridge across it.

50—There was only one way over the River Laig, and that was by the ferry-boat run by a grumpy old man called Innes. Black Bob watched the boat cross the river from the far side and draw in at the little stone pier, then he drove his sheep down to it. But as Bob made for the boat there was a shout from old Innes. "Hoi, what's this?" he said gruffly. "Where do you think you're going? There should be a shepherd with you. Go away! Shoo!"

51—The old ferryman thought that Bob's master would turn up soon, and he waited for about five minutes. But, of course, there was no sign of any shepherd, so the man took another load aboard, then set off across the river. It looked as if Black Bob would have to make a long detour. Then as Bob turned away he heard a familiar sound—the bleating of a flock of sheep. There, coming down the road to the pier, was a shepherd driving fourteen sheep.

52—Tom Gray, the shepherd, drove his sheep off the road and sat down to wait for the ferry-boat returning. And his back was to Bob. As quietly as a shadow, the collie drove his four sheep in amongst Gray's flock. Then Bob stole away out of sight. In half an hour old Innes came back, and the two men started to drive the sheep into the ferry-boat. The danger now was that Gray would notice that there were eighteen sheep. Bob watched anxiously.

Who pays the fare for Black Bob's sheep?

53—Bob's luck was in. Gray was so busy gossiping to the ferryman that he didn't see the four strangers in his flock. The collie waited until he saw all the sheep aboard, then he plunged into the river. The sheep were on the ferry-boat all right, but poor Bob would have to swim across. The collie was in midstream when he heard Innes start up the engine—and Tom Gray hadn't noticed the four extra sheep. But in a few minutes the fun started.

54—"Here's my fare," said Tom. "A shilling for me and three and six for fourteen sheep." "Wait till I count," said old Innes. "Looks more than fourteen—aye, there are eighteen sheep here." The shepherd stared in amazement. "Well, four of them aren't mine, so I'm not paying for them," he said. "They must be yours," argued Innes. "But they're not," protested Gray. So it went on. And they were still at it when Bob reached the far side of the river.

55—What an argument it was. Old Innes was determined he was going to collect the fare for eighteen sheep and Gray was equally determined that he was going to pay only for his own fourteen. The ferryman broke off the argument long enough to steer his boat in to the jetty. Then they went at it again. However, Bob didn't wait for the business to be settled. Behind the men's backs he clambered aboard and began to separate his sheep from the others.

56—Quickly Black Bob cut out the four sheep and sent them off down the road. Both the ferryman and the shepherd turned round and saw him. "Can you beat that?" Innes muttered, seizing Gray's arm. "I turned that collie away from the ferry just before you came along." "Then he must have mixed these four sheep amongst mine to get them across!" Innes laughed. "Yes, he fooled us, so he deserves to get them over for nothing."

57—Black bob drove the sheep through the little village just beyond the ferry, and soon they were in the open country. Bob was feeling hungry, so he kept his eyes open for a safe place where he could leave the four prize sheep while he went off to look for a bite to eat. Then Bob saw a good place, a stone-walled fank, or sheep pen, just off the road. The collie drove the sheep in there and closed the gate before setting off to try to catch a rabbit.

58—Bob found some rabbits at the top of a hill. But they were very close to their burrows. At the first sign of alarm they would bolt, and would reach safety before Bob could get near them. However, Andrew Glenn had taught Black Bob a cute trick when it came to rabbit catching. Bob broke a branch off a nearby bush with his teeth. Holding this in front of him, he began to make his way across the clearing towards the unsuspecting rabbits.

59—It was a useful trick, for the branch hid Bob from the rabbits, and in this way he was able to get quite close without being seen. Then, with a sudden rush, Bob was on them. Next second a rabbit lay dead at his feet. Just as Bob was about to pick it up he heard an angry roar. The collie looked round in alarm. Striding towards him was a big burly gamekeeper, carrying a double-barrelled shotgun—and the shotgun was pointed at Black Bob.

60—The keeper, Sid Crowe by name, thought that Bob was a dog belonging to some poachers in the district. "Get out of this, you brute," he shouted. Black Bob knew only too well what guns could do. He had seen his master using one back home in Selkirk, so he slunk away and left the rabbit. He wasn't going to argue with a shotgun. But Bob didn't go very far. From the shelter of a rock he watched hungrily as the keeper picked up the rabbit.

61—A few minutes later Sid Crowe set off towards his cottage on the far side of the hill, taking the rabbit with him. Following him, but keeping carefully out of sight behind bushes and clumps of heather, was Bob. When Sid reached home he put the rabbit in a meat safe beside a mutton chop. But Sid Crowe didn't see the two brown eyes watching him from the garden gate. These eyes belonged to Black Bob—a very hungry Black Bob.

62—As soon as Sid went into the house, Black Bob nipped smartly into the back garden and had a look at the meat safe. The door was kept shut by a little brass bolt, and the bolt was too high up for Black Bob to reach. How was Bob to open it? The collie looked around and saw the very thing he was looking for—a walking stick leaning against the cottage wall. Black Bob picked up the stick in his mouth. Then he set about pulling back the bolt.

63—It was a tricky job. Three times Bob got the handle of the stick curled round the bolt and each time it slipped off. At the fourth attempt, the bolt slid back. Black Bob quickly pulled the door open. There was his rabbit- and the big juicy chop as well. After a bit of a struggle, Bob managed to pull the rabbit and the chop out of the safe, then away he ran across the moor as fast as he could go. He had got back his rabbit—with interest.

64—Black Bob ran on till he was well clear of Crowe's cottage. Then he stopped and listened. There was no sound of pursuit, so the collie sat down and ate the chop and the rabbit. Within ten minutes he had finished them and was trotting down the hill, ready for the road again. But a shock awaited Bob. When he got back to the fank where he had left the sheep he jumped on top of the wall. His four prize sheep had vanished!

65—It was a queer mystery. The gate was still shut and there was no gap in the wall through which they could have escaped. Black Bob was puzzled. Where could the sheep have gone? Bob set about finding out. As he was nosing around the mound in the centre of the pen he noticed for the first time that there was now a huge, gaping hole in the side of it. It was quite a deep hole and the sides of it were lined with large flat stones.

66—Black Bob did not know it, of course, but this was a Pict's house dating back to the days when this wild race inhabited Scotland. For centuries it had been there, undiscovered until Black Bob's sheep climbed on to it. The weight of the four sheep made the earth and stones covering it collapse, and the sheep had fallen into the underground stone house. Bob jumped into the hole, and he saw by the prints in the earth that the sheep had gone into a tunnel.

67—Black Bob went into the darkness of the tunnel. It, too, had been made by the Picts. The walls were carefully built up of flat stones, and bits of ancient urns and platters littered the floor. There was a damp, musty smell about the place and a constant drip of water from the roof. It was almost pitch dark, but as Bob's eyes became accustomed to the gloom he saw the four sheep in front of him. They were standing there, one behind the other.

68—The sheep had been unable to climb up out of the hole, so they had come down the tunnel looking for a way out. But there was no escape this way. Part of the roof had fallen in and completely blocked the tunnel. Black Bob saw that the tunnel was too narrow for him to squeeze past the sheep, so there was only one thing he could do. He scrambled on to the back of the nearest sheep and, creeping from back to back, made his way to the front.

69—Here Bob found the barrier of earth and stones that had brought the sheep to a stop. At once he set to work scraping away the rubble. Beyond this heap there might be a way out. It was Bob's only hope. The sheep could not climb out of the hole. They were trapped unless Bob could find another way up to the surface. It was hard work for Black Bob, but, digging furiously and pawing boulders out of the way, the collie toiled on.

70—Meanwhile, in a cottage not far away from the sheep pen, two ploughmen were sitting down to a cup of tea. They were Ned Dick and Sam Hughes. Suddenly Sam turned and stared down at the stone floor. "Hear that scraping noise, Ned?" he asked. "It's coming from under the floor." Ned nodded. "It'll be rats," he said grimly. "Let's get them." He got a crowbar and began to lever up the big stone slab nearest to the noise.

71—Ned was able to lift up the corner of the slab, and big Sam got his fingers under to lift it away. Ned took a tighter grip on his crow-bar, ready to deal with the rats. But it was no rat that came out of that hole under the slab—it was Black Bob! Sam and Ned could hardly believe their eyes-especially when four sheep came scrambling out after the collie. Bob had found the way out of the tunnel, right under the cottage floor.

72—Sam and Ned investigated the tunnel and the old Pictish house. They saw now how Bob and his sheep had got to the cottage, but that didn't explain where they had come from. Ned decided to make inquiries. "Put the sheep in the empty field along the road," he said, slipping a rope through Bob's collar. "We'll keep the collie till the morning and find out where he's come from." Bob struggled to get free. He didn't want to lose his sheep again.

73—All night long Black Bob was kept a prisoner in the cottage, but whenever it was light enough to see, he got up and looked around. The door was bolted and all the windows were securely fastened except one. The ploughman had jammed a piece of wood under the sash to keep it open and let some fresh air into the room. It was a long piece of wood—long enough for Black Bob to press down on the end of it with his forepaws and use it as a lever.

74—The window creaked noisily. Black Bob hesitated. Would the noise wake the sleeping ploughmen? The collie's luck was in. Their lusty snoring went on uninterrupted. Two minutes later the window was open far enough for Black Bob to squeeze through. He climbed out on to the water butt just outside, and from there he jumped to the ground. Just up the road he saw the field where the ploughmen had put his sheep, and he hurried towards it.

75—But when Bob reached the gate he found that it was secured by a chain. Bob could have chewed through a rope or unfastened a catch, but he could do nothing about the chain. However, he wasn't licked. The field was surrounded by a wall known in Scotland as a drystane dyke, because no mortar or cement was used to keep the stones in place. Near the gate was a weak spot where some of the stones were loose, so Black Bob made for this.

76—Black Bob jumped on to the wall and started to knock away the stones to enlarge the gap. It was hard work, for some of the stones were heavy, and it took all Bob's strength to dislodge them. Then suddenly part of the wall collapsed and a big stone crashed down on Bob's paw. The collie yelped with pain, but he didn't let the accident delay him. He kept pushing aside the stones until at last the gap was big enough for the sheep to get through.

77—It didn't take Bob long to round up the sheep and drive them through the hole in the wall. Then he headed towards Selkirk again. But a few miles farther south a car stopped on the road beside Bob. Two men got out and came towards the collie. It was McLean, the man who had taken Glenn to hospital, and his farmer friend. They had been able to pick up Black Bob's trail by making inquiries at the villages he had passed through on the road south.

78—Black Bob didn't know his master had asked these men to look for him and that they would help him. He gave a sharp bark and sent the sheep scampering down the road. The men gave chase, but this only made Bob run faster than before. Eventually the men ran back to their car and climbed in, hoping to overtake Bob in it. They were out of luck. A little way down the road was a big lorry. It had broken down in the middle of the road.

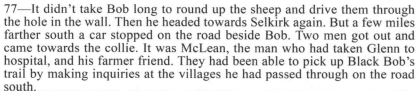

79—Black Bob had no difficulty getting his four sheep past, but it was a different matter for the two men in the car. In the end they had to help the lorry driver to put his lorry into a field before they could get past. By then Bob was out of sight, but the men drove on until they came to a bridge. Here they were faced with a problem. Just in front was a crossroads. The men got out of the car and looked around. Which way had Bob gone?

80—The men could see no sign of Black Bob and the sheep, so they were convinced that Bob had taken one of these three roads. But which one?- that was the puzzle. They stood on the bridge pondering over this. And all the time Bob was just a few yards away—under their feet! Black Bob had driven the four sheep down the bank into the stream and then coaxed them under the bridge. He was hiding there until the two men went away.

81—After a few minutes the car drove off and Bob emerged from his hiding-place. Bob, however, had learned a lesson. He left the road and took to the moors, for he knew he wouldn't be easily spotted there. All that day he headed south, and it was late in the afternoon when he heard a car in the valley road far below him. Bob watched from the shelter of a rock as two men got out of the car and began talking to a passing cyclist.

82—It was McLean and his friend. They were still looking for Bob and were asking this cyclist if he had seen a collie with four sheep. But the cyclist hadn't seen Bob and presently the men got into the car and drove away again. Bob waited until it was out of sight, then he ran over to get his sheep on the move again. Suddenly he stopped, amazed at what he saw. There were five sheep now, and a moment ago there had been only four.

83—The stranger was a white-faced sheep, vastly different from the four black-faced sheep Bob was looking after. It was a stray which had wandered away from its flock and, seeing four sheep grazing on the hillside, joined up with them. But it didn't stay there long. Black Bob rushed at the stray and quickly separated it from the others. He worked his way round behind it, and, with a frightening bark, sent the sheep scampering away down the hill.

84—Bob then went back to his four sheep and got them on the move. But Bob did not hurry them. He couldn't. His foot which had been crushed under the stone was bothering him. It was painful when he put his weight on it, so for most of the way he hopped along on three legs. On a quiet stretch of road Bob stopped to drink from a spring. He didn't notice the single sheep that trotted out of a wood and followed the others. The stray had returned.

Who rang the bell?

85—Whenever Bob saw it he chased it away. But that didn't do any good. The stray sheep came back again. And it kept coming back, no matter how often Bob chased it away. In the end Bob gave it up. In this open country there was no way of giving the stray the slip, so he let it run with the others. Darkness was falling by this time, but Black Bob kept crippling along. Towards midnight they arrived in the little village of Bannoch.

86—At the far end of the village Bob came to a stop. Here was a chance to get rid of the stray sheep. On one side of the road was a little stone cottage surrounded by a fairly high wall. On the other side of the road was the grocer's shop with a pile of empty boxes stacked in the yard beside it. The street was deserted. Bob pulled one of the boxes out of the yard and across the road. Then he laid it along the bottom of the wall round the cottage garden.

87—Next Bob singled out the stray sheep and herded it towards the wall. The sheep, agile though it was, could never have jumped the wall, but the box made all the difference. With Bob chasing it, the stray leapt on to the box, then over into the garden. Bob followed and ran up to the front door. Here he gave the bell a hefty tug, a trick Glenn had taught him long ago. Then Bob hurried away, and sent his four sheep scampering along the road.

88—Thus Bob got rid of the stray sheep at last, for it couldn't get out of the garden. And though Bob didn't know it, he had left it in good hands. It was in the garden of Sandy Fraser, Bannoch's policeman. But it was a shock for Sandy. He came rushing out in his pyjamas when he heard the bell and stared goggle-eyed. Next day he found out where the stray came from and sent it back. But he never found out who rang his doorbell.

89—Black Bob and the sheep rested for the night just outside Bannoch, and as soon as dawn broke they set off again. But they did not make very good progress, for Black Bob's paw was even more painful now. Suddenly Bob stopped. Tied up at the bank of the nearby river was a boat. Here was a chance for Bob to rest his paw. The collie turned the sheep on to a path that led down to the river, then cleverly coaxed them aboard the boat.

90—There was a big house not far away, and no doubt someone from there used the boat for fishing. But at that time in the morning there was no one about, and Bob got the sheep aboard without any trouble. Next he started to chew through the rope mooring the bow of the boat to the bank. Bob used his injured paw to steady the rope, and with his strong white teeth he soon ripped apart the strands. In less than five minutes he bit right through it.

91—Bob then chewed the rope at the stern, and as soon as it parted, the boat started to drift away from the bank. Black Bob leapt aboard. They were off. The boat swung out into midstream, and for mile after mile they drifted along, passing farms where the ploughmen stopped their work to stare at the dog and four sheep alone in a boat. At length they came to a town. Here there was great excitement. People lined the bridge to see this strange sight.

92—About a mile below the town Black Bob had a bit of bad luck. The boat ran aground on a bed of shingle near the river bank. Black Bob realised he could not get the boat into deep water again, so there was only one thing to do—continue the journey on foot. Bob herded the sheep out of the boat, then, still limping, he scrambled out after them. But they hadn't done badly. They had come nearly fifteen miles in the boat and rested Bob's sore paw.

93—Black Bob decided they had come far enough for that day, so, although it was still early he let the sheep graze, and took the chance to rest his paw. Next morning they set off again, but it was hilly country, and, hampered by his sore paw, Bob had to go slowly. Finally on the shoulder of a hill the collie flopped down, tired and panting. Presently the sound of a train whistle echoed up from the valley. Down below was a little railway station.

94—For a while Bob lay and watched the engine shunting waggons in a siding. Then it rattled away down the line. Bob's instinct told him that Selkirk lay in that direction. He rounded up the sheep and herded them down the hill towards the station. There was nobody in sight as Bob drove his sheep into the yard and on to the platform. There were four waggons, one of them with the door in the side open. Bob drove the sheep into it.

95—Inside the waggon were some packing cases. The collie drove the sheep behind these and settled down to wait. And it was a long wait. It was two hours later before he heard footsteps approaching. A porter was coming along the platform. He stopped at the waggon in which Bob and the sheep were hiding. But it was only to close up the side of the waggon. He didn't see the five stowaways hiding behind the pile of packing cases.

96—Then followed another long wait. But at last the waggon jolted. An engine was being hitched on, and soon the string of waggons left the siding, with Bob and the four sheep aboard. Once again Bob had found a way of travelling without hurting his foot. Suddenly a panic seized Black Bob. In his doggie way he sensed that there was something very far wrong. He looked over the side of the waggon. They were going in the wrong direction.

A puzzle for two porters

97—Poor Bob! He was going back the way he had come—and much faster. It was maddening. This was the worst thing to happen since he left his master nearly a week ago. But there was nothing Bob could do, so he settled down to wait. An hour later the train stopped at Sandford Junction, and two porters came along to unload the waggons. What a shock they got when they opened one and saw Bob and the four sheep amongst the boxes!

98—"That's queer," said one. "Sending sheep in an open waggon?" "Aye, and there's a dog with them. We'll have to look into this," said his mate. While the men began to scan the slip of paper which listed the contents of the waggon, Bob took the chance to drive the sheep down the ramp and on to the platform. The men did not pay much attention to him, for the list made it clear that Bob and the sheep should not have been in the waggon.

99—As Bob was driving the sheep away down the platform one of them suddenly ran off. Bob went after it. But the sheep wasn't trying to escape. It only ran as far as a water tap on the wall near the booking office. The animal was thirsty. Black Bob stopped chasing it and ran off down the platform. He soon found what he was looking for—a bucket. Bob carried this back to the tap. By now all the sheep were clustered round it.

100—Black Bob drove the sheep away from the tap and placed the bucket underneath it, then he reared up on his hindlegs and placed a forepaw on the tap. Back at his house near Selkirk, there was one exactly the same as this, and Andrew Glenn had taught Bob how to turn it on. So Bob pushed and prodded with his paw until at last the tap moved. Water gushed out into the bucket, and when it was full Black Bob quickly turned off the tap again.

Disaster on a speeding trolley

101—Then Black Bob stood back while the sheep drank their fill. Only when they were satisfied did Bob think about a drink for himself. He was very thirsty, too, so he filled up the bucket again and lapped up the water. Meanwhile, Tom Robertson and Sam Jones, the two porters, were in a quandary. They phoned the station where the waggons had come from only to find that no one there knew anything about Black Bob and his four prize

102—"Still," said Tom, "I think we should send them back. The sheep must have got on the train there. The people at the other end should find out where they're supposed to be going. It's nothing to do with us." "Aye," agreed Sam. "But there's not a train till tomorrow morning." "No, but there's that hand trolley in the siding," answered Tom. "The very thing," said Sam. So the two men took the four sheep round to the trolley.

103—At one time the trolley belonged to a wealthy landowner who ran a private railway on a nearby estate. Recently he had closed down the railway and handed over the trolley to the railwaymen at Sandford Junction. It was usually the men who repaired the tracks who went out on it, but today, as it happened, it wasn't in use. Bob went aboard the trolley willingly enough, and soon the collie and the sheep were bowling back down the line again.

104—It was Tom Robertson who went with Bob and the sheep. He was a big burly chap, and he fairly sent the trolley speeding along the line. But this was the first time Tom had been on the trolley, and he didn't realise how fast it was going—and just ahead was a sharp bend. The trolley was going far too fast to take the corner. It tilted and shot off the tracks. Black Bob, Tom, and the four sheep were all sent flying head over heels.

A fright for Fatty Mick McFee

105—When Black Bob recovered he got to his feet and looked about him. He was shaken, but not badly hurt. The sheep were all right. In fact, one was already nibbling the grass alongside the track. Tom, however, had not been so lucky. He was lying where he fell, and not a movement did he make. Bob ran over and peered anxiously at the porter. In his doggie way he realised there was something far wrong with Tom. He needed help.

106—The nearest building was a farm about a mile away, so Black Bob started to hurry towards it, going as fast as he could with his sore paw. But as Bob was running past a haystack he heard a queer sound coming from the other side of it. He stopped and peered round the stack. A big burly tramp was sleeping there, snoring lustily. Black Bob barked loudly right in the tramp's ear. The man woke up with a start and glared at the collie.

107—"Go away," he muttered sleepily. "I'm tired." And Fatty Mick McFee, as the tramp was called, flopped back amongst the hay again. It didn't look as if Bob would get much help from him. Then Bob noticed that Fatty wasn't wearing his boots. The fat tramp's feet were bothering him. Black Bob grabbed one of the boots and began to run away. This brought Fatty leaping to his feet. "Hoi, come back with my boot," he yelled.

108—But Bob didn't take the boot back. He ran on, keeping ahead of Fatty, and all the time leading the fat tramp towards the railway line. Only when Bob reached the senseless porter did he stop. Fatty came up, puffing and blowing. He looked at Tom. "I see now why you pinched my boot," he said to Bob. "This fellow's hurt and you wanted help. Is that it?" The fat tramp scratched his head. "But there's not much I can do," he muttered.

Black Bob has earned his supper

109—Then Fatty McFee had an idea. Lying on the ground near Tom was his porter's cap. Fatty picked it up and saw that Tom's name was written inside it. "Here, boy," he said to Bob. "Take this to the station." With that he pointed along the line. Bob barked. "Go on then," said Fatty, giving Bob the cap. "Take it, lad, and be as quick as you can." Obediently Bob took the cap in his mouth and raced away along the railway line towards the station.

110—Black Bob ran his fastest, and in a matter of ten or twelve minutes reached the railway station. Sam Jones was pushing a barrow along the platform when Bob arrived, but he stopped when the collie reared up and showed him the cap. The porter took the cap from Bob and looked inside it. "This is Tom Robertson's cap," he muttered. "Has something happened to him? Where is he?" Bob ran off and led him to the scene of the crash.

111—Here Fatty and Sam Jones, the porter, were faced with a problem. How were they to move Tom? Then Fatty had a brainwave. "We could make a rough and ready stretcher," he said. "Just button up our jackets and put two branches through them." They did this. Then, with Tom lying on the make-shift stretcher, they carried him home. Black Bob rounded up the four sheep and followed Fatty and Sam as they trudged over the moor.

112—When they reached Tom's house they sent for a doctor. He found that Tom's head was badly cut, but there was no serious injury. So, later that day, he was allowed to get up and have a meal. Mrs Robertson insisted on Fatty joining them. Black Bob was there, too. He had a great time playing with Harry Robertson, the porter's son. But the collie knew he would have to be on his way very soon again—heading once more towards Selkirk.

Black Bob's scaffolding escape

113—Black Bob, however, found that it was difficult to get away from the Robertsons. Tom decided to wait until the following day and send the collie and the four sheep back down the line by train. When young Harry heard this he asked if he could take Black Bob up to his bedroom and let him sleep there. Black Bob didn't want to do this. He was keen to get going, but rather than upset Harry he allowed the wee lad to pull him up the stairs.

114—The wee lad crawled under the blankets and then patted the bed. "Here, boy," he coaxed. "You sleep here." Bob jumped up beside him, but though Bob lay there with his head between his paws he was just dozing. His half-closed eyes were watching Harry, just waiting for the little lad to fall asleep. Bob did not mean to stay there any longer than he could help. His sore paw was nearly all right now, and he wanted to be on his way again.

115—For half an hour Bob waited. Then when he was sure Harry was fast asleep, Bob jumped lightly off the bed. It was a warm night in early June, and the window of the room was open. Bob made for it, still keeping a watchful eye on Harry in case the boy woke up. Black Bob climbed outside on to the roof, then stopped. He was two storeys up—fully fifteen feet above the ground. Then Bob noticed some scaffolding just below the window.

116—The house was being repaired, and the workmen had left the scaffolding in position, for they were returning on the following day. But more important—they had also left their ladder leaning against the platform. Very few dogs can climb ladders and fewer still can descend them. But Black Bob's master had trained him well. The collie jumped from the roof on to the scaffolding. Then, rung by rung, he carefully made his way down the ladder.

A Kitten appears and Black Bob disappears

117—Black Bob reached the ground safely and made for the moor where the sheep had been left to graze. Tom Robertson thought they would be safe there until they were put on the train the next day. The moon had come out from behind some clouds, so Black Bob found them easily enough. He had expected to find the sheep grazing or perhaps asleep, but they were doing neither. They were staring sheeplike at a little black and white kitten.

118—The kitten was a stray. Even when Bob chased the sheep away, it still just sat there, not knowing where to go. Gently Bob picked it up by the loose skin on the back of its neck and carried it towards the Robertsons' home. Back up the ladder he went and into the bedroom where Harry was sleeping. He crept quietly across the floor and put the kitten on the bed beside the little boy. Here in the warmth the little stray kitten curled up and went to sleep.

119—Only then did Bob sneak away again. In the morning Harry would be disappointed to find Bob had disappeared; but he would soon forget that in the excitement of finding a new pet. And that is just what happened. When Harry woke, he could see no sign of Bob. Then he saw the kitten. His eyes lit up. He picked up the kitten and dashed downstairs. "Look," he cried, excitedly. "I found this little kitten sleeping on my bed. Can I keep it?"

120—At first Mr and Mrs Robertson couldn't promise this, for, of course, they had to find out if the kitten belonged to anyone. But as the day wore on and nobody claimed the kitten, they decided to let Harry keep it. The boy was thrilled, and soon forgot about Bob. Everyone was puzzled by Bob's sudden disappearance, for they could find no trace of him anywhere. The reason was that Black Bob was already many miles away, heading for Selkirk.

121—During the next three days Bob and the four sheep covered many miles. They skirted the town of Callander, and they were in the hills near Kilsyth when suddenly Bob heard a cry coming from the other side of a wall. Black Bob leapt over the wall. He was just in time. Little Susie Randall had disturbed a weasel. Its angry whistle brought others, and now half a dozen of the little slinking terrors were swarming towards the terrified girl.

122—Before the weasels could touch her, Bob was in amongst them. Four quick snaps and four of them lay dead. The other two scurried into hiding in the cracks of the wall. The little girl soon got over her fright, but her troubles weren't over. Susie had wandered so far from home that she was lost. She was a stranger in the district, for she was spending a holiday there with her grandmother, who lived in a little cottage down in the valley.

123—Susie was anxious to get home again, but she didn't know which way to go. She decided to follow this friendly black and white collie. So she took hold of Bob's collar as he set off down the hill. But for the last half hour big black clouds had been sweeping over the hills. Suddenly a deafening thunderclap rent the air. Seconds later the rain started. It came lashing down in torrents. In no time Black Bob, Susie and the four sheep were all soaked.

124—Bob and Susie struggled on, wet and bedraggled. Overhead the lightning streaked across the sky and the thunder crashed and echoed amongst the hills. Black Bob looked around to see if there was a place where they could shelter from the storm. Just to the left he saw a cave. He drove the sheep towards it. Susie followed. But when they reached the cave Black Bob did not stay in it. He raced away, leaving the sheep and Susie.

Why does Bob steal a lamp from a crippled old lady?

125—The little girl was soaked to the skin and shivering with cold, so Black Bob was going off to try to get help. By now it was evening, and it was growing dark as Bob sped down into the valley. He ran for two miles before he saw lights burning in a little cottage. The collie ran up to the front door and barked for all he was worth. Black Bob heard someone moving inside the cottage, then the door was opened by an old lady in a wheelchair.

126—The old lady was Susie's grandmother, but she didn't realise Bob was there to get help for the little girl. "Shoo, get away, you brute," she shouted. Then she steered her chair back into the passage. She was going to shut the door. Bob stood back. He wouldn't get much help from this crippled old woman. But before Mrs Randall could shut the door she had to put down her lamp. Like a flash Bob streaked through the doorway towards it.

127—Old Mrs Randall gave a scared cry. She thought Bob was going to attack her. But she was a plucky old lady, and as Bob dashed inside she whacked him across the shoulders with her stick. Black Bob winced, but did not stop. He seized the lamp, turned, and went racing out before Susie's grandmother could stop him. Through the garden and away up the hillside he ran, making for the cave where he had left little Susie and the four sheep.

128—Wee Susie was very pleased to see Bob with the lamp. In fact, that oil lamp was probably the best thing that Bob could have brought to that lonely shelter in the hills. Susie managed to light a fire from it, using the dry bracken and sticks she found in the cave. Outside the rain poured down, but Bob, Susie and the sheep were snug and comfortable. Soon they were all sound asleep except Black Bob. The collie stayed awake—ever watchful.

129—When dawn broke, Black Bob rose and stretched himself. Susie was still sound asleep, but the fire was burning low. Once during the night Bob had crept off downhill to a nearby wood to fetch some sticks for the fire, so away he went again. It was still raining, but in the thickest part of the wood Bob found some fallen branches that were fairly dry. The collie picked up as many of them as he could carry in his mouth, and set off up the hill again.

130—When Black Bob got back with the sticks he dropped them on the fire. Then away he ran again. Three times in all the collie fetched sticks from the wood, and by that time the fire was burning nicely. Bob would have liked to carry on with his journey south, but he did not want to leave the little girl alone in this lonely spot. So the collie settled down by the fire to wait until Susie awoke. Time passed, but Susie, tired out after her adventure, slept on.

131—Meanwhile there was a stir in the nearby village. Susie's grandmother had become very worried when the wee girl didn't come home. None of the neighbours had seen Susie, so she sent for the police and told them about her missing grandchild. And there was something else worrying old Mrs Randall. "You see," she said to the policeman, who was studying the missing girl's photograph, "a mad dog attacked me last night. It may have hurt Susie."

132—Little did Mrs Randall know that the mad dog, as she called it, was really Black Bob, the champion sheepdog. The policeman did not know this either, and to him it looked as if Mrs Randall was right. This mad dog might have something to do with Susie's disappearance. The policeman didn't waste any time. He got in touch with the men who lived nearby, and soon organised a search party to scour the hills for Susie and the mad dog.

Saved by Susie's voice

133—Gamekeepers, farmers, policemen and Susie's little brother, Steve, all joined in the hunt. They spread out in a long line, searching every bush and every rock for the missing little girl. It was an hour later when Black Bob heard them coming up the hill. He ran to the mouth of the cave. Little Steve was the first to see him. "Come on," he shouted, waving his arms excitedly, "here's the dog." Grimly the men closed in on Black Bob.

134—From where they were the men could see no sign of Susie. She was still asleep in the shadows of the cave. But they had no doubt this was the dog that attacked Mrs Randall. One of the gamekeepers raised his shotgun to his shoulder and took aim at Black Bob. His finger was tightening on the trigger when suddenly there was a shout from inside the cave. "Stop! Stop!" cried a panic-stricken girlish voice. "Don't shoot that doggie."

135—The men's voices had wakened Susie just in the nick of time. She ran out of the cave. The surprised gamekeeper lowered his gun. Here was little Susie, safe and sound, and clearly very friendly with the black and white collie. Susie explained how it all came about; how Bob took her into the cave; and how he brought her an oil lamp, with which she lit a fire. The panic was over, and at the first chance Bob sneaked away with the sheep.

136—Just about the same time that all this was happening a big bearded shepherd was striding along the road to his cottage near Selkirk. It was Andrew Glenn, Bob's master. The shepherd had got out of hospital and made for home, hoping that Bob and the sheep would be there. Glenn paused when he reached the gate. If Bob was home he would surely come to meet him. But there was no welcoming bark to greet Andrew Glenn.

155

Will Bob's sheep be sold?

137—After leaving Susie, Black Bob headed south-east. His instinct told him he was getting nearer home, and for two days he hurried the sheep along at a good speed. But Bob's troubles began again when he reached the town of Inveravon. The streets were busy, and buses, cars and lorries went hooting past, scaring the sheep badly. They panicked first this way, then that, and Black Bob had a hard job keeping his tiring flock together.

138—The trouble was, of course, that these sheep from lonely Birsay weren't used to traffic like this. In a matter of five minutes they saw more traffic than they'd seen during the whole journey south along the quiet Highland roads. Finally in desperation Black Bob turned them into an alley where there was no traffic. Farther along this alley was a gateway in the wall. Black Bob wanted to rest the sheep, so he drove them through the gate.

139—Perhaps Bob expected to find a quiet spot where he could keep the sheep till nightfall. By then the streets wouldn't be so busy. But Bob was mistaken. The gateway led into an auction mart, thronged with farmers buying and selling sheep, cattle and pigs. Before Bob could turn the sheep back a man came up. He drove Bob away with a stick and then herded the sheep into a pen, for he thought they had been brought to the market to be sold.

140—In the end the sheep weren't sold. They were pointed out to the auctioneer when the sale was over, and since he had no idea where they had come from, he decided to treat them as strays and tell the police about them. When all the people were gone he tried in vain to drive Bob away. But the collie wasn't to be parted from the sheep he had looked after for so long. The man gave up, and Black Bob was left in the empty yard with the sheep.

141—Bob had a good look round the place to see if there was any way of getting out. It seemed hopeless. The one and only gate was securely locked, and the wall was much too high to jump over. Then Bob saw a pile of timber stacked against the wall. He climbed up on to this and looked over. His doggie eyes sparkled at what he saw. There was a lorry parked nearby, and Bob recognised the driver. He was Tom Small, a carrier from Selkirk.

142—Quickly Bob climbed back down the timber pile and raced to where his sheep were penned. Here was a great chance to get out of the yard and on his way to Selkirk. But he would have to hurry. The gate on the sheep pen was kept shut by two pieces of rope. Bob tore these ropes with his teeth. Then he pushed open the gate and drove the sheep out. Now came the tricky part-driving the sheep up on to the pile of timber and along the top of the wall.

143—One by one they climbed, gingerly stepping from plank to plank, with Bob close behind, coaxing them on. At last they reached the flat top of the wall. Black Bob herded them along this till they were right above the lorry. Then a quick bark from the collie sent them leaping down. Bob was right behind them. A few minutes later Tom Small came out of a shop and got into the cabin without so much as a glance at the back of the lorry.

144—Meanwhile, Andrew Glenn had been phoning all the police stations round about Selkirk to see if they had any news of Bob. As luck would have it, he got in touch with Inveravon just after the auctioneer reported finding Bob and the sheep. So Glenn boarded the first train for Inveravon. Unfortunately the shepherd didn't notice a lorry passing under a bridge just as the train rumbled across it. It was Tom Small's lorry with Bob and the sheep on it.

A scare for two scallywags

145—For mile after mile the carrier's lorry sped along the roads towards Selkirk, with Bob and the four sheep nestled comfortably amongst the crates. This was the easiest part of their long and weary trek. At this rate they would be in Selkirk in a very short time. Already they were in country that Bob recognised. They flashed past farms he had visited with Andrew Glenn, and then, about halfway to Selkirk, Tom pulled up at a wayside cafe.

146—Tom jumped out of the cab and walked into the cafe without even glancing at the back of his lorry, so he did not see Black Bob and the sheep. And two tough-looking loafers hiding behind a fence on the other side of the road also failed to see the collie. It so happened that from where they were Black Bob couldn't be seen. But the long wooden crate at the rear of the lorry was in full view of the two toughs, and they were very interested in it.

147—"Come on, Jake," whispered the smaller of the two men. "That looks as if it might be a crate of cigarettes. Let's grab it." Bent double, the two men sneaked alongside the lorry, carefully keeping out of sight of anyone who might happen to glance out of the cafe window. But they didn't manage to keep out of sight of the sharp-eyed Black Bob. As soon as the men laid hands on the crate Black Bob leapt at them, teeth bared and snarling.

148—This sudden attack was too much for the loafers. Though they wanted the crate, they weren't going to stay and fight Bob for it. They fled. Black Bob leapt down from the lorry and went after them, barking and snapping at their heels. For two or three hundred yards Bob chased them. Then he pulled up. But the crooks kept right on running at top speed. It would be a long time before they tried to steal anything from Tom Small again.

149—When Bob got back to the cafe he found Tom Small standing outside it. The carrier had come out to see what the noise was all about, and now he recognised Bob at once. "Hullo, Bob," he smiled. "I don't know how you and these sheep came to be on the back of my lorry, but it's a good job you were there. I saw what you did. Good lad!" Black Bob wagged his tail and looked towards the lorry. He wanted to get on the way to Selkirk again.

150—"I've heard you were lost," went on Tom. "so I suppose you want a lift home? Well, up you go, lad." Meanwhile Andrew Glenn had reached Inveravon and got in touch with the auctioneer. They went along to the market, only to find that Bob had vanished. The men were baffled until Glenn found Bob's pawprints on the planks. "Bob drove the sheep up here and somehow or other got them down on the other side," said Glenn.

151—Glenn was right. But he couldn't guess that Bob had made the sheep jump down on to the carrier's lorry and at that very moment was bowling along towards Selkirk. Suddenly Bob ran to the rear of the lorry. The crate had been moved by the men who tried to steal it, and it was no longer secure. Bob jumped on to it to try to steady it. Then came disaster! The lorry hit a stone. There was a terrific jolt, and both Bob and the crate went flying.

152—Bob hit the road with such a jar that every ounce of breath was knocked out of his body. For a minute he lay there, absolutely motionless. Then he slowly got to his feet. Away down the road was Tom Small's lorry. It was trundling along as if nothing had happened, for the carrier didn't know that Bob and the crate had fallen off the back of his lorry. Here was a fine state of affairs. It looked as if the sheep would reach Selkirk before Black Bob did!

153—Black Bob realised there was no time to waste. He must chase the lorry and let Tom Small know that the crate had fallen off. And, more important, he must get back to the sheep. Quickly he pulled off the label tied to the crate. Then, with the label firmly gripped between his teeth, Bob raced after the lorry. From the top of a hill he saw that the road went round in a loop. So Black Bob left the road and raced across the open country.

154—The short cut saved Bob a lot of time. He didn't make up on the lorry, but he reached the road only seconds after the lorry passed. The collie kept on running, but he was being left behind when a lucky thing happened. The lorry pulled up at a garage and Tom got out. He glanced at the back to see if Bob and the sheep were all right, but, of course, Bob wasn't there. And Tom got another shock when he noticed that a crate was also missing.

155—A minute later Black Bob came racing up, still carrying the label in his mouth. He ran to Tom and held out the label. "It's the label off the crate that was on the back of the lorry," muttered the carrier. "It must have fallen off in the last few miles. Do you know where it is, lad?" Black Bob barked excitedly and looked back down the road. "You seem to know," said Tom. "Well, just wait till I get some petrol, then we can go back and pick it up."

156—When Tom got his petrol tank filled up he set off back down the road, with Bob sitting beside him. As they drew near the spot where the crate had fallen off, Black Bob pawed at Tom's sleeve. "Right-ho, Bob," said Tom, "I see it." He turned the lorry round in a side road and steered it alongside the crate. Then he got out and started to heave the crate on to the lorry. Black Bob jumped up on the back and helped Tom as much as he could.

157—They got the crate safely stowed on the back, and soon they were speeding down the road to Selkirk. Black Bob stayed on the back this time. He wanted to be able to keep an eye on the sheep. About ten miles beyond the garage there was a side road leading off to the right. But Tom made no move to turn. He was heading straight on. When Bob realised this he leaped at the little window in the back of the cabin, barking furiously.

158—The road that Tom was following would take them far away from Bob's home, for the collie's instincts told him that the way to the cottage lay up this road to the right. When Tom heard Black Bob barking he stopped the lorry and got out of the cab to see what was wrong. He stared in surprise as Black Bob drove the four sheep off the lorry and started to hurry them up the side road—the road which he knew would lead him to his master's home.

159—Tom let him go. He knew that Bob would find his way home from there, so the carrier drove off, marvelling at Bob's cleverness. Several hours later Bob turned the sheep off the road and headed into the hills. Home was only a few miles away now. Suddenly Bob stopped. Leaning against a rock, he saw a shepherd's crook. Only part of it was showing, but Black Bob recognised it at once. The crook belonged to Andrew Glenn, his master!

160—Black Bob gave a bark and raced towards the rock, excited at the thought of meeting his master again after all this time. The sheep wandered on by themselves. Bob had forgotten them completely in this mad, exciting moment. When he reached the rock he reared up and peered over the top of it. As he did so Black Bob gave a mournful whine. It was his master's crook, of that the collie was certain. But his master wasn't there.

161—Beside the crook lay Andrew Glenn's pipe, jacket and cap. Bob sniffed the pipe. It was still warm, so Black Bob knew his master could not be far away. The collie climbed on top of the rock and scanned the hillside, but nowhere could he see any sign of the shepherd. So Bob jumped down and started to circle the rock with his nose to the ground. If only he could pick up his master's scent he would soon find out which way he had gone.

162—Suddenly Bob gave an excited bark. He had found his master's trail. It led down the hill towards an old deserted cottage. But as Bob was approaching the old well near the cottage he heard a shout coming from it. And the voice was Andrew Glenn's. The shepherd had gone to the well to try to get a drink. Unknown to him, however, the stones on the parapet were loose, and when Glenn leaned over they collapsed and he fell into the well.

163—Glenn had managed to climb up part of the way, then stuck for want of foot-holds. And when Bob looked over the parapet, there was Glenn clinging precariously to a tiny crack. In spite of his danger Glenn gave a glad cry. "Good lad, Bob," he shouted, "you've turned up at last." But the shepherd had been hanging there a long time. His hands were numb. Then, even as Bob watched, Glenn's fingers slipped and he plunged back into the well.

164—Black Bob looked round to see if there was anywhere he could get help for his master. But he was out of luck. Nobody lived in the old cottage, and there wasn't another house for miles. Then Bob remembered about Glenn's stick leaning on the rock at the top of the hill. That might be of some use. He ran up the hillside and picked it up. With the crook firmly gripped between his teeth, Black Bob raced back down to the well as fast as he could.

Home again and happy

165—When Bob reached the well he dangled the crook over the parapet. Glenn saw it. "Good lad," he shouted excitedly. "That's the very thing. Stay there—I'm coming." With that Glenn started once again to climb up the side of the wall. It was slow work, but Glenn kept going hopefully. With Bob and the crook to help him this time, he should manage to climb these last few difficult feet, even though there was no foot-hold of any kind.

166—As Glenn drew near the top Black Bob hooked the handle of the crook over the edge of the parapet. Then Glenn grasped the end of the long stick and gradually put his weight on it. The crook held. Hand over hand Glenn climbed up. The strain on his arms, already aching, was terrible. Bob did all he could to help his master. He leaned as far over as he dared and grabbed the sleeve of Glenn's shirt in his teeth. Then he pulled with all his strength.

167—What a struggle it was to get up these last few feet. Glenn was exhausted by the time he managed to get his hands over the edge of the parapet. For a minute he hung there, panting. Then with a final effort he heaved himself over the edge. Fondly he patted Bob's head. "You were just in time, lad," he muttered. "Goodness knows how long I would have been down that hole if you hadn't turned up." Bob wagged his tail happily.

168—"What about the four prize sheep, Bob?" asked Glenn after a while. "Are they all right?" Bob ran off and rounded them up. "Good, Bob," said Glenn. "I'll bet it was hard work bringing them all that way by yourself." Then the shepherd put on his jacket and they set off for home. It had been a long, weary trail. Black Bob was tired out, gaunt and haggard, but he had done a good job in bringing the four sheep safely home to Selkirk.

Plucky Pals
BOB and NICK

BLIND MATTY'S GUIDE DOG

Andrew Glenn and Black Bob were coming down from the hills one afternoon when Bob suddenly stopped, pricked up his ears, and stared down towards the road as though astonished by what he saw.

"Hullo, what have you seen—a hare?" asked the shepherd, also stopping. "No, it's Old Blind Matty striding along behind a dog! It must be the new guide dog that he was talking about the other day. We'll go to meet them, but be sure you behave yourself, Bob!"

Bob wagged his tail and trotted along beside his master until they were on the roadway. By that time the blind man was only fifty yards away,

and they could see that he was holding with one hand a thick strap attached to the dog's collar. He was walking fearlessly, as though quite certain the dog would not lead him into trouble.

Blind Matty was a close neighbour of Andrew Glenn's, and was an old-age pensioner who had lost his eyesight in an accident many years before. His cottage was tiny, and he had taught himself to move about inside it and do all the housework and cooking. But he had never been able to get any distance outside because of his blindness. Often Andrew Glenn had taken pity on him and called to take him out for a walk in the fine weather, but the shepherd had not much time for this sort of thing. That was why he had been so pleased when he had heard that kind friends were going to present Blind Matty with a guide dog.

165

"Hullo, Matty, I see you've got your dog!" he called out.

"He's wonderful, Mr Glenn," said Matty. "They say it cost a hundred pounds to train Nick, and he's worth it. Now I can go anywhere without bothering my neighbours, even through traffic. Do I hear Black Bob with you? Think he'll be friends with Nick?"

The two dogs were looking at each other but neither bounded forward. Both were too well trained for that. Nick stood with his master still holding the harness. His tail was wagging, and so was Bob's. It was clear that they had taken to one another.

"Yes, I'm sure they will," said Glenn. "And now there's no reason why you shouldn't come down and visit me some evening. Don't wait to be invited. Drop in any time."

The blind man thanked Glenn, then went on his way to his own cottage whilst Glenn and Black Bob hurried home for their tea.

TROUBLE FOR NICK

It was four mornings later, when Bob and his master were leaving home for their day's work, that they met Angus Soutar, a shepherd from farther up the glen. His expression was grim, and his eyes smouldered with rage. His dog, Tasker, was not with him, which was a good thing, for Bob and Tasker were enemies.

"Have any of your sheep been attacked lately?" asked Soutar.

"No," replied Andrew Glenn.

"Well, you're lucky. Some brute of a dog is running amok and attacking my ewes. Tom Millar tells me he's lost five the last three nights. I'm off to the police station in the village to report it. I advise you to carry a shotgun in the future."

Andrew Glenn was very disturbed by what he had been told, and was anxious to see whether his own flock was safe. When a dog took to sheep-worrying all the shepherds had to be on the alert. One crazy dog could do a great deal of damage.

"I'll certainly keep my eyes open for any strange dog," said Bob's master. "We've not had such a thing happen for years."

Whoof-whoof! The barking came from behind them. The two shepherds turned and saw a brown retriever outside Blind Matty's cottage. It had spotted Black Bob and was barking at him.

"What dog's that?" demanded Angus Soutar suspiciously. "I've never seen it before."

"It's Matty's guide dog," Glenn told him.

"Huh!" The other shepherd was glaring. "How long's he had it?"

"Four days now. It arrived on Tuesday and it's a great help to Blind Matty," replied Glenn.

"Then I bet that's the dog that's worrying the sheep!" rasped Soutar. "It arrived four days ago and we've only had trouble the last three nights. That proves it!"

"That proves nothing!" said Glenn. "That dog cost a hundred pounds to train. It's not a common mongrel that's likely to run wild. Don't be spreading rumours that it's responsible for the sheep-worrying!"

"I bet it is, and I'll tell the police when I'm down there," snapped Angus Soutar, and he turned away without another word.

Bob's master stared after him.

"If he starts rumours about Nick it's going to cause trouble for Blind Matty, Bob. I think we'll have a word with him."

He headed for the cottage, and Bob joyfully sped ahead to meet his friend. Very soon they were rough-and-tumbling on the grass outside the cottage. Glenn shouted to Blind Matty, and the old man came to his door.

"Hullo, Mr Glenn. I thought I heard Nick romping with someone. Today I'm going to let Nick take me into Selkirk."

"That's fine!" said the shepherd. "But I want to ask you something, Matty. Do you ever let Nick out at nights?"

"Well, yes," confessed the blind man, "I let Nick out between ten and midnight to let him get some exercise. It's only fair, as he's tied to me all day."

Andrew Glenn looked grim.

"Well, I wouldn't for the next few nights, Matty. There's a lot of sheep-worrying going on and the local men are looking for a strange dog. If they see Nick running loose they may shoot him."

"But they couldn't do that! Nick's not interested in sheep!" protested Blind Matty.

"I don't think that he is," said Bob's master, looking at the two dogs playing on the grass, "but don't take any chances."

Blind Matty promised to take the advice, and also accepted an invitation to come to supper on the Sunday night. Then Andrew Glenn called Bob to him and doubled back to reach his sheep-pens.

A SHOT IN THE DARK

It was Sunday evening, and Blind Matty and Nick were at Andrew Glenn's cottage. The men were having tea, while Nick and Black Bob ate together in a corner of the kitchen.

Suddenly Black Bob lifted his head and growled. At the same time Glenn heard the click of the gate leading to the garden.

"Visitors!" exclaimed Glenn. "I wasn't expecting anyone."

Now they could hear the tramp of feet coming up the garden path and the low murmur of voices. Andrew Glenn made for the door and opened it. Immediately Black Bob darted outside, and somebody shouted:

"There it is! . . . No, it's Black Bob. Don't shoot!"

"Who's there?" called Andrew Glenn.

Back came the voice of Angus Soutar:

"Have you got Blind Matty and his dog there, Glenn?"

By now Glenn's eyes were getting accustomed to the darkness, and he recognised his callers as six of the local shepherds and their dogs. Standing alongside Angus Soutar was Tom Millar.

"Yes, but what do you want?" Glenn asked sharply.

"We want that dog of his—that sheep-worrier!" came the stern reply.

Blind Matty came to Glenn's side.

"That's a lie!" he said hotly. "Nick has never gone sheep-worrying!"

"Yes, he has!" It was Tom Millar who was speaking. "We have watched your cottage for the past two nights and you haven't let the brute out. There has been no sheep-worrying during these two nights, but the three nights before that we all lost sheep. That proves it. Where is the brute?"

"Look here——" began Andrew Glenn, and just then Nick ran out through the door to see what Bob was doing.

Instantly somebody cried:

"There's the retriever! Get him! He won't worry any more of our sheep."

To Glenn's dismay Angus Soutar raised a shotgun to his shoulder. There was a flash and a bang, and a yelp from Nick. The retriever had been hit by a shot in the leg, and was now limping away down the garden path, whining miserably.

"The other barrel, Angus!" shouted one of the other shepherds, and again Soutar raised the gun to his shoulder.

Nick was clearly seen in the moonlight, an easy target, but before the man could fire there was a flash of movement. Black Bob came leaping upwards. His forepaws hit the barrel of Soutar's gun, knocking it sideways. Soutar staggered, knocked off his balance by the blow.

"Drat your dog, Glenn," he shouted. "But it won't do any good. I'll get that killer."

He raised his gun to his shoulder again, but by this time Bob had raced to the bottom of the garden and was right behind Nick—in a direct line between Soutar and the retriever. He was shielding his wounded pal with his own body.

"Shoot, Soutar!" growled one of the other shepherds.

"If you shoot Black Bob you know what will happen to you, Soutar!" called Andrew Glenn fiercely. Muttering angrily, Soutar lowered his gun. He knew he could not hit Nick without risking hitting Black Bob. "You ought to be ashamed of yourselves, hounding a blind man's dog like this. Get out of my garden!"

As the men argued, Black Bob hustled Nick through the gap in the hedge. The clever collie realised that he must get his friend away quickly to some place of safety, for the six shepherds were determined to kill the retriever.

Nick was limping and bleeding. He did not know the district, but he let Bob lead him up the slope away from the river. The hills represented their only safety.

Behind them the voices of the men grew fainter. Andrew Glenn was arguing with the shepherds for as long as possible, knowing that every minute he kept them there gave the dogs a better chance.

As the dogs hurried up the hillside Black Bob was peering anxiously into the darkness ahead. Nick's wound needed attention, and there was only one person who lived out here in the hills. That was Red Kelly, an old Irish packman who went around the countryside selling cottons, threads and bootlaces. He was very poor and lived in a tumbledown shack. Black Bob knew he was up there now because he had seen Red Kelly passing the cottage that morning. So now Bob was guiding Nick towards the shack.

It was about a mile from Glenn's cottage, and as they drew nearer Black Bob was delighted to see a light in the solitary window. Red Kelly had a candle burning.

Five minutes later they were outside the door. By then Nick was limping worse than ever.

Black Bob rose on his hindlegs and rattled the latch of the door.

"Who's there?" came the voice of Red Kelly.

"Whoof-whoof-whoof!" barked Bob, though not loudly enough for the sound to carry down the hill.

There was a shuffle of feet inside the shack, and the door was opened by a little old man whose red face matched his hair. He peered out.

"Well, if it isn't Black Bob, Mr Glenn's dog!" he cried. "Bejabers, what are ye doin' here at this hour o' night? Come in. Come inside!"

Nick would have drawn back, but Bob pushed him with his shoulder, and the Irishman saw the retriever for the first time in the candlelight.

"What is it, a friend that ye've brought to see me?" he exclaimed, then saw the red patch forming on the floor where Nick stood shivering. "So it's wounded ye are! Ye poor baste, now how did that happen? Is that why Bob brought ye here?"

He closed the door, then got down on his knee and examined the wound. Very gently Red Kelly felt all round it with his fingers.

At last the Irishman stood up.

"No bones broken," he muttered. "Ye'll be all right in a day or two."

Red Kelly bathed the wound in a bowl of warm water and bandaged it with strips of cloth torn from an old shirt. As he completed this task Nick reached out and licked his hand.

Black Bob was now standing at the door, his ears cocked. He was listening in case the shepherds were coming towards the shack. They knew all about Red Kelly's home and would come here sooner or later. So it wouldn't do to stay here too long although Nick badly needed a rest.

Red Kelly tried to coax the wounded animal with some soup and bread, but Nick had already eaten a good meal that evening and only wanted to lie still.

For the next hour Nick rested and Black Bob mounted guard at the

Black Bob rattled the latch on the door of Red Kelly's shack. The old Irishman would help Bob's injured pal.

door. Then suddenly Bob growled and scratched madly at the woodwork. He heard men coming.

"Now what is it?" asked the Irishman, springing from the chair where he had been dozing. "Someone comin', is it?"

He opened the door, and heard the voices of men and the barking of dogs. Next moment Bob and Nick blundered against his feet as Bob pushed his pal out of the shack. The collie realised that he had to find a new hide-out for his friend. Nudging Nick in the right direction, he led him further along the hilltop, towards some trees and rocks.

As he did so he heard somebody shout out:

"There they go! Quick—after them!"

Black Bob and Nick had been spotted. The grim hunt was on.

At once Black Bob dived into some bushes. Nick followed, though not so quickly. There was another shout from the pursuing shepherds.

"They've gone into these bushes. They'll lie low there and try to hide. That wounded dog can hardly walk."

The speaker was right about Nick, but he was wrong in thinking that the dogs were going to hide there. Bob led the way through the bushes and down the slope on the far side. There was a stream at the bottom. The two dogs crossed this then hurried into the shelter of the rocks on the far side.

By now their pursuers had arrived at the bushes.

Convinced that Bob and Nick were hiding there, the shepherds began to search, trampling down the smaller growths with their feet and sending their dogs into the thickest clumps. It was ten minutes later before they finally decided that the runaways weren't there.

By this time Bob and Nick were half a mile away, crossing a bog. It was tricky going, but it was worth the risk. Black Bob realised that the men would not attempt to follow them over this dangerous ground in the darkness.

When at last the two dogs reached dry land again Bob led Nick into a dry little cave amongst the boulders. There the two dogs lay down side by side. And all night long Bob lay there, watching and listening, while Nick slept.

THE CUNNING OF ANGUS SOUTAR

At dawn Black Bob was up and out of the cave. There was a little stream close to the cave and he knew that Nick could manage to crawl as far as that to drink, but he would not be able to hunt for any food.

Bob did not intend neglecting his duties to his master, but he meant to leave Nick a supply of food, so he went hunting for a rabbit. He finally ran one to earth about half a mile away, and carried it back to Nick, who was awake by now.

There was nothing more that Bob could do. Nick was well hidden for the time being and had both food and water. With a final bark to show

Nick was too badly hurt to hunt food for himself, so Black Bob brought him a rabbit.

that he was coming back, Bob again left the cave, this time racing across the hill and down the slope towards the cottage.

He was at the back door when Andrew Glenn opened it to fetch some water. The shepherd's eyes brightened.

"Bob, so you're back! What have you done with Nick? Soutar and the others are still hunting for him, and Blind Matty is very worried."

Black Bob stood there slowly swinging his tail and looking up at his master with big, unwinking eyes. That was the only way he could speak. In his own doggie way he was doing his best to tell Glenn that the retriever was safe.

The shepherd understood and patted him on the head.

"Good for you, Bob!" he whispered. "You've done the right thing, for I'm sure it's some other dog that's been doing the mischief."

Then he took Bob inside and made sure that he had something to eat and drink before they started work.

It was a clear, crisp morning, and as they passed along the hillside Bob looked downwards and growled.

A wisp of smoke rose from Blind Matty's cottage, but what had made Bob growl was the sight of a man standing under the trees directly opposite the cottage. It was Angus Soutar, and his dog was at his side. It was a brown dog, a terrible fighter. Soutar had a shotgun under his arm.

"Huh!" grunted Andrew Glenn, looking in the same direction. "He's waiting there in case Nick comes back to his home. I hope Nick doesn't do that, Bob!"

Glenn did not realise that Nick was in too much pain to move far.

Whenever Glenn had the chance during the day's work he stopped to look down into the glen to see if Soutar was still on guard. Furthermore, he listened for the sound of a shot anywhere in the hills. None came, and he was satisfied that Nick had not been found.

But what Black Bob and Glenn did not take into account was the full cunning of Angus Soutar. The man guessed that Bob had hidden Nick

Half a dozen angry shepherds were hunting for Bob and Nick–

somewhere and that he would visit the wounded retriever again, so just before sunset, when he knew that Glenn would cease work, he sent Tasker, his dog, up the hill to keep watch.

"Find Black Bob!" were his orders, and the snarling Tasker slunk away. He climbed up a long gully until he caught sight of Andrew Glenn and Black Bob as they parted on the hilltop.

"All right, Bob, go and see your friend, but don't get into trouble!" the shepherd was saying, and he patted Bob before watching the collie dash away towards the east.

Glenn did not see Tasker slinking after Bob, taking advantage of every bit of cover. There was something about the way Tasker moved which reminded one of a poacher's dog. He never ran; he always slunk. Even when he fought he always crept up behind his victims from the rear and pounced on them unawares.

The wind was in the wrong direction for Bob to pick up Tasker's scent, and Bob was in such a hurry to reach the cave that he did not once look back, so he was unaware that he was being followed.

Red Kelly lends a hand

– would the two dogs manage to escape?

flash. Black Bob chased him to the top of the slope, then stopped. He realised that they had been discovered. Tasker was now on his way back to his master. Presently he would lead Angus Soutar up to the cave. Nick would be shot.

Nick must not be there when Soutar and the dog arrived!

So Black Bob pursued Tasker no longer. He returned to the cave and pushed and prodded Nick until he got him outside. Then he led him up the slope away from the cave.

Up there on the more rugged slopes of the hills Bob knew of a fox's earth. Bob had killed the fox some weeks before, so he knew there was nothing living there now. It was not as comfortable as the cave which they had just left, but it would serve its purpose.

Nick limped along at Bob's side, and they had gone a hundred yards or so when a figure loomed up to the east of them. A low whistle sounded. Bob stopped and so did Nick. They stared at the stationary figure. The man whistled again, then called softly:

"Black Bob! Are ye there, Black Bob? I've got somethin' for ye!"

Immediately Bob recognised the voice of the Irish packman. Red Kelly was out on the hillside looking for them.

Black Bob at once leapt forward and raced to the Irishman's side.

"Ah, there ye are, lad!" muttered Red Kelly. "I thought ye'd be somewhere around with that poor crathur who was wounded. I've got something for him to eat. It's only a bone, but there's plenty of meat on it."

He placed it at Bob's feet, and Bob reached out and licked his hand, as Nick had done the night before. He wanted to thank the kindly old packman.

Away down in the glen a dog was barking excitedly. Bob recognised it as the bark of Tasker. At that moment he was probably leading his master towards the cave. There was no time to be lost.

He reached the cave just as it was getting dark, whined to tell Nick that it was a friend, and hurried inside. Nick greeted him gladly, and seemed a little better. He had eaten some of the rabbit and did not seem to be thirsty.

It must have been ten minutes later that Bob jerked his head towards the cave mouth. He could see nothing because of the darkness under the trees, but his keen ears had detected the slightest rustling sound. It had not been made by the wind.

He crept to the entrance and peered out. Something was moving out there, Bob was certain. Then the wind brought a whiff of animal smell to Bob, and instantly he recognised it as the scent of his old enemy—Tasker.

With a rush and a growl he was outside and speeding towards the other dog, but Tasker saw him coming and was away down the hillside in a

With a last look at Red Kelly, Bob snatched up the bone and raced back to where Nick was waiting. The retriever sniffed the bone hungrily, but there was no time for eating then. Bob kept the bone, and hurried Nick up the hill.

It became very steep. More than once Bob had to push Nick with his shoulder to help him up the slopes, for Nick couldn't put much weight on his bad leg. Finally they came to the gully where the fox's old hide-out was, and Bob slid down to the bottom to show Nick the way to come.

Nick paused at the top. It was dark down there and he did not like the look of the place. Perhaps it was only because Bob had the bone that the retriever finally followed down into the burrow.

There Black Bob gave him the bone, and for a long time the collie lay there listening to his friend's white teeth tearing at the meat.

The moon was up when at last he left Nick and headed for home.

As he passed near the cave where they had originally hidden there was a chuckle from some bushes nearby. Bob shied away, but it was only Red Kelly who was sitting there on a boulder in the moonlight. He came towards Bob and patted him on the head and fondled his ears.

"You're a clever lad, Bob, and your master should be proud of ye! Now I know why ye wanted to get away from that cave. Twenty minutes after ye'd gone a man with a gun and a dog arrived and went straight to it. When the man found nothing there he beat his dog for wasting his time! It's a real laugh ye'd have had if ye'd been here, Bob."

Bob, of course, couldn't understand what Red Kelly was saying, but he wagged his tail happily, and set off down the hill.

The Irishman watched Black Bob carefully descending the slope to the glen, then slowly went back to his shack. The lateness of the hour did not worry Red Kelly, for he often did a little poaching, and even now he had under his jacket a rabbit which he had snared that night.

DEADLY DANGER AT THE LAKESIDE

For a whole week Black Bob watched over his pal and guarded him. Every night he visited Nick, and usually brought him food.

There had been no more sheep-worrying. The other shepherds had given up the hunt for Nick, but Angus Soutar and Tom Millar still spent all their spare time seeking him, and they still took it in turns to watch old Blind Matty's home.

Twice Tasker had almost led them to Nick's hide-out, and once it was only the quick thinking of Red Kelly that saved Nick.

It happened one day when Bob was out on the hills with his master. They had been working hard all morning herding sheep to some fresh pastures, and at midday Glenn called a halt.

"It's time for something to eat, Bob," said the shepherd, and he sat down behind a rock out of the wind. Glenn took some sandwiches from his pocket and put two down on the heather in front of Bob.

"There you are, lad," he said. "That will keep you going till tea time."

Bob sniffed the sandwiches. They smelt good and he was starving. But not far away Nick was lying in the old fox hole and he hadn't eaten anything since last night. He would be hungry, too.

The collie looked up at his master. Glenn was eating. After that he would light his pipe and then have forty winks before starting the afternoon's work. There was plenty of time to go and see Nick.

Black Bob picked up the sandwiches and ran off. In ten minutes he was at Nick's hiding place. Nick hobbled to the entrance of the burrow, his tail swishing from side to side with pleasure. He soon gobbled up the sandwiches Bob had brought, then the two pals went down to the nearby lake for a drink of water.

While Nick was drinking, Black Bob looked all around. There were some ducks swimming on the lake but there wasn't another living thing in sight. All seemed safe. Then suddenly there was a flash of light away to the west. It came from the direction of a hill known as The Slug, so called because it was a long and low shape with two huge rocks sticking up at one end like horns. And it was from near these rocks that the flash came.

A moment later a man and a dog stepped out from behind the rocks. Bob growled. The figures were a quarter of a mile away, but the collie recognised them—Soutar and his dog.

Soutar had been hiding there all morning watching the hills through his binoculars for some sign of Bob or Nick. And at last his patience had been rewarded. He came hurrying down the slope towards the lake.

It was the sun glinting on the glass of Soutar's binoculars that Bob had seen. It was a good job he had spotted it. If he hadn't, Soutar and Tasker might easily have got within gunshot before Bob and Nick noticed them.

There was no time to waste. Not since the night that Nick was shot had Soutar been as close as this. Quickly Bob led Nick away along the lakeside. Nick needed no urging. He had recognised his enemies and was hobbling along as fast as he could.

They kept to the shore until they came to a stream bubbling into the lake. Bob led the way into the water and upstream away from the lake. Bob knew that a short distance ahead the stream ran through a deep gully, and once in there they would be out of sight of Soutar and his dog. But just before they reached the gully a shot rang out behind them. Soutar had fired in desperation, realising that they would soon be out of sight. Luckily he was too far off. The pellets came nowhere near Bob and Nick.

For two hundred yards Bob and Nick followed the stream, then Bob led the way into a clump of birch trees that grew all the way up the side of a slope. He could hear Tasker's bark more clearly now. Soutar and his dog were drawing nearer. It was going to be difficult giving them the slip in broad daylight.

When Bob and Nick emerged from the trees at the top of the slope, the collie paused, wondering which way to go. Then suddenly he ran forward. Striding towards them was Red Kelly.

"What's up wi' you two today?" demanded the Irishman. "Someone chasing you? I thought I heard a shot."

Just then the sound of Tasker's bark and Soutar's voice urging him on came from the clump of birches that had concealed Bob and Nick.

"Soutar, is it?" muttered Red Kelly angrily. He looked around.

"Look, in there with you," he whispered, pointing to a drainage ditch that had been cut along the side of the slope. "Hurry now."

At once Bob and Nick jumped down into the ditch. There was no water in it though the bottom was still muddy. A moment later Soutar and his dog burst out of the trees.

"Have you seen Black Bob and a brown retriever, Kelly?" demanded Soutar.

"To be sure and I did," said Kelly. "And what would you be after doing to them?"

"You know fine," shouted Soutar. "Stop wasting my time. Which way did they go?"

"Wasting your time," said Red Kelly indignantly. "And if it isn't you that's wasting my time, and me in a hurry to get home and get a bite to eat."

Soutar was livid with rage by this time, but little did he guess that Red Kelly was deliberately delaying him to give Bob and Nick time to sneak away along the ditch.

"For the last time, Kelly," roared Soutar, "which way did they go?"

It was then that the old Irishman really foxed Soutar.

"That way," said Red Kelly, pointing in the direction of Glenn's cottage. "Most likely they're heading for home."

Soutar and Tasker hurried off in the direction indicated by Red Kelly.

Red Kelly chuckled. He knew quite well that Bob and Nick had gone the other way—back towards the lake. Once again the old Irishman had done Bob and Nick a good turn, for the two dogs saw no more of Soutar and Tasker that day.

However, Bob realised that the old fox hole was no longer a safe hiding place for Nick, so he led his pal to another hide-out. It was only a hollow in a sandy bank but it was dry and in a quiet spot.

Black Bob went racing back to where he had left his master. He worked hard all afternoon, but at night returned to see Nick.

ON THE TRAIL OF THE SHEEP-WORRIER

And so it went on, with Bob hardly getting any sleep, and starving himself into the bargain so that his pal could have plenty to eat. The strain began to tell on Bob and he began to look lean and scraggy.

Andrew Glenn noticed this, and one day he said:

"The sooner this stops the better, Bob! You can't go on like this. I wish we could find the real sheep-worrier, but ever since Nick was wounded there has been no further trouble. Soutar is saying that's definite proof that Nick is the guilty one. He says that as soon as Nick is better he'll start attacking sheep again. If he does, not even you will be able to save him."

Black Bob always watched his master's face when Glenn talked with

A grim game of hide-and-seek in the hills

Soutar wanted to know which way Bob and Nick had gone. Red Kelly pointed to the east, but all the time he knows the pals were heading in the opposite direction.

hide-out where he had left the retriever, Nick was not there. It was the first time he had ever failed to be there when Black Bob arrived. Had the retriever gone back to try to reach Blind Matty? Or had he merely got hungry and gone hunting for something to eat?

Bob scouted around with his nose to the ground, trying to pick up Nick's scent, but there had been heavy rain during the day, and he could not pick up the trail.

Then he remembered about Red Kelly. Perhaps Nick had gone to the packman's shack. The two had become very fond of each other.

Away went Black Bob to the shack, but even as he scratched at the door he could smell that Nick was not inside.

Red Kelly opened the door; and looked down at Black Bob.

"Hello, Bob," said the old Irishman. "Where's your friend?"

But Bob ran inside and sniffed around the shack to discover if Nick had been there. He could find no sign of the retriever, and when he rushed outside and began sniffing round the back of the shack, Red Kelly realised Bob was looking for Nick.

"So ye've lost him!" he exclaimed. "That's what brought ye here? Ye thought he might be with me? I've not seen him at all, but I'll come with ye and search."

He put on his battered hat and they left the shack together. While Black Bob sniffed the ground and the air, and relied on his powers of scent, the Irishman whistled and shouted.

There was no response, and Black Bob did not pick up any trail until they had gone about a mile. Then he began to run round in circles with his nose to the grass. Nick had passed that way recently. The trail was

him, but this was beyond him. He did not understand more than that his master was worried, and he tried to please him by doing extra well at his work.

The night after that talk he got a shock, for when he went to the latest

174

fresh. Now Bob was trying to find out which way the retriever had gone.

"Do you think he passed this way?" asked Red Kelly, watching Bob anxiously. "Maybe he's headed for home—feelin' that he's strong enough to get there?"

Suddenly Bob started off at such a pace that the Irishman found it hard to keep up with him.

Nick may have been heading for Blind Matty's cottage, but he did not know the district well enough to go straight there. The trail Black Bob was following led along the hillside towards the pens where Farmer Grant's sheep were kept at night. Bob had helped to drive them into those very folds at sunset.

It was true that Nick could get down to his master's cottage that way, but it was a long way round.

Then when they were still a hundred yards from the pens, the sheep began bleating loudly. Instantly Black Bob stiffened. That sounded as though the sheep were frightened. There was a crashing sound as though they were trying to leap over the hurdles. Something was far wrong.

Bob shot forward and Red Kelly ran behind. As he drew nearer to the pens Bob sensed that there was something inside with the sheep. The sheep-worrier?

Black Bob got a shock when he went to Nick's hide-out—the retriever was no longer there!

175

Anger gripped Bob. He fairly raced over the turf, and just as he reached the near corner of the pen something leapt over the top and landed a little ahead of him.

It was a brown dog, and even at that distance Bob could see tufts of wool hanging from its jaws. It had been worrying the sheep.

The dog saw Bob and turned to flee. As it dashed away in the starlight Bob recognised it. The dog was Tasker, Angus Soutar's dog!

Never had Bob run faster, and Tasker realised that he couldn't outdistance Bob. The collie was gaining fast. Suddenly Tasker turned about and bared his teeth.

Bob did not hesitate. He went in as straight as an arrow. But Tasker was not there. He had leapt aside at the last moment, and as Black Bob flashed past the other dog gashed Bob's flank with his teeth.

But if Tasker could dodge quickly, Black Bob could turn with lightning speed. He did so now, rushed in low, and got Tasker by the throat. Over they rolled, Tasker snarling and growling, Bob making no sound.

Tasker was strong, and heavier than Black Bob. He tore at Bob with his four legs, but he could not break that grip. All the time they were fighting Red Kelly was dodging around them, encouraging Bob. He dared not try to separate the two. He knew that it was a fight to the death.

Once Tasker managed to get to his feet and dragged Black Bob several yards along the ground, but Bob would not let go. His teeth were locked in the other's throat.

At last the bigger dog collapsed, and the fight was over. Bob had slain the sheep-worrier.

A SHOCK FOR SOUTAR

Black Bob lay there for some minutes, licking his wounds and recovering his breath, while the packman fussed around him and told him that he was a champion fighter.

Bob had just got to his feet when a shot sounded down in the glen, then another.

At once Bob turned about and ran to the top of the slope. The shots had come from the direction of Blind Matty's cottage. Had Nick tried to get back to his master and been shot by one of the watchers? Bob went leaping down the hill, his weariness and wounds forgotten.

"Hi, wait for me!" panted Red Kelly, and scrambled after him.

Black Bob ran his fastest for the second time that night. As he drew nearer the cottage he saw two men hurrying down the road in front of him. They were Angus Soutar and Tom Millar, and they both had shotguns.

"You missed it, Angus," panted Tom Millar. "It's just gone into the cottage."

"Ay, but I won't miss it next time," muttered Soutar. "We're going into the cottage to get it. I'll shoot that sheep-worrier if it's the last thing I do."

The men strode up the garden path and pushed open the front door.

"We're coming in to get your dog, Matty," shouted Soutar. "We know it's here."

Just then there was a savage growl and Black Bob came hurtling through the darkness. He dashed across the garden and rushed at the legs of the men, snapping and snarling like mad.

Soutar and Millar leaped back in alarm, and at once Bob jumped on to the doorstep and turned to face them, barring the way into the cottage. And so fierce and savage did he look that neither Millar nor Soutar would move a step nearer.

Blind Matty by this time had found his way to the door.

"What's going on?" he demanded. "What do you want?"

"Call off Black Bob and we'll soon show you," growled Soutar. "We've come to get your dog."

"But he's done nothing," said Matty.

At that moment there was the sound of running feet, and Red Kelly came up the garden path. Close behind him was Andrew Glenn. The shepherd had heard the sound of the shots fired at Nick and had raced to Blind Matty's cottage, guessing something was wrong.

"What's the trouble?" panted Red Kelly when he reached the front door.

"It's the sheep-worrier, that dog of Blind Matty's," growled Soutar. "It came back home. We shot at it but missed. Now it's inside and Black Bob won't let us get after it!"

Brave Bob bars the way

Angus Soutar and Tom Millar were after Nick, but Bob stopped them. Snarling fiercely he barred the way into the cottage.

"But it's crazy ye must be!" protested the old Irishman. "The sheep-worrier's up there on the hill—dead. Black Bob killed it. I saw him. We caught it in the act of leaving one of the pens. We left it there dead."

"What?" demanded Andrew Glenn. "A dog been after my sheep! That must be the real sheep-worrier. Come on!"

He turned and headed for the hillside, and the others followed him, all except Red Kelly, who was too breathless to run any farther.

Ten minutes later the bloodstained Bob led the three men to the dead dog near the pens, and at sight of it a shout went up from Glenn and Tom Millar:

"Tasker! It's your dog, Soutar. It was your dog all the time."

At first Angus Soutar refused to believe it, but when they found sheep-wool between Tasker's teeth, and when they saw the two injured sheep in the pen, he had to admit that they were right.

All three helped with the wounded sheep. There was no doubt that Tasker had done this sort of thing on other occasions, and the newcomer to the glen, the guide-dog, had got the blame for it.

The plucky pals are safe at last

Even surly Soutar had the decency to admit that he had been very wrong, and that it was a good thing Bob had not let them get at Nick.

That night a mystery had been solved and a right had been wronged, and most of the credit for this had to go to Black Bob, but for whose cleverness Nick would have paid the penalty more than a week earlier, and Tasker's evil ways might not have been discovered for months to come.

So Blind Matty had the joy once again of a loyal dog to act as his eyes, and Black Bob had the friendship of the dog which he had saved. Whenever they could get together the two dogs did so, and many an expedition the plucky pals made into the hills. But no longer did they have to slink from hiding place to hiding place. They had no enemies now and were free to romp as they pleased.

178

BLACK BOB AND THE BLACK PROWLERS

IN a little stone cottage near Selkirk lived Black Bob, the famous sheepdog. Bob was known throughout the length and breadth of the land for his skill at handling sheep. Whether he was looking after stubborn rams or frisky lambs, it was all the same to Black Bob. He knew just how to deal with them, for years of practice had given him a great understanding of the ways of sheep. Time and time again he had won cups and trophies at sheepdog trials and everyone admitted that he was far ahead of other dogs in cleverness and knowledge. And the credit for Bob's success was largely due to his master, Andrew Glenn. It was Glenn who had trained Bob from his puppy days and made him a champion.

Glenn was the shepherd on a large sheep farm and he and Bob looked after the hundreds of sheep that roamed the hills. It was a big job. The sheep had to be clipped and dipped in summer and tended throughout the storms and blizzards of winter. In addition they had to be guarded at all times from the dangers of foxes, wild-cats and killer dogs. Sheep-stealers, too, were a worry to Bob and his master, and many sleepless nights they spent, patrolling the hills and watching for the thieves. So although Bob and Glenn lived in a quiet and lonely part of the country they saw plenty of excitement. And one of Black Bob's most thrilling adventures was his encounter with the Black Prowlers.

2—It was a warm afternoon in March and Black Bob and his master were rounding up some sheep on the hillside near their cottage. Black Bob managed to get the sheep herded together and moving down the hill. But there was a young lamb with them and it was a bit frisky. It dodged away from the others and walked out on to the trunk of a tree that had been blown down in a storm and was now lying half-submerged in the river.

3—When the lamb reached the end of the trunk it came to a stop and stood looking down into the water. Black Bob followed slowly, for he did not want to panic the lamb in case it lost its footing on the narrow tree trunk. Nearer and nearer he came, and before the lamb could dodge he suddenly nipped forward and grabbed it by the loose skin on the back of its neck. Then, taking care not to hurt it, Black Bob carried it back to the bank.

4—Andrew Glenn, meanwhile, went on down the hillside. He knew it was a tricky job Bob was tackling, but he had full confidence in his clever collie. When Bob ran up with the lamb the shepherd patted him. "Good lad," he said. "We'll have to keep an eye on the little rogue in future." But Bob saw to it that the lamb gave no more trouble. He watched its every move until it was safely shut in the sheep-pen with the others.

5—Glenn and Bob went home then. They had tea and spent the rest of the evening sitting by the fireside. After Glenn went to bed, Bob settled down to sleep. But it wasn't a deep sleep. In the middle of the night Bob heard an unusual sound from far away. Bob knew that Glenn never shut the scullery window, so Bob pushed it open and clambered out on to the sill. He could see nothing from there, so he ran to the garden wall and climbed on to it.

6—Black Bob looked towards the sheep-pen. A full moon was peeping through the clouds, and Bob could see that the gate of the pen was still shut. Everything seemed to be all right there. But what Bob did not see were the three black shapes loping silently through the night. With their tongues lolling from slavering jaws they looked a fearsome sight. But they weren't making for the sheep-pen. The Black Prowlers were coming up behind Bob.

7—Black Bob never saw his attackers. There was a rush in the darkness behind him and next second Bob was knocked clean off the wall. As he fell he hit his head on a stone. He lay there unconscious for the rest of the night. Next morning Glenn was surprised when he found that Bob wasn't in the cottage, but he wasn't very worried, for Bob sometimes let himself out. When breakfast was ready Glenn went outside and whistled shrilly.

8—But there was no answering bark, no sound of paws racing up to the front door. Glenn hurried down the path. He gasped when he saw the still body sprawling limply over a trough. For one horrible moment Glenn thought Bob was dead. But when he picked Bob up he felt the collie's heart beating. Quickly he carried Bob into the house. There, in the warmth, Bob recovered and opened his eyes to find his master bathing the bruise on his head.

9—Glenn saw there wasn't much wrong with Bob, so they had something to eat then went along to the sheep-pen. Glenn stared in amazement at what he saw there. The gate was torn off its hinges and the sheep had vanished. "So that's it," he said grimly. "Sheep-stealers! That's why you were hurt, lad. You must have heard them some time during the night, but they beat you up when you went outside. This is a bad business, Bob."

10—Andrew Glenn made up his mind to report his loss to the police right away, so he set off with Bob for the police station in the village. On the way there they met Farmer Findlay. He, too, had lost some sheep. And, stranger still, Grip, his big mastiff, was missing. Findlay took Glenn and Bob to see the empty kennel. "Someone unfastened the chain," said Findlay, "but I don't know how they managed it. Grip's mighty fierce."

11—"I know," said Glenn. "Many's the time he's jumped at me when I've come into the yard. All we can do is report it to the police. They may be able to do something." When Glenn and Bob reached the police station. Bob waited at the gate while his master went inside. Billy Pearson was a little way down the street at the time with Snap, his dog. It was a friendly little terrier, and it came running back down the road when it saw Bob.

12—Snap and Bob were capering about when a rough-looking man in a crumpled brown suit came along on a bicycle. He was a stranger to the village, and Bob had never seen him before. He stopped opposite the two dogs and took a long look at Bob. Then he glanced all around him before taking a tin from his pocket. "Here, lad," he said. And, picking a round, black thing like a sweet from the tin, he threw it down in front of Bob.

13—Black Bob was a well-trained dog and did not gulp the sweet down at once. He sniffed it first, for it was not like the sweets he usually got from his master. While he was examining it, Snap suddenly dashed right under Bob's nose. The excitable terrier didn't wait to sniff the sweet. Snap swallowed it with one gulp. The stranger gave a grunt of annoyance. It was clear he had meant the sweet for Bob, but Snap had rushed in and taken it instead.

14—The man looked in his tin but there were no more pellets in it. Angrily he slammed it shut and put it back in his pocket. He shook his fist at Snap. "You're a greedy little pest," he muttered. Then he turned his bicycle and cycled off down the road that led past the end of the police station. Snap gave a queer bark and started to run after him. A few minutes later Andrew Glenn came out of the police station and set off home. Bob followed at his heels.

15—It was after tea when Billy Pearson came running up to Glenn's cottage. "Is Snap here?" he asked anxiously. "No," said Glenn. "I haven't seen him." "But Bob was playing with him this morning," said Billy. "I thought, maybe, Snap had followed him home. Where can he be, Mr Glenn?" Andrew Glenn looked puzzled. Another dog had vanished. Was there any connection between the missing dogs and the missing sheep?

16—The kindly shepherd patted Billy's shoulder. "Don't worry, son," he said. "Snap is sure to turn up soon." When Billy had gone home Glenn picked up his shotgun. "Come on, Bob," he said. "If these sheep-stealers come again tonight we'll be ready for them." So for the next few hours Glenn and Bob patrolled the hills. Near midnight, Glenn was resting on a wall when Black Bob gave a growl and dashed off into the darkness.

17—Black Bob had heard a queer sound—the same sound as he had heard before, and he was going to see what was causing it. There was a full moon peeping below the edge of a bank of cloud, so it was quite light as Bob loped along. Suddenly Bob came to a stop, and a growl rumbled in his throat. His hackles rose as he saw, silhouetted against the moon, a pack of dogs racing along the skyline. There was something ghostly and unreal about them.

18—Black Bob realised he could not tackle these brutes alone. He raced back to his master and pulled at Andrew Glenn's coat. The shepherd knew what Bob's actions meant. "Right, lad," he said. "Lead on." Bob ran off, following the scent of the hounds, with Glenn hurrying along behind him. On the edge of a cliff Bob came to a stop. Below were the hounds—and they had rounded up four sheep belonging to a neighbouring farmer.

19—"Dogs stealing the sheep," muttered Andrew Glenn. "Come on, Bob, we'll follow them." By the time Bob and Glenn climbed down the cliff the hounds were out of sight in the hills, for they had been well trained and were driving the sheep in a close, compact bunch. Bob was able to follow their scent, and it led the collie and his master to an unused quarry. Here they saw the sheep in a roughly-made pen, but there was no sign of the hounds.

20—Glenn was puzzled for a moment. He couldn't make out why the hounds had left the sheep here, nor who had made the pen. Then the shepherd suddenly realised what was happening. "These sheep have been left here for someone else to collect," he muttered to himself. "In that case we won't worry about the hounds in the meantime, Bob. We'll wait to see who comes for the sheep." So Bob and Glenn climbed down and hid near the pen.

21—All night long they waited and nothing happened. There wasn't a sound except an occasional bleat from the sheep. Glenn began to wonder if anyone was going to come for the sheep. Maybe he and Bob had been seen and the sheep-stealers had changed their plans. Then as dawn broke, Glenn heard the sound of a car engine. A few minutes later a van drew up on the road near the quarry. A man got out and walked towards the sheep.

22—Glenn was disappointed. It was only a laundry van, and it didn't seem likely that it had anything to do with the sheep-stealers. As the man drew near, Glenn moved out of his hiding place. "Well," he said, "what are you doing here?" The man turned round, startled. He hadn't seen Bob and Glenn until now. "Oh, hello," he said, "I saw these sheep and wondered what they were doing in the quarry. But I suppose they belong to you?"

23—"As a matter of fact, they don't," said Glenn. "They've been stolen." Then he told the laundry man what had happened. "I see," said the man. "I thought it was a bit queer when I saw them here. It's not often you see sheep penned in a quarry." While Glenn and the man were talking, Black Bob went over to the laundry van. It had a familiar smell about it. The side door was slightly open, so the collie went inside and had a look round.

24—Inside were some big laundry baskets, and hanging from the corner of one of them was a piece of sheep's wool. No wonder the van had a familiar smell—it was the smell of sheep. Bob pulled the piece of wool off the basket and ran outside. Glenn was on the point of saying good-bye to the laundry-man when Bob ran up to him. But Glenn paid no attention to Bob just then. It was only when the van drove away that he looked at his collie.

25—"What's bothering you now, Bob?" said the shepherd. Then he noticed the piece of wool which Bob was holding up to him. "So you've found a piece of wool. But there's nothing remarkable about that. There must be hundreds of pieces like that lying around. I don't know what you're getting so excited about." Bob ran a little way down the road, but still Andrew Glenn didn't realise that Bob had found the wool in the back of the laundry van.

26—Finally Andrew Glenn threw the piece of wool away. "I'm sorry, Bob," he said. "But I don't know what you're trying to tell me. I think we might as well take these four sheep back to Farmer Craig. The sheep-stealers won't come and collect them now that it's broad daylight." So Bob and Glenn let the sheep out of the pen and drove them back towards the farm. When they reached the farm road, little Billy Craig came running to meet them.

27—Billy began to romp with Bob, chasing him through the stackyard, and playfully pulling his ears and tail. Andrew Glenn, meanwhile, was talking to Farmer Craig about the sheep-stealing. None of them saw the furtive figure slinking through the stackyard. It was the man with the crumpled brown suit and untidy hair whom Bob had met in the village the day before. On hands and knees he crept round the stacks, making for Bob and Billy.

28—The man got within a few yards of Bob, then he fumbled in his pocket and brought out one of the little black pellets. "Here, lad," he hissed. As Bob turned, the man held out the pellet. "Go on, take it, boy," he coaxed. But Bob didn't take it. He backed away snarling fiercely. Bob remembered the queer way Snap had behaved after taking one of these pellets, and the collie's instinct told him that this untidy stranger was up to no good.

29—As the man crept nearer, Bob suddenly let out a fierce growl and snapped at the man's fingers. The stranger jumped back hurriedly, dropping his cap as he did so. Bob started to bark fiercely, and the rough fellow decided to clear out. He ran away swiftly and Bob watched him go. Then he lifted the cap the man had dropped, trotted over to his master, and held it out to him. "Here, Craig," said Andrew Glenn. "Bob's found an old cap of yours."

30—But the farmer shook his head. "It's not mine," he said. "Then whose is it?" muttered the shepherd. "Where did you find it, lad?" Bob at once turned, and by pulling at Glenn's coat persuaded his master to come with him on the trail of the ugly stranger. For miles they followed it, then suddenly Bob growled. Below were the sheep-stealing hounds. One of them was holding open the gate of the pen while the other four drove out Glenn's sheep.

31—It was all done quickly and without a single bark from any of the dogs. They were well trained. There was no doubt about that. Then, without warning, three of the brutes stopped chasing the sheep and made for Glenn and Bob. The shepherd got ready to defend himself and Bob took up a position near him. Next second the hounds arrived. It was a fierce fight. Glenn kept lashing out with his crook while Bob tackled the hounds that Glenn missed.

32—The brutes seemed fearless. Time and again they rushed in. Then a lucky blow from Glenn hit one of the hounds on the head. It fell unconscious. At the same time Bob pinned down one of the others. When the brute managed to break free, it fled. The other dog followed it. Glenn bent down to examine the unconscious dog. "This is Grip," he muttered. "Farmer Findlay's dog that vanished two nights ago. How does he come to be mixed up in this?"

33—Glenn decided to leave Grip there for the time being, for just then his sheep were more important. By now they had been driven over a ridge and were out of sight. Bob and Glenn hurried to the top of the ridge, but there was no sign of the sheep or the hounds. The only thing in sight was a van. And Bob just couldn't pick up a trail. The hounds and sheep had vanished. Finally Bob and Glenn returned to where they'd left Grip. He was no longer there.

34—A week passed and still the raids went on. The situation was serious. By this time over a hundred sheep had been stolen. Finally the shepherds could stand it no longer. They decided to band together to hunt down the thieves. So one morning Glenn and three of his friends set off carrying haversacks packed with food. They were prepared to spend the next twenty-four hours hunting the sheep-stealers. Bob, of course, went with them.

35—The men did not tramp aimlessly over the hills. They worked to a plan. Glenn was convinced that the sheep were being carried off by road, so the men patrolled the hills near the roads in the hope that they might come across some sign of the sheep-stealers. Glenn's plan worked. Late in the afternoon they were near the railway viaduct when they saw four hounds driving off some sheep. Bob and the shepherds worked their way towards them.

36—They crossed the river at some stepping-stones and made for the hounds, which were now driving the sheep along the side of a wood. "If they nip into the wood we'll lose sight of them," said Glenn. "I'll send Bob on to try to head them off." He signalled to Bob and at once the collie went racing away. But Bob was too late. The hounds saw him coming. They left the sheep and made for a gap in the wire-netting fence surrounding the wood.

37—Black Bob got there a minute later and cautiously crawled through the gap in the fence. Then he peered into the matted tangle of trees and bushes, trying to catch a glimpse of the hounds. But he saw no signs of the dogs, nor did he hear any sound that would lead him towards them. Black Bob was puzzled. The hounds had made a very quick getaway. The only thing the collie could do was to try to pick up their scent and follow them.

38—Bob sniffed around and managed to get on the trail of the hounds. Then, nose to the ground, he set off through the trees. But he had only gone a few paces when suddenly there was a movement in some bushes. Next second a sack was thrust violently over Bob's head. Bob struggled and fought, but all to no avail. Big, strong hands were holding the sack firmly over Black Bob's head, and though he tried hard, he couldn't escape.

39—Glenn and the shepherds made sure that the sheep were all right then they climbed over the fence into the wood. They saw no signs of the hounds or Bob, so they began to search the wood, beating every bush that could be used as a hiding place. The main road ran through this wood, and when the men reached it a van passed them. It was the laundry van that Glenn had seen at the quarry. Glenn gave the two men in the cab a friendly wave.

40—Right through the wood went the four shepherds, strung out in a line so that the hounds couldn't double back and get behind them. They reached the far side of the wood without finding a trace of the hounds or of Black Bob. Beyond the wood was a flat stretch of country with no cover of any kind, so the hounds couldn't have gone that way without being seen. The men were baffled. They couldn't make out what had happened to Bob and the hounds.

41—Black Bob, meanwhile, was in big trouble. He was in the back of the laundry van—the same van that had passed Glenn—and in the big baskets around him were the four strange hounds. The man who had captured Bob in the sack was one of the sheep-stealers, and he had carried Bob through the wood to where the laundry van was waiting. That was the sheep-stealers' secret. They used this van to transport the hounds and the stolen sheep.

Dirty work in a laundry

42—A few miles along the road the van stopped and a man climbed into the back. It was Beefy Brand, the roughly-dressed stranger. Beefy had caught Bob and put him in the van, and the collie realised by now that this man was one of the sheep-stealers. Beefy dragged Bob outside, but he kept a firm grip of the rope while he opened the hampers. As the four dogs jumped out, Bob got a shock. One was Snap, Billy Pearson's missing terrier.

43—Beefy spoke a few words to the van driver, then he set off through a wood, dragging Bob along with him. The other four dogs followed Beefy obediently. The fat man seemed to have a strange power over them. Presently they came to an old shack. At one time it had been used by woodmen, but now it served as a hideout for Beefy and his dogs. For the rest of the day Bob was kept a prisoner in the hut, along with a dozen other dogs.

44—Near midnight Beefy took Bob and three of the other dogs away through the wood. An hour's walking brought them to a laundry on the outskirts of a village near Selkirk. Beefy went up to a door and knocked. The door was opened by a man wearing a skull cap. Beefy followed the man into the laundry. "I've caught this collie belonging to the man called Glenn," said Beefy. "Good," said Smythe, as he was called. "Give him a pill."

45—Beefy opened a tin and threw a little black pellet to each of the dogs. Bob made no attempt to eat his pill, but the other dogs gobbled theirs up. Bob sensed there was something evil about these pills. He was right. They were made of a special chemical, and if a dog ate one it would do anything to get more. That was the secret of Beefy's power over these hounds. They did as they were told in the hope that they would get more pills.

46—Beefy was determined to get Bob under his power like the other dogs. He got Smythe to take a firm hold of Black Bob, and then he forced the pill into the collie's mouth. Beefy watched for a minute, but Bob made no move to spit out the pill. "That's fine," gloated Beefy. "He must have swallowed it by now. This dog won't annoy us any more. He'll do what he's told now." But Beefy Brand was wrong. Black Bob hadn't swallowed the pill.

47—The other dogs were now prancing round Beefy, eager to get more of the pills. "Give them some more," said Smythe. "You're going to steal that prize ram tonight, and you'll have to keep the dogs well under control to do it." "Right," said Beefy, and he took out his tin. While he was giving the dogs more of the pills, Bob slipped away to a corner of the room. Then, unseen by the two sheep-stealers, he spat out the little black pill.

48—Bob's distrust of these men overcame any desire to eat this queer-tasting pill. But Beefy and Smythe didn't know this. They went into the office. On the wall was a large map. "The ram's up at White's Farm here," Smythe pointed. "When you get it, hurry over the hill and tie it up in the gorse near this corner on the Selkirk road. Dickson will come along in the van for it later. Make no mistakes about this. It's a very valuable beast."

49—Every detail of the theft was worked out and it seemed foolproof. Who would think of looking in a laundry van for a stolen sheep? With this trick the sheep-stealers had been very successful. About two in the morning when Beefy set out he took Bob with him. But it was not a cowed, harmless Bob who would obey every word in order to get more pills. Black Bob was on the alert, waiting his chance to upset the sheep-stealers' carefully laid plans.

50—Presently Beefy and the four dogs arrived at White's Farm. Beefy soon located the prize ram in a field and signalled to the dogs. Away they went, without a sound, and got the ram moving. Black Bob pretended to help them, and not for one moment did Beefy suspect that the collie was not in his power. But the ram was stubborn. Suddenly it stopped and refused to move. Muttering angrily, Beefy started to drag it along the path.

51—Beefy was no fool. He could have set the dogs on it, but he didn't want this valuable ram to go charging through the darkness in a panic in case it fell and injured itself. So Beefy tugged and wrestled with the ram all the way to the Selkirk road. Here a member of the gang had already left some brushwood hurdles and driven a stake into the ground. While Beefy was tying the ram to the stake Bob took the chance to slip away.

52—Bob's luck was out. One of the dogs saw him and gave a growl. Beefy cursed when he saw Bob running off. "After him," he ordered. Obediently the three dogs set off after Bob. But the collie dodged through a wood and jumped into a stream. He waded through the water for some distance, then climbed out on the other side. Looking back, Bob saw Beefy and the dogs trying to pick up his trail. They were baffled, for the water had destroyed Bob's scent.

53—Black Bob made for his master's cottage at top speed. It was several miles away, and it took Bob some time to get there. Being a countryman, Andrew Glenn seldom locked the door, so Bob lifted the latch and let himself into the cottage. He barked loudly, then started tugging the clothes off his master's bed. Andrew Glenn woke with a start. He saw from Bob's actions that there was something amiss and he dressed quickly.

54—Then Bob led Glenn off on the long walk to the spot where Beefy had left Farmer White's prize ram. But luck was against him. He got there just in time to see a laundry van start to drive off down the road. Nearby were the brushwood hurdles which Beefy had put round the ram to hide it, but of the ram itself there was no sign. It was quite clear what was going on. Farmer White's prize ram was in the back of the laundry van.

55—Glenn, of course, didn't know this until Bob led him over to the brush-wood hurdles. When Glenn saw the stake and the rope attached to it he realised there was something fishy happening. Then Bob started to chase the van. Glenn followed, too, but they were left far behind. Presently the road began to zig-zag over the hills. Bob left the road and took a short-cut across country. On the far side of the hills he saw the van outside a cottage.

56—The van driver was coolly delivering the weekly parcel of clean laundry at this cottage, and all the time there was a stolen ram in the back of the van. No wonder the sheep-stealers had been so successful. Nobody would suspect that this van had anything to do with the missing sheep. When Bob reached the van he heard faint sounds from inside one of the baskets. He jumped up and started to chew through the rope holding the lid down.

57—Black Bob ripped and slashed at the rope with his strong teeth. He was in a desperate hurry, for the laundry man might return at any moment. The last strand parted just as the driver returned to the van. Quickly Bob dodged out of the way. "Hey, what are you up to?" shouted the driver. He soon found out. The man reached the back of the van just as the ram came hurtling out of the basket. With a frightened yell he staggered back.

58—For the next few seconds there was pandemonium. When Black Bob came rushing round the end of the van the ram was thundering down the road in a panic, and Dickson, the van driver, was scrambling to his feet. A little farther off was Andrew Glenn, racing up at top speed. Dickson realised the game was up. He turned. He couldn't get through the gate because of Mrs Wright, who was standing there screaming, so he vaulted over the wall.

59—Andrew Glenn realised by now that this laundry van was being used by the sheep-stealers and that it was important to catch the driver. "Go on, Bob," shouted Glenn. "Catch him, boy." But Bob was already over the wall and speeding round the corner of the cottage after the driver, who was racing across the drying green. Bob saw that the man was heading straight for a clothes line lying on the grass. The collie made a quick grab for it.

60—Bob snatched up the clothes rope and threw himself back on his haunches. The rope twanged taut just as the van driver drew level with it. The man didn't have time to stop. The rope caught him across the front of the legs and he went flying headlong. Black Bob dropped the rope and ran over to stop the man from getting up. But he need not have worried. Dickson had fallen with such a wallop that he was too dazed to try to escape.

61—He lay there groaning as Glenn came running up followed by Big Hughie Wright, who had come out of his cottage to see what the rumpus was about. Bob left them and went after the runaway ram. It had left the road and was now racing across the moor. Bob managed to overtake it and turned it back towards an empty hen-run alongside the cottage garden. Skilfully and quickly, Bob drove the ram through the open doorway.

62—Once the ram was inside, Bob shut the door and pulled the wooden snib into place. The ram would be safe there until it could be returned to Farmer White. Meanwhile Dickson had been talking. He had told Glenn and Hughie that he was taking the ram to a place on the Berwick road, where it would be handed over to another member of the gang. Glenn and Hughie decided to catch this rogue, too, so they tied Dickson to the seat of his van.

63—Their plan was to hide in the van while Dickson drove to the meeting place. Then, provided Dickson didn't warn his pal, they would stand a good chance of surprising the second sheep-stealer. When Dickson was securely tied, Hughie, Glenn and Bob hid in the baskets in the van. Then Dickson drove off and about half an hour later he stopped at a side road. A big float was waiting there and its driver came over to the van.

64—"Is the stuff in the back?" he asked. Dickson hesitated. Then he heard a movement in the basket behind him, the one in which Big Hughie was hiding. That decided Dickson. He remembered what Hughie had threatened to do to him if he gave the game away. He nodded to the lorry driver. "Yes," he muttered. "It's there all right." "Good," said the lorry driver. He went round to the back of the van and began to open the door.

65—There were tiny spaces in the sides of the big hamper and Glenn was able to see what was happening. He saw the door opening and the burly figure of the driver standing there. The shepherd leapt upright and brought the lid of the basket crashing down on the lorry driver's head. Never was a man more surprised. He was taken completely unawares by the sudden blow. Startled, shocked, and stupefied, he fell on his back in the roadway.

66—That one blow put paid to Martin, the lorry driver. Before he could get to his feet Glenn leapt out of the basket and grabbed him. Big Hughie was close behind Glenn, and between them they forced Martin into the back of the van. Then Glenn told Dickson to drive the van down to the police station in the village. Here Constable Moffat took charge. After hearing Glenn's story, the constable locked his prisoners in a cell.

67—Glenn then suggested to Constable Moffat that it might be worth while taking a look at the laundry which employed Dickson. "That's not a bad idea," said Moffat. "The rest of the gang may work there." So Glenn, Bob and the constable went to the laundry. The first building they came to was the boiler-house. The two men looked inside, but there was nobody about. Black Bob, however, was sniffing at a heap of small coal.

68—There was a familiar scent coming from that coal—the scent of sheep. To Black Bob, who had spent all his life amongst sheep, the scent was unmistakable. He climbed on to the heap and began to scrape away the coal. Glenn stared at his collie in surprise. "Come down," he said. "You'll get in an awful mess." But a moment later Glenn saw the reason for Black Bob's queer behaviour. Buried under the coal was a big laundry basket.

69—Glenn and Moffat at once lent a hand and soon they had uncovered the whole top of the basket. Then they lifted the lid and there, hidden in the basket, were two sheep. Andrew Glenn recognised them by the marks on their ears. "These belong to Farmer Findlay," he said. "They must have been stolen. There's no doubt this laundry is mixed up with sheep-stealing." Moffat nodded grimly. "Yes," he said. "Let's see the manager."

70—Bob, Glenn and the policeman went across to the office and there they met Smythe, the manager. He was a strange-looking man because of the black skull cap he wore. "I know nothing about stolen sheep," he said, when Moffat started to question him. "The van driver must have hidden these sheep there. But have a good look round." While Moffat was searching Smythe's desk, Bob wandered off to a rack containing some laundry parcels.

71—Moffat found no papers of any kind in the desk which might show that Smythe was connected with the sheep-stealers. "There's nothing here," said the policeman. "We might as well go." Smythe smiled sourly and showed them to the door. But, meanwhile Bob had found a parcel which was different from all the rest. Smythe's scent was on it. Black Bob picked it up and ran outside. When Smythe saw the parcel he took to his heels and fled.

72—Andrew Glenn quickly realised that Smythe's flight had something to do with the parcel Bob had found. He and Moffat raced after Smythe. They caught up with him some distance away. Then, while Moffat held Smythe, Glenn opened the parcel. In it Glenn found bundles of bank notes, and a note-book containing a record of all the sheep that had been sold to unscrupulous dealers. This was proof that Smythe was the leader of the thieves.

73—On the way to the police station with Smythe, Bob started to tug at Glenn's jacket. Glenn realised that the collie was wanting to show him something. "I'll go and see what's bothering Bob," said the shepherd to Moffat. "I'll see you later." Bob at once started to lead Glenn over the hills towards Beefy Brand's hideout—the old hut in the wood. But Beefy's dogs gave the alarm, and the sheep-stealer saw Glenn and Black Bob approaching.

74—Beefy brand was desperate. He realised by now that the game was up. There was only one way he could escape. Beefy opened the door and shouted an order to the hounds. At once they made for Glenn and Bob. Then Beefy ran off through the trees, counting on the dogs to keep Glenn and Bob from following him. His plan worked. Glenn realised that these brutes weren't normal. Quickly he scrambled into a tree. Bob turned and fled.

75—Black Bob wasn't scared. If his master had ordered him to do so, Bob would have fought those hounds. But the clever collie realised that the best thing to do was to lead the hounds away from Glenn, and give his master a chance to follow Beefy. So Bob ran at top speed with the hounds trailing after him. When Bob reached the edge of the wood he saw a big farm nearby. He ran towards it, hoping to give the hounds the slip amongst the buildings.

76—Bob reached the farm well ahead of the hounds and leapt the gate into the yard. Just ahead he saw a ladder leading up to a hay-loft. Bob glanced back at his pursuers. They hadn't reached the gate yet, and the wall hid him from their sight. Bob started to climb the ladder, but he wasn't quick enough. Before he reached the loft, the hounds came leaping over the gate into the yard. They saw Black Bob and at once set up a chorus of excited barks.

77—Black Bob looked around the loft. He was trapped. There was no other way out. He could hide amongst the hay, but the hounds would find him there easily enough. Then Bob saw above him a wide wooden beam running across the loft. The collie climbed on to a pile of hay, and from there he managed to scramble up on to the beam. He was just in time. As he lay flat along it, the hounds came hurrying up the ladder into the loft.

78—Whining eagerly, the dogs scattered and began to look for Bob amongst the hay. They were completely baffled. They couldn't make out where Bob had gone. And not one of them thought of looking upwards. Very silently Black Bob wormed his way along the beam towards the door. Then, waiting until the hounds were looking in another direction, Bob dropped lightly to the floor. Still without making a sound he started to climb down the ladder.

79—In a few seconds Bob had reached the bottom of the ladder. He did not run off at once. He took hold of the bottom of the ladder and gave it a sharp tug. The ladder clattered to the ground. The noise brought the hounds rushing to the door of the loft. But they were too late. They were well and truly trapped. It was much too far to the ground for the hounds to jump, so they just had to stay in the loft, barking and yowling.

80—Bob left them there and ran back to the wood. Here he found his master trying to follow Beefy's trail. Glenn was glad to see Bob. "Good boy," he said. "So you managed to dodge them." Then he pointed to Beefy's footprints in some soft earth. "Seek him," he coaxed. Black Bob ran off with his nose to the ground. He managed to follow Beefy's trail and as they drew near the village, they caught sight of Beefy heading for the railway station.

81—There was a hunted, panic-stricken look in Beefy's eyes. He was wanted by the police for many other crimes besides sheep-stealing, and he knew capture would mean a long prison sentence. Just then a train pulled in at one of the platforms. Beefy realised there wasn't time for him to go over the bridge so he started to climb over the station wall. "Go on, Bob. Hurry!" shouted Andrew Glenn. "Stop him before he gets aboard that train."

82—Black Bob raced towards the station at top speed. The wall was too high for Bob to jump so he made a beeline for a five-barred gate. He cleared it with a single bound and landed in the station yard. Bob could see no sign of Beefy as he raced up the steps on to the bridge But when Bob reached the top he spotted the sheep-stealer dashing along the crowded platform towards the train. Bob raced down the steps on to the platform.

83—By the time Bob reached the platform Beefy had vanished amongst the passengers entering and leaving the train. Bob dived into the crowd but he found he couldn't make his way quickly enough through the jostling throng to catch up with Beefy. There was only one thing to do. Black Bob scrambled up on to the tender of the engine. The driver and a nearby porter let out startled yells, but before they could do anything, Bob was out of reach.

84—He ran quickly over the coal and jumped on the first carriage of the train. From there he had a good view of the crowded platforms, and as he ran along the carriage roofs he kept a sharp look out for Beefy. Bob was halfway along the train when suddenly he gave an eager bark. He had caught sight of Beefy opening the door of a compartment. In another second he would have been out of sight. With a snarl, Bob threw himself at Beefy.

85—Beefy let out a howl of fear when he saw this vengeful fury of a dog that had upset his plans so often. He threw Bob to the ground, but almost at once Bob was on his feet again. He seized Beefy's jacket between his teeth and hung on grimly. The crowd scattered as Beefy swung round, beating at Bob with his fist and trying to dislodge him. But Bob kept his grip, and he was still holding on to the sheep-stealer when Andrew Glenn came panting up.

The Black Prowlers will raid no more

86—Beefy realised then that he was licked and he waited quietly until Constable Moffat was sent for. Beefy was taken along to the police station. He was searched and in one of his pockets they found a flat box containing some of the black pellets that he used to control his dogs. He glowered angrily at Bob as the collie sniffed the pellets. "That's right," growled Beefy. "Have a good look at them. If you'd eaten one of these I'd never have been caught."

87—While Constable Moffat was questioning Beefy, there was a phone call from a nearby farmer. He sounded puzzled. And no wonder! He had found Beefy's pack of dogs in his loft. Glenn guessed that it was Bob who had trapped them there and told Moffat what had happened. Later on, Bob, Glenn and Moffat went to the farm, and on the way they called on three folk who had lost dogs recently. Farmer Gray, Farmer Findlay and Billy Pearson.

88—When they arrived at the farm, the dogs were still in the loft. But there was nothing wild or fierce about them now, because the effects of Beefy's pellets had worn off. In fact three of the dogs were yelping excitedly at sight of their masters. One was Snap, Billy Pearson's little fox terrier. When it got out of the loft it jumped up and down in front of Billy, barking all the while in a fever of excitement at meeting its young master again.

89—None of the dogs was any the worse of having been under Beefy's control, and it was arranged that they should all be returned to their owners. All the farmers thanked Glenn and Bob before they left, for they realised that it was due to Bob's cleverness that the sheep-stealers had been caught. Billy Pearson and Snap were the last to leave, and Andrew Glenn smiled as they romped off towards the village. Another great adventure was over.

A DOG'S LIFE

THE BLACK BOB INDEX
INTRODUCTION

This chronological index of the strips and stories that have featured Black Bob is split into two sections. The first section outlines his appearances in the text story format and the second, much larger section, his appearances in the picture story format. All of Black Bob's picture serials and most of his picture completes had their origins in the tabloid pages of *The Weekly News* where, from October 1946 to September 1967, he appeared in a half page, nine-panel strip every week. And, in turn, virtually all Black Bob strips that appeared anywhere other than the *Weekly News* were reprints from that paper in one form or another, with some *Weekly News* serials even being cut into self-contained sections for use in a number of locations over a number of years. It is especially important to note that when Black Bob was reprinted in the pages of *The Dandy* comic from 1956 to 1968 a good deal of editing of the original *Weekly News* nine-panel strips was necessary to accommodate the single eight-panel page adopted by *The Dandy* at this time. A problem that was subsequently rectified for Black Bob's later serialised appearances in *The Dandy* when a two-page, nine-panels per page format was introduced from 1969 to 1982. It should also be pointed out that, for reasons of space, and beyond their original appearance, this index only charts the history of the text stories and picture strips where any reprinting amounted to a page, or more, of the original and does not include montages made up of individual illustrations from various sources as are often found in editions of the yearly *Beano/Dandy* celebration volumes. To give an example of how the index works, here are the details of the 1948 *Weekly News* series 'Birsay Island' (PS6). After its initial appearance in the *Weekly News* this series was split into two self-contained parts and republished in the Black Bob Book for 1951, the first half titled as i) Brave Bob's Island Adventures and the second as ii) Ten Pell Mell Days for Black Bob. The strip was then reprinted twice in *The Dandy* comic first, in 1958, iii) D844-867 and then, in 1977, in iv) D1858-1869 before finally the Ten Pell Mell Days segment of the strip, as published in the Black Bob Book for 1951, turned up in the celebratory *Beano/Dandy* volume v) 'Crazy about Creatures' (2009). Also, all artwork contained in the strips and stories that follow was the work of Jack Prout except in the examples indicated otherwise.

TEXT STORY DETAILS

TS1) **Kidnapped** D280(25/11/44) - 287(3/3/45) adapted as PS1.

TS2) **Amnesia** D298(4/8/45) - 305(10/11/45) adapted as PS2.

   i) **Favourites from the Forties** (2003) 1 episode (18/8/45).

TS3) **From Shropshire to Selkirk** D314(16/3/46) - 323(20/7/46)

TS4) **Black Bob's Double** D327(14/9/46) - 338(15/2/47) adapted as PS4.

TC1) **Guide Dog Bob** DMC1947. Art - James 'Peem' Walker.

TS5) **Blind Billy** D344(24/5/47) - 352(13/9/47) adapted as PS5.

TC2) **Bob's Cliff-ledge Rescue** DMC1948. Art - James 'Peem' Walker.

TS6) **The Bad Shepherd** D359(20/12/47) - 368(24/4/48) adapted as PS8.

TS7) **The Perky Pup** D374(17/7/48) - 380(9/10/48) adapted as PS3.

TS8) **Alabama Johnny** D391(12/3/49) - 399(2/7/49)

TS9) **The Scarface Gang** D403(13/8/49) - 410(1/10/49)

TS10) **The Siberian Wolf** D415(5/11/49) - 426(21/1/50)

TC3) **The Mad Dog of Tinker's Hill** BB1950

TC4) **The Danger Light on Bradman's Bridge** BB1950

TC5) **Stop that Tiger** BB1950

TC6) **The Mad Bull** D419(22/4/50)

TS11) **Tex Mason's Horses** D445(3/6/50) - 456(19/8/50)

TS12) **Luke Fragg's Circus** D466(28/10/50) - 480(3/2/51)

TC7) **The Feud at the Clattering Crags** BB1951

TC8) **Black Bob and the Towsy Tinkers** BB1951

TC9) **Black Bob's Plucky Pals** BB1951

TS13) **Spitfire, the wildcat kitten** D490(14/4/51) - 501(30/6/51)

TS14) **The Mysterious Prowler** D519(3/11/51) - 532(2/2/52)

TS15) **Mr Nobody the Hypnotist** D543(19/4/52) - 553(28/6/52)

TS16) **Cripple Dick Duncan** D565(20/9/52) - 574(22/11/52)

TC10) **Black Bob and the Terrible Tucker Twins** BB1953

TC11) **The Wreck on Red Man's Reef** BB1953

TS17) **Andrew blind in France** D586(31/1/53) - 597(2/5/53)

TS18) **The Phantom Robber of Thirlwood** D623(31/10/53) - 640(27/2/54)

TS19) **Castaways on Mysterious Island** D653(29/5/54) - 664(14/8/54)

TC12) **Black Bob on the Danger Trail** BB1955

TC13) **The Midnight Mystery at Frenchie's Inn** BB1955

TS20) **The Skyman** D684(1/1/55) - 694(12/3/55)

TS21) **Salvador the Lion Tamer** D709(26/6/55) - 720(10/9/55)

   i) **Crazy about Creatures** (2009) final episode.

TC14) **The Flight from the Roaring Rip** BB1957

   i) **Great Stories from the First Fifty Years** (1990)

TC15) **Plucky Pals Bob and Nick** BB1957

TC16) **Black Bob and the 40 Thieves** BB1959

TC17) **The Bravery of Bonehead Fred** BB1959

TC18) **Black Bob and the Shepherd Crook** BB1961

TC19) **The Forbidden Lands of Snarly Sharp** BB1961

TC20) **That Shepherd's a Crook** BB1965

TC21) **The Feud at No-Man's Farm** BB1965

TC22) **The Vengeance of the Roaring Rockets** DB1966

TC23) **Battling Bighorn** DB1967

TC24) **Reckless Robbie** DB1968

TC25) **Blind Bob** DB1969

ABBREVIATIONS USED IN THE INDEX

TS = Text Series
TC = Text Complete

PS = Picture Series
PC = Picture Complete
CS = Comic Strip
WN = The Weekly News
D = Dandy Comic

DMC = Dandy Monster Comic
DB = Dandy Book
BB = Black Bob Book
DBSS = Dandy/Beano Summer Special

DSS = Dandy Summer Special
CC = Classics from the Comics
BCL = Beano Comic Library

THE BLACK BOB INDEX
PICTURE STORY DETAILS

PS1) **Kidnapped** WN(5/10/46) - (25/1/47)
adaptation of TS1.
i) **The Bravery of Bob** BB1950
ii) D754(5/5/56) - 762(30/6/56)
PC1) **The Rebel Sheep** WN(1/2/47)
i) **Black Bob's Blizzard Battle** BB1950
PC2) **The Championship Cup** WN(8/2/47)
i) **Black Bob and the Mud-Pie Boys** BB1950
PC3) **The Stockyard Fire** WN(15/2/47)
i) **Black Bob and the Schoolboy Scallywags**
BB1951 Due to severe weather conditions no issues
of the Weekly News were published for the weeks
(22/2/47) or (1/3/47).
PS2) **Amnesia** WN(8/3/47) - (21/6/47) adaptation of
TS2.
i) **Faithful Old Friend** BB1950
ii) D763(7/7/56) - 778(20/10/56)
iii) D1192(26/9/64) - 1207(9/1/65)
PC4) **The Mad Alsatian** WN(28/6/47)
i) **Black Bob and the Mad Alsatian** BB1950
PC5) **The Telephone Linesman** WN(5/7/47)
i) **Black Bob and the hair-raising hat-trick** BB1951
PS3) **The Perky Pup** WN(12/7/47) - (16/8/47) adaptation
of TS7.
i) **Black Bob and the Perky Pup** BB1950
ii) **Black Bob and the Perky Pup** DMC1951
iii) D815(6/7/57) - 819(3/8/57)
iv) D1891(18/2/78) - 1893(4/3/78)
PC6) **The Dammed Burn** WN(23/8/47)
i) **Black Bob and the Three Jack Tars** BB1951
PC7) **The Wild Bull** WN(30/8/47)
i) **Black Bob and the Wild Welsh Bull**
DMC1951
PC8) **The Electric Cable** WN(6/9/47)

i) **Black Bob and the Electric Peril** BB1950
PC9) **The Phone Call** WN(13/9/47)
i) **Black Bob and the phone-call fire call** BB1950
PS4) **Black Bob's Double** WN(20/9/47) - (29/11/47)
adaptation of TS4.
i) **Black Bob the Outlaw** BB1951
ii) D790(12/1/57) - 800(23/3/57)
iii) D1870(24/9/77) - 1875(29/10/77)
PS5) **Blind Billy** WN(6/12/47) - (13/3/48) adaptation
of TS5.
i) **Black Bob and Blind Billy** BB1953
ii) D801(30/3/57) - 814(29/6/57)
iii) D1850(7/5/77) - 1857(25/6/77)
PS6) **Birsay Island** WN(20/3/48) - (28/8/48)
i) **Brave Bob's Island Adventures** BB1951
ii) **Ten Pell Mell Days for Black Bob** BB1951
iii) D844(25/1/58) - 867(5/7/58)
iv) D1858(2/7/77) - 1869(17/9/77)
v) **Crazy about Creatures** (2009) **Ten Pell Mell Days
for Black Bob**.
PS7) **Bob is Lost** WN(4/9/48) - (5/2/49)
i) **Black Bob and the Trip-Rope Trap** DMC1951
ii) **Black Bob and the Little Brown Bomber**
DMC1952
iii) **Wandering Bob** BB1953
iv) D884(1/11/58) - 904(21/3/59)
v) D1839(19/2/77) - 1849(30/4/77)
PC10) **The Farmer's Children** DMC1949 **Not
reprinted.**
PC11) **The Football Team** WN(12/2/49) **Not reprinted.**
PC12) **The Bath-Chair** WN(19/2/49)
i) **Black Bob and the Never-say-Die Sergeant**
BB1951
PS8) **The Bad Shepherd** WN(26/2/49) - (28/5/49)

adaptation of TS6
i) **Black Bob all alone** DB1953
ii) **Ten Hard Weeks for Black Bob** BB1953
iii) D905(28/3/59) - 918(27/6/59)
iv) D1876(5/11/77) - 1882(17/12/77)
PC13) **Bob in the Belfry** WN(4/6/49)
i) **Black Bob's Ding-Dong Rescue** DB1953
ii) D989(5/11/60)
PC14) **Buried Alive** WN(11/6/49)
i) **Black Bob's Black-faced Battle** DMC1952
PC15) **The Billy Goat** WN(18/6/49)
i) D930(19/9/59)
PC16) **Slick Mick** WN(25/6/49)
i) **Black Bob and the Bandit Boy** DMC1952
PC17) **The Ragman** WN(2/7/49)
i) D931(26/9/59)
PC18) **The Burglar** WN(9/7/49)
i) DBSS1963
PC19) **The Cap Trick** WN(16/7/49)
i) **Black Bob and the Red Raider** DB1955
PC20) **The Valet** WN(23/7/49)
i) Odd Job Bob DB1954
PC21) **The Homing Pigeon** WN(30/7/49) **Not reprinted.**
PC22) **The Flower Show** WN(6/8/49)
i) **The Black Joker** DB1955
PC23) **The Railway Siding** WN(13/8/49) **Not reprinted**
PS9) **The Nicker** WN(20/8/49) - (3/12/49)
i) **Black Bob and the Nicker** DB1953
ii) **BLack Bob and that nuisance the Nicker**
BB1955
iii) D868(12/7/58) - 883(25/10/58)
iv) D1883(24/12/77) - 1890(11/2/78)
PS10) **The Onion Johnny** WN(10/12/49) - (21/1/50)
i) **Black Bob and the hunted Onion Johnny**

DB1960
PC24) **Black Bob and the Sheep Stealers** DMC1950
   Not reprinted.
PS11) **Return to Birsay** WN(28/1/50) - (22/7/50)
   i) **Black Bob and the Bold Sea-Dog** DB1954
   ii) **Black Bob and the Storm-along Battler** DB1954
   iii) **Black Bob's Big Job** BB1955
   iv) D933(10/10/59) - 953(27/2/60)
   v) D1944(24/2/79) - 1956(19/5/79)
   vi) DB1991 with amendations.
PS12) **The Salmon Poachers** WN(29/7/50) - (23/9/50)
   i) **Black Bob against the Salmon Poachers** BB1957
   ii) D954(5/3/60) - 962(30/4/60)
   iii) D1957(26/5/79) - 1961(23/6/79)
PS13) **The Gaucho** WN(30/9/50) - (9/12/50)
   i) **Clever Bob the dog detective** BB1955
   ii) D919(4/7/59) - 929(12/9/59)
   iii) D1962(30/6/79) - 1967(4/8/79)
PS14) **Tommy Watt** WN(16/12/50) - (9/6/51)
   i) **Two brave runaways on the long,long road
   to London** BB1957
   ii) D963(7/5/60) - 988(29/10/60)
   iii) D1731(25/1/75) - 1743(19/4/75)
PS15) **The Bighorn Ram** WN(16/6/51) - (25/8/51)
   i) D781(10/11/56) - 789(5/1/57)
   ii) D1894(11/3/78) - 1899(15/4/78)
PC25) **The Sea-lion** WN(1/9/51)
   i) D1208(16/1/65)
PC26) **The Old Lady's Budgie** WN(8/9/51) **Not reprinted.**
   Art George Ramsbottom
PC27) **The Thieving Jackdaw** WN(15/9/51)
   Art - George Ramsbottom
   i) D1308(17/12/66)
PC28) **The Wee Terrier** WN(22/9/51)
   Art - George Ramsbottom
   i) **Black Bob and the Black Scamp** DB1956

PC29) **The Mad Elephant** WN(29/9/51)
   Art - George Ramsbottom
   i) D1307(10/12/66)
PC30) **Fishy Business** WN(6/10/51) Not reprinted.
   Art - George Ramsbottom
PC31) **The Professor and the Black Cat** WN(13/10/51)
   Art - George Ramsbottom
   i) D1309(24/12/66)
PC32) **Bob Baffles Burglars** WN(20/10/51)
   Art - George Ramsbottom
   i) D1209(23/1/65)
   ii) D2924(6/12/97)
PS16) **The Dog Dealer** WN(27/10/51) - (15/3/52)
   i) D822(24/8/57) - 842(11/1/58)
   ii) D1900(22/4/78) - 1910(1/7/78)
PS17) **The Black Prowlers** WN(22/3/52) - (31/5/52)
   i) **Black Bob and the Black Prowlers** BB1957
   ii) D990(12/11/60) - 1000(21/1/61)
PS18) **Professor Rusack** WN(7/6/52) - (4/10/52)
   i) **Black Bob and the Flying Thief** DB1956
   ii) **Black Bob on Roaring Reef** DB1956
   iii) **You can't bluff Black Bob** DB1957
   iv) **Black Bob and the 10 o'clock prowler** DB1959
PS19) **Billy the Boxer** WN(11/10/52) - (11/4/53)
   i) **Black Bob's Pell-Mell Pal** BB1959
   ii) D1133(10/8/63) - 1158(1/2/64)
   iii) D1912(15/7/78) - 1922(23/9/78)
PS20) **Betty Ross** WN(18/4/53) - (1/8/53)
   i) D1083(25/8/62) - 1098(8/12/62)
   ii) D1923(30/9/78) - 1929(11/11/78)
PS21) **Ill in Canada** WN(8/8/53) - (27/2/54)
   i) **Black Bob's Day of Danger** DB1957
   ii) **Black Bob and the Canadian Killer** DB1958
   iii) **Black Bob's Canadian Christmas** DB1959
   iv) D1175(30/5/64) - 1189(5/9/64)
   v) D1930(18/11/78) - 1943(17/2/79)

PS22) **Kate Lindsay's Cottage** WN(6/3/54) - (24/4/54)
   Art - George 'Dod' Anderson
   i) **The Secret of Kate Lindsay's Cottage** DB1965
PS23) **The Cornish Smugglers** WN(1/5/54) - (17/7/54)
   i) **4 Dangerous Days for Black Bob** BB1959
   ii) D1113(23/3/63) - 1124(8/6/63)
   iii) D1725(14/12/74) - 1730(18/1/75)
PS24) **Buffer the Ram** WN(24/7/54) - (18/12/54)
   i) **Rammer on the Rampage** DB1958
   ii) D1001(28/1/61) - 1019(3/6/61)
   iii) D1707(10/8/74) - 1717(9/10/74)
PS25) **Bob in Spain** WN(25/12/54) - (26/2/55)
   i) **Black Bob the Bandit-Buster** BB1959
   ii) D1125(15/6/63) - 1132(3/8/63)
PC33) **Black Bob in the House of Hate** DB1955
   Not reprinted.
PS26) **The Farm Manager** WN(5/3/55) - (4/6/55)
   i) **The Boot for Black Bob** BB1961
   ii) D1159(8/2/64) - 1172(9/5/64)
   iii) D1968(11/8/79) - 1974(22/9/79)
   iv) CC67-73
PS27) **The Wild Goats** WN(11/6/55) - (6/8/55)
   i) **Black Bob and The Battling Billy Goat** DB1962
PS28) **The Dirty Dog** WN(13/8/55) - (1/10/55)
   Art - George Ramsbottom
   i) **Black Bob and the Dirty Dog** DB1961
PS29) **The Canadian Mine** WN(8/10/55) - (25/2/56)
   i) **Bullet-Proof Bob** BB1961
   ii) D1697(1/6/74) - 1706(3/8/74)
PS30) **The Canadian Farm** WN(3/3/56) - (9/6/56)
   i) **Black Bob and the Blind Mountie** DB1960
   ii) **Black Bob in the Wild West** DB1961
   iii) D1650(7/7/73) - 1657(23/8/73)
PS31) **The Spanish Galleon** WN(16/6/56) - (1/9/56)
   i) **Bad Luck Gold in Battle Bay** BB1961
PS32) **The Runaway Pup** WN(8/9/56) - (29/12/56)

i) D1047(16/12/61) - 1063(7/4/62)
PS33) **The Kidnapped Girl** WN(5/1/57) - (6/7/57)
   i) D1020(10/6/61) - 1046(9/12/61)
   ii) D1744(26/4/75) - 1757(26/7/75)
PS34) **The Roman Remains** WN(13/7/57) - (16/11/57)
   i) D1064(14/4/62) - 1082(18/8/62)
   ii) D1758(2/8/75) - 1769(18/10/75)
PS35) **Mystery Boy Danny** WN(23/11/57) - (1/3/58)
   i) **The Hide-Aways on Hee-Haw Hill** BB1965
   ii) D1718(26/10/74) - 1724(7/12/74)
   iii) CC8
PS36) **The Highland Cattle Rustlers**
   WN(8/3/58) - (7/6/58)
   i) D1099(15/12/62) - 1112(16/3/63)
PS37) **The Gipsy Boy** WN(14/5/58) - (18/10/58)
   i) D1324(8/4/67) - 1342(12/8/67)
PS38) **Cripple Billy** WN(25/10/58) - (27/12/58)
   Art - George 'Dod' Anderson
   i) **Cripple Billy and the Towsy Tinkers** DB1964
PC34) **Crook to catch a Crook** WN(3/1/59)
   Not reprinted.
PS39) **Bob in Argentina** WN(10/1/59) - (18/7/59)
   i) D1257(25/12/65) - 1283(25/6/66)
   ii) D2097(30/1/82) - 2110(1/5/82)
   iii) **Crazy about Creatures** (2009) 1page.
PS40) **Dusty the Pup** WN(25/7/59) - (17/10/59)
   i) **Black Bob and Hungry Hector** DB1963
PS41) **Blind Bob** WN(24/10/59) - (11/6/60)
   i) **Poor Blind Bob** BB1965
   ii) D1680(2/2/74) - 1696(25/5/74)
PS42) **Andrew Glenn's Double** WN(18/6/60) - (27/8/60)
   i) D1644(26/5/73) - 1649(30/6/73)
PS43) **Bob in Australia** WN(3/9/60) - (26/11/60)
   i) **Black Bob's Black Master** BB1965
   ii) D1802(5/6/76) - 1808(17/7/76)
PS44) **The Diamond Smugglers** WN(3/12/60) - (15/4/61)

i) D1625(13/1/73) - 1634(17/3/73)
   ii) CC103-109
PS45) **The Tucker Twins** WN(22/4/61) -(28/10/61)
   i) D1545(3/7/71) - 1558(2/10/71)
   ii) CC77-92
PS46) **The Apprentice Farmer** WN(4/11/61) - (9/6/62)
   i) D1228(5/6/65) - 1255(11/12/65)
   ii) D1786(14/2/76) - 1801(29/5/76)
PS47) **Professor Mills** WN(16/6/62) - (17/11/62)
   i) D1284(2/7/66) - 1306(3/12/66)
   ii) D2111(8/5/82) - 2122(24/7/82)
PS48) **The Great Dane Mystery** WN(24/11/62) - (27/7/63)
   i) D1344(26/8/67) - 1378(20/4/68)
   ii) D2066(27/6/81) - 2083(24/10/81)
PS49) **Bob in Holland** WN(3/8/63) - (18/1/64)
   i) D1379(27/4/68) -1402(5/10/68)
   ii) D2084(31/10/81) - 2096(23/1/82)
   iii) CC48-61
PS50) **The Wildcat** WN(25/1/64) - (25/4/64)
   i) D1618(15/11/72) - 1624(6/1/73)
   ii) CC94-100
PS51) **The Island Twins** WN(2/5/64) - (7/11/64)
   i) D1494(11/7/70) - 1507(10/10/70)
PC35) **Black Bob and the Homeless Pups** DSS1964
   Not reprinted.
PS52) **Lulu the Poodle** WN(14/11/64) - (3/4/65)
   i) D1559(9/10/71) - 1569(18/12/71)
   ii) CC23-32
PS53) **The Mystery Mansion** WN(10/4/65) - (14/8/65)
   i) D1570(25/12/71) - 1579(26/2/72)
PC36) **Bob to the Rescue** DSS1965 Not reprinted.
PS54) **The Rowdy Campers** WN(21/8/65) - (9/10/65) **Not reprinted**.
PS55) **The Flre Raiser** WN(16/10/65) - (1/1/66)
   i) D1446(9/8/69) - 1451(13/9/69)
PS56) **The Trained Falcon** WN(8/1/66) - (1/5/66)

i) D1635(24/3/73) - 1643(19/5/73)
   ii) CC37-45
PS57) **The Football Farmhand** WN(8/5/66) - (2/7/66)
   i) D1658(1/9/73) - 1661(22/9/73)
PC37) **Dusty the French Bullpup** DSS1966
   Not reprinted.
PS58) **The Wild Alsatian** WN(9/7/66) - (7/1/67)
   i) D1517(19/12/70) - 1528(6/3/71)
   ii) CC121
PS59) **The Bad-Tempered Bobby** WN(14/1/67) - (20/5/67)
   i) D1580(4/3/72) - 1589(6/5/72)
   ii) CC111-120
PS60) **Bob and the Setter** WN(27/5/67) - (2/9/67)
   Not reprinted.
PC38) **Dixie the Dalmatian** DSS1967 **Not reprinted.**
PC39) **Gabby Gibson the Bully** DSS1968 **Not reprinted.**
PC40) **The Alsatian Thief** DSS1975 **Not reprinted.**
PC41) **The Chicken Thieves** DSS1976 **Not reprinted.**
PC42) **Young Tim Taylor** DB1977 **Not reprinted.**
PC43) **Mrs Hobbs' Siamese Cat** DSS1977 **Not reprinted.**
PC44) **The Government Treasure** DB1978 Not reprinted.
CS1) One Menace and his Dog BCL33 (1983)
   Art - Dave Sutherland
   i) **Side by Side** (1999) 3 pages.
CS2) Shepherd Crook BCL84 (1985) Not reprinted.
   Art - Henry Davies
   Note) A further series titled '**Young Bob**' which
   appeared in the Dandy in 1989
   (2465-2468) and a strip titled '**Young Black Bob**'
   which appeared in the
   Dandy Book for 1990 are not strictly part of the
   true **Black Bob** series.
   Both were drawn by Keith Robson.

BLACK BOB'S ADVENTURES

BLACK BOB USUALLY STARTS THE DAY'S WORK BY RUNNING DOWN TO THE VILLAGE FOR HIS MASTER'S MILK AND NEWSPAPERS.

BOB HAS DONE MANY BRAVE DEEDS — FOR INSTANCE HE SAVED TED GRAY WHEN THE WEE LAD FELL THROUGH THE ICE ON A POND.

IT WAS A GREAT DAY FOR BOB WHEN HE CORNERED A CROOK. BOB BACKED A HORSE AND CART AGAINST THE DOOR OF A TELEPHONE KIOSK AND TRAPPED THE ROGUE INSIDE.

ANOTHER ROGUE WHO WAS NO MATCH FOR BOB WAS ALF BATES. THE CLEVER COLLIE SAW THROUGH THE CROOK'S DISGUISE AND CAUGHT HIM.

OLD SANDY TAIT IS A GREAT FRIEND OF BOB'S. SANDY CAN'T GET OUT OF BED, SO BOB OFTEN GOES TO HIS COTTAGE AND HOLDS UP A MIRROR WHILE SANDY SHAVES.

A ROCKY MOUNTAIN RAM CAUSED BOB A LOT OF TROUBLE. IT WAS A FIERCE BRUTE AND RAN WILD IN THE HILLS FOR MANY WEEKS BEFORE BOB HELPED TO CATCH IT.